An Arm and a Leg

by

Olive Balla

An Arm and a Leg

Cover Art by *Tina Lynn Stout*

The Wild Rose Press, Inc.
PO Box 708
Adams Basin, NY 14410-0708
Visit us at www.thewildrosepress.com

Publishing History
First Mainstream Mystery Edition, 2014
Print ISBN 978-1-62830-607-1
Digital ISBN 978-1-62830-608-8

Published in the United States of America

He pulled a handkerchief from his pocket and polished the clear, vacuum-sealed glass dome, pleased to note hardly any deterioration in the mummified flesh beneath.

"Beautiful, absolutely beautiful." He smiled and nodded, as if the thing under the dome was whispering the secrets of the universe to him…

In near-worshipful silence, Bellamy walked among the bits and pieces the rest of the world would view as monstrosities. No matter where he was or in what activity he was engaged, his Pretties were never far from his mind. But this was more than a collection—it was an extension of him. Not because of any malformation of his own person, but because of the rarity of his carefully selected pieces.

An image of Frankie O'Neil sprang into his mind. She of the tiny hands and feet. She of the striking eyes. Rare eyes, glowing at him from the picture frame in which O'Neil had kept her photo.

How best to preserve those eyes—one sky-blue, the other amber-yellow? Formaldehyde? No, that didn't prevent decay, it only slowed it. And alcohol would alter the cell structure such that bits of flesh would loosen and peel away, destroying the face's loveliness. No, no…that would be unacceptable.

Cryonics was the answer—a complex procedure ending in the head's being submerged in liquid nitrogen and maintained at absolute zero… He'd be the proud owner of the only known example of that rare condition called heterochromia iridium. It would be the crowning glory of his collection.

Dedication

To the men in my life:
my husband Victor
and
my sons Kevin, Patrick and James O'Donnell
—my fiercest cheerleaders

Acknowledgments

Thanks to:
Dr. Dennis Burns, Professor of Pathology;
APD Detective Christine Munsey;
Author Bonnie Tharp;
Proof Reader Susan Welch;
Beta Readers Vivian Maheu and Nancy St. John.
And special thanks to my amazing editor,
Ally Robertson

Chapter One

Alone.

In an empty house.

Certainly not what Frankie O'Neil had intended. But then, not much of her life had turned out as she'd intended. She stood in the center of the room that would become her den, sighed and chewed on her thumbnail.

She should be filled with euphoria at the purchase of her first home. Should be flitting from room to room, arms and hair flying in joyous celebration. And she would have been, had there been someone special with whom to share it.

But that chapter of her life was done. Done and best left in the past. Especially since it was her fault, her failure that had brought her here. Step right up folks and take a gander at the life lesson in her solitary habitat.

At least, Frankie told herself, she was making progress. She was moving forward, getting on with her life, making better choices. Just, by gosh and by golly, getting better and better every day and in every way. She snorted at her bastardized version of the old mantra, the derisive sound reverberating through the empty room.

The house itself was the perfect oasis. With eighteen-inch-thick adobe walls, arched doorways, and a heavy pole-beamed ceiling common to Albuquerque during the early 1900s, Frankie had loved the eighty-year-old house on sight. The lot on which it sat, a tad over an acre, was located just where the Albuquerque city limits curved upward toward the Sandia Mountains. Those mountains, bathed red in the afternoon sun, had called to her, and she'd plunked down most of the cash inherited from her Uncle Mike as a down payment. She'd had just enough money left to buy curtains and a few items of furniture.

The ringing Big Ben doorbell interrupted her thoughts. The unexpectedly loud sound reverberated through the empty space and sent her heart rate into the stratosphere.

Making a mental note to dial down the bell's volume, she pushed an auburn curl behind her ear, stood on tiptoes and peered through the peephole. She slid back the deadbolt and opened the door.

"Hey, Little Brother, you're up early this morning."

"Hi, Sis. Got a minute?"

"Sure." Frankie stepped to the side, pulled the door open wider and held it while her brother crossed the threshold. "Come in out of the cold."

Tim O'Neil tossed his car keys into a wooden bowl on the floor next to the front door and headed toward the living room. His usually squared shoulders sagged, and his short brown hair looked like a well-worn pot scrubber. His shirt and trousers, always immaculately pressed, looked as if they'd spent several weeks stuffed inside a too-small box. With red-rimmed gray eyes and a stubble-stippled face, he bore little resemblance to the well-known and respected doctor he was in the process of becoming. The oddly-shaped, ratty duffel bag he carried added to the down-and-out image.

He crossed to the stucco fireplace and sat cross-legged on the bare, red brick hearth in front of it. The duffel he placed on the floor beside him.

"Still no furniture?" His voice echoed through the hollow space.

"Everything was supposed to be here yesterday afternoon." Frankie pursed her lips. "But some of it's been back ordered. At least the electricity's on and I have appliances. Most of my clothes and things are still in boxes in the garage." She shrugged. "I told the furniture store to hold the new stuff until after I get back."

"About that." Tim ran his hand through his hair several times, mussing it even more. "I know it's your vacation, but I'd like to tag along just for a couple of days."

"Of course, it's your cabin too." Frankie looked more closely at her brother's ragged face. "If I didn't know you better, I'd swear you've just come off a bender. What's going on?"

"Nothing I want to talk about." He hunched his shoulders in his bullheaded mode.

"Okaaay." Frankie's voice became playful in an effort to lighten her brother's mood. "Let me guess, you decided to drop out of medicine and travel the world to find yourself."

She was surprised to see the strain around Tim's mouth when he raised his head and swiveled it toward her. "What part of 'I don't want to talk about it' don't you understand?"

Frankie's smile dissolved like an effervescent cold remedy in water. "What the hell. Where's all the defensiveness coming from?"

Tim blew out a long breath through puckered lips. "Look, I didn't come here to get into an argument." He stood, lifting the duffel by its straps. The weight of whatever was in the bag pulled the nylon handles taut. "Maybe this wasn't such a good idea."

Frankie stepped toward her brother and touched his arm. "Lighten up. You know you're welcome to come with me. I won't ask again, but if you want to talk, I'm here."

Tim's face relaxed a bit and he breathed out a long sigh. "I'm sorry, Sis. Got a lot on my mind."

"No harm done. At least your timing's good. Let's get a move on. I want to get to the cabin by mid-afternoon."

She walked to the hall closet. Careful to position herself between Tim's line of vision and the boxes, cans, and bags of food stacked there, she opened the door only enough to slip an arm inside and retrieve her nylon windbreaker. It wouldn't do for Tim to catch a glimpse of her collection of provisions. He'd just start asking questions, and she was neither in the mood to come up with a reasonable explanation nor to scramble for words to defend herself. People get hungry, plain and simple.

Sliding her eyes in her brother's direction, Frankie whispered a sigh of relief to see he'd moved out of view. She opened the closet door wider, stood on tiptoes, and pulled down the pet carrier for Collette, a cat she'd agreed to babysit for a musician friend on tour with the Albuquerque Symphony Orchestra.

After managing to corner the animal, she put the grumbling kitty into the carrier, slipped her hand through the handles and headed back toward the living room. Tim was just returning from the direction of the kitchen—the duffel bag was gone.

"Hope it's okay for me to leave that in your freezer for a couple of days."

"Sure." Frankie shot a quizzical look at her brother. "What is it?"

"Just something I picked up. It's too big for the tiny thing above my fridge. I'll get it when we come back on Monday."

"*Mi casa es su casa.*" Frankie moved through the house, checking locks and making sure lights were turned off. "I'll get the Jeep while you get your stuff," she yelled from the kitchen.

After Frankie backed out of the garage, Tim stood at the open passenger door and stared into the idling vehicle's interior. "Holy crap, Sis. Planning on feeding the Denver Broncos?" He scrunched his small travel bag into a ball and struggled to find an empty space. "And since when do you eat those god-awful canned sausages?"

Frankie cleared her throat. "They're protein. Never know when we'll lose power at the cabin and have to survive on non-perishables, especially this time of year." Grateful her brother could neither see her face nor read her mind, she attempted a light-hearted chuckle. "I'd hate to have to raid a squirrel's nest for breakfast."

"Ouch." Tim flapped his hand. "Damn. Jammed my thumb on a case of freaking tomato sauce. Tomato sauce and sardines, now that sounds yummy."

After a couple of minutes and several muttered imprecations, Tim finally managed to stuff his bag into a tiny space atop two boxes of ramen noodles. He climbed in and buckled up as Frankie backed into the street.

They delivered the cat to a pet boarding establishment and headed north on Interstate 25. A pickup merged onto the highway behind them, its front bumper so close to the Jeep's rear that its grill was hidden from Frankie's view. She goosed the accelerator to put some distance between the two vehicles.

Scenery flowed past the windows in flashes of color. The tan and ochre of the high desert gave way to green-splotched hills peppered with wildflowers and piñon trees. The dry, herbal fragrance of prairie grass, juniper, and sage brush became the loamy, earthy smells of scrub oak and conifers. Fluffy thunderclouds flattened and condensed into a low-hanging gray ceiling. A few tentative drops of rain turned into a torrent, and the fragrance of precipitation in the mountains seeped through the air vents.

Traffic thinned as they turned onto the Santa Fe Bypass and the road to Eagle Nest. Thankful for the Jeep's four-wheel drive, Frankie turned onto the muddy unpaved road that would take them the remaining few miles to the cabin. Again, she picked up speed to open distance between them and the only other vehicle on the road.

The beginnings of alarm buzzed up her neck when the other driver also sped up. She slowed to allow the guy to pass, but he slowed as well. Jerking her eyes back and forth between the highway in front of her and the images in the rearview mirror, she alternately sped up and slowed down, only to have the other vehicle duplicate her moves.

"Do you know someone who drives a dark green pickup?" Frankie turned her head slightly toward her brother.

"A green pickup?" Tim's face reflected surprise. His voice sounded high-pitched and tight. "Are you..." He started to swivel his head back over his shoulder.

The move was never completed. The sharp report of a rifle sliced through the silence, and the front and rear windows exploded almost simultaneously. Red and pink liquid sprayed the dash in front of Tim as the sudden smell of copper suffused the air. Without comprehending the reality of what she was seeing, Frankie looked first at the dripping dashboard, then at her brother.

"Tim? Tim?" Whimper became shriek as it moved through her lungs and exploded through her open mouth. She stared at her brother's bowed head. This wasn't real. None of this was happening.

Another shot slammed Frankie's self-preservation, fight-or-flight instinct into high gear, and she floored the gas pedal.

Tires threw up chunks of brown mud in an effort to gain traction on the rain-soaked dirt road. After what seemed an eternity, the wheels' impotent whirring stopped and the tires bit into more solid soil. The Jeep shot forward.

Between frantic glances at the road, Frankie looked at her brother sitting slumped against the seatbelt, bright red drops falling into his lap. His bowed head bobbed up and down as the Jeep flew over rises and plummeted down gullies. Gorge rose in Frankie's throat. Her chest tightened and her vision blurred.

"Tim? Oh God, oh God, oh God..." She brushed

her brother's shoulder with the fingertips of her right hand, half afraid she'd further hurt him but needing the contact.

Tim breathed out a final, long sigh. The soles of his shoes did a tap dance against the floorboard as his nerves fired off their final salvos. That sound—the sound of death—would have in reality been barely audible, but to Frankie's ears it became a pounding jackhammer.

Chapter Two

"No. No, no, no…" Frankie cried the word over and over, as if by force of will she could make the universe stop whatever was happening. She swallowed hard against the panic that threatened to make her vomit, while shoving the recognition of what Tim's wounds meant into the recesses of her conscious mind.

Another shot shattered the outside mirror on the driver's side. Frankie's eyes jerked to her rearview mirror. The pickup had nearly closed the gap between them.

Slowing barely enough to keep from rolling the vehicle, she made a sharp turn onto what looked like a trail in the woods. Relief filtered into her panic-stricken brain when the pickup fishtailed and then stalled as the driver took the same turn while going too fast.

Frankie jammed her foot on the accelerator with all her strength in hopes she could somehow make the Jeep go faster. Fast enough to become airborne. Fast enough to reverse time.

The Jeep sped cross-country down gullies and over ridges toward Taos and the nearest hospital. She fought to maintain control of the whipping steering wheel as the vehicle gee'd and haw'd. Every bump jogged pieces of the shattered windshield loose. Brickled bits of glass rained onto the boxes of food, where they slid and tick-tacked with every frantic turn.

But after only a few miles, the engine sputtered and died. The odor of gasoline filled the interior, and the light on the dash indicated an empty gas tank, the evident victim of a stray bullet.

Her stomach dropped, even as her brain refused to admit what the empty tank meant. For several seconds she gripped the steering wheel, her neck and shoulders rigid.

She turned the key in the ignition over again and again, pumping her foot on the gas pedal. She pounded her left hand against the steering wheel, willing the useless vehicle to roar back to life. But the Jeep only responded with a sputtering cough that soon gave way to a series of impotent clicks.

Frankie's heart set up a drummer's paradiddle in her chest. The pulse in her temples throbbed in cadence, her breathing came in shallow gasps. The Sangre de Cristo Mountains, host to years of happy family campouts, now surrounded her like a troop of malicious hump-backed ogres.

Sodden pine needles muted her footfall as she stumbled out of the Jeep. The rain-slick carpet made for treacherous walking, forcing her to step carefully as she walked around the vehicle to the passenger's side. She unbuckled her brother's seatbelt, pulled him toward her and struggled to gently lower him to the ground.

Her eyes were drawn to Tim's face. The air whooshed out of her lungs at the sight. Was it only minutes ago they'd been laughing at childhood antics? And now Tim lay unmoving at her feet, her clothes soaked in his blood.

A keening moan bubbled up from somewhere inside, and she swallowed hard. If she gave in to the urge, she might never stop screaming. And hysteria would serve no purpose now.

Gripping Tim's still-warm hands, she struggled to pull him toward the thick underbrush. Her feet kept slipping out from under her and she often fell to her knees. Each time, she hoisted herself back up.

In a few hours, the sun would fall behind the trees and the forest would become dark as a galactic black hole. While she would welcome the concealing darkness, it would also blot out any familiar landmarks. And an inability to find a landmark in the mountains could result in a number of outcomes, none of them good. She dragged her brother's body in the direction she hoped the cabin lay.

An hour or so later, the burble of water flowing over stones buoyed her courage. She could follow what she knew to be the only stream in this part of the forest almost to the cabin's back door. Offering thanks to the Creator, she pulled Tim's body toward the sound of rushing water.

The adrenaline infusion had long since worn off by the time she reached the river, and her back felt as if it would be permanently cocked at a forty-five degree angle. Every muscle in her body ached and twitched.

She dropped Tim's now-cool hands and straightened her back, gritting her teeth at the resulting pain. No use in racing against the clock any more. No use praying for Tim's life to be spared. No more pretending not to recognize what the coldness of his body meant.

Frankie locked her trembling knees in place and surveyed the still unfamiliar surroundings. A few feet from where she stood lay a slab of sandstone about three feet wide and eight feet long. Overhung with sod and tree roots, the flat stone formed the floor of a shallow cave that ran parallel to the river. Well above water level, it would serve her purpose perfectly. She dragged her brother's body down to the ledge and positioned it on the sun-warmed stone.

Somewhere along the way Tim's shoes had come off, uncovering dark socks, one with a hole in the toe. Something between a sob and a moan hissed through her lips at the sight of Tim's big toe peeking through the tear. She'd teased him about those toes, told him they were big enough to merit smaller, tacked-on shoes all their own—like an add-on to a one-room house. Those two thick, wide big toes he proudly claimed made swim fins unnecessary.

Sunlight slanting through the pines mottled the scene, and the merest whisper of a cool breeze stirred Tim's hair. Frankie sobbed at the normalcy of the sight. At the memory of summer fishing trips, winter snowboarding, and high school basketball games during which his hair had ruffled in exactly the same way.

After removing her windbreaker, she pulled off her blue cardigan, then put the jacket back on over her white turtleneck. Hands trembling, she wrapped her brother's head in the soft folds of her sweater, careful to cover his ruined face.

She caved in the soil that jutted out over the shelf. The rich, wild smell of forest earth mingled with the fragrance of the evergreens and fall wild flowers.

Her ears tuned to pick up sounds of pursuit, Frankie found two large fallen tree branches and pulled them on top of the makeshift grave. Then she spent precious minutes collecting river rocks for a cairn at the head of the mounded earth.

In spite of the crisp autumnal mountain air, perspiration poured down her face. It stung her eyes and pasted her hair against her forehead. The salty fluid worked its way along the crease of her lips, even as her mind registered the danger the moisture represented.

She knelt beside Tim's grave and patted the fragrant, muddy soil. "I'll be back."

Shivering, she turned and headed upstream. She could feel her body heat evaporating in waves. Her water-repellent windbreaker protected her from the rain, but her cotton turtleneck underneath was soaked in perspiration. She had to find the cabin within the next couple of hours or be forced to find a place to hole up for the night. The prospect brought fresh panic bubbling up her throat.

Stiff-legged and aching, her body reluctantly followed her command to keep moving. She focused on trying to ignore the knots in her leg muscles and the growing cramp in her side.

The sight of a familiar outcropping of rock brought a prayer of gratitude to her lips. In minutes she would drink fresh water and could use the cabin landline to call for help. She would tell the police about the men in the green pickup. Then she'd go back for Tim.

But before she could step into the clearing around the cabin, the sound of a rifle shot pulled her up short. Adrenaline again erupted, and the tiny hairs on the back of her neck moved as if alive. She pressed herself against the trunk of a large pine tree and willed her body to fuse with it. The sound of angry voices hit her like a slap.

"I told you not to shoot, dammit." A masculine

voice crescendoed into a bellow.

Someone mumbled a response, the words unintelligible.

"I don't care what you thought. Bad enough you took the first few shots. And now look what you've done. Thanks to you, they've gone to ground, and we're well and truly screwed."

Frankie turned back in the direction from which she'd just come. In spite of her racing heart, she made herself walk for several yards before giving in to the urge to run. Then she ran pell-mell, heedless of direction, and long after her burning lungs told her to stop.

After several minutes that seemed like hours, she stopped to listen for sounds of pursuit. She stooped over at the waist, put the palms of her hands on her bent knees for support, and sucked in great gulps of air. Except for her gasping breaths, no other sound broke the silence. No thumping footfalls, no voices arguing over how best to proceed. No evidence of the two murderers intent on… Intent on what? On catching her? On killing her? What in God's name were they after?

Frankie straightened her back and scanned the area, hoping to spot one of the hundreds of landmarks she'd memorized from the annual two-week forest survival training her uncle Mike had put her and Tim through during their growing-up years. Just one landmark to tell her where she was standing, that's all she needed.

She should have paid attention to where she was going—shouldn't have allowed panic to blind her to everything but the thought of putting distance between her and Tim's murderers.

Her eyes strained, pulling at their muscle-moorings, as if by sheer effort they could pierce through the dense foliage and thick underbrush. Gorge rose in her throat.

She turned around again and again as renewed panic clawed its way through her chest. Lost. Like a death knell, the words rang through her mind: lost and alone.

A gentle rain started up again as she considered her options. The good news was that the rain would keep most mountain predators and creepy-crawlies snuggled in their warm homes for a while. Although poisonous snakes would not yet have gone into hibernation, they tended to shy away from human contact unless cornered. And she had no intention of being either the cornerer or the corneree.

A shiver ran across her shoulders as she remembered Uncle Mike's stories of ill-prepared hikers who got lost in these mountains. Some of them, usually the ones who ignored the hikers' cardinal rule by not telling at least one other person where they were heading, had never been seen again. And then there were the stories of bodies so gnawed by animals they were only identifiable through their DNA. But the most horrific story of all was about the hiker who became pinned under a boulder and had to sever his own arm with a penknife to escape.

Frankie adjusted the hood of her nylon jacket. She was grateful for its protection from the rain, but underneath it, the perspiration-absorbing fibers of her cotton shirt pressed against her body, cooling it and making her a perfect candidate for hypothermia.

And hypothermia impaired judgment. It made thinking difficult and increased the probability of an accident. She could fall victim to it and not even realize what was happening.

Calm yourself, Frances. Fear sucks up your energy, and you'll need every scrap of it before this is over. Remember what I taught you and you'll find a way. The standing-right-next-to-her sound of her dead uncle Mike's voice pulled her back from the edge of hysteria. She clung to its echoes, assuming it was only a memory stirred up by terror.

Snippets of her uncle's survival speeches floated through her mind as she worked her memory for the skills he had taught her and Tim. Her first job was to get out of the drizzling rain. She scanned her surroundings and spotted two fairly large boulders propped against each other, forming a kind of lean-to.

Watchful of any other creatures that might have had the same idea, she approached the rock shelter. She picked up a long stick, poked it as far into the recess as she could and shook it around, banging it against the stone walls. When nothing moved or scurried out of the enclosure, she dropped to all fours and crawled in.

Hunkering down with her back toward the opening, she curled into a ball. She pressed her knees against a semi-soft mass of what she assumed to be a pile of needle-covered branches and tried to get comfortable. She had to cock her head at an angle and push it up against one of the boulders, but at least the ground beneath her was dry.

Frankie focused on her breathing. After a few minutes, she was surprised to find herself warming up. Her body stopped shivering, and she fell into an uneasy sleep.

Dark dreams periodically jerked her awake, and

she jumped, banging her head, elbows, and knees against the boulders. She dozed off and on, while the temperature outside the stone teepee dropped.

Sometime during the night the rain stopped. Its cessation pricked Frankie's subconscious, and she jerked awake.

A coyote howled from what sounded like only a few yards away, and she held her breath. It was a useless tactic, of course, since the coyote didn't need to hear her breathing to know she was there. He'd probably smelled her long before she heard him calling his mate to dinner. Smelled her covered in Tim's blood.

When the coyote inexplicably neither howled again nor showed up with a knife, fork, and bib, Frankie breathed a sigh of relief. Coyotes are generally afraid of people, but the smell of blood and her own weakened condition would have been a temptation to any carnivore trying to find a meal during New Mexico's worst drought on record.

She'd been lying on her right arm, and now it was numb. In an effort to get into a more comfortable position, she moved the arm as much as she could in the confines of her shelter until feeling began to return. Her body complaining like a circus contortionist with arthritis, Frankie tried to straighten her legs a bit.

Then the mass that formed the back wall of her shelter moved.

Had the early-hibernating bear either had cubs or been in a foul mood, Frankie could have been history. But the drowsy creature moved slowly, seemingly unconcerned about the pitiful human's proximity. Grateful for the lethargic bear's unwillingness to leave its cozy bed, she rolled out through the shelter's opening. With her adrenaline-charged body again primed to break the land-speed record, she forced herself to walk slowly for several yards in the nearly complete darkness before breaking into a run.

When it became apparent that she'd made good on her getaway, she stopped and studied the now cloudless sky. She marveled at how close the stars appeared against their black velvet background as she searched the Little Dipper's handle for the North Star Polaris.

As thousands of humans throughout past millennia had done, she used Polaris to get her bearings. With a returning infusion of confidence, she began to walk.

For what seemed like hours, she forced one foot in front of the other while her vision blurred and her thigh muscles twitched. Surely she'd come across a road at some point. Or even an animal trail that she could follow to water.

Her thickened tongue stuck to the roof of her mouth. All she could think about was water. She imagined its coolness trickling down her throat. She could almost feel the warm wetness of it washing over her in the city swimming pool where she and Tim had spent hot summer days. And she could hear ice cubes clinking together in a tall glass full of it. She picked up two small stones, rubbed the mud off them, and put them into her mouth to encourage her salivary glands to do their job.

Trees often blotted out her view of the heavens. During those times, she continued on in what she assumed to be the correct direction until she again caught sight of Polaris and adjusted her bearing accordingly.

She stepped into a familiar-looking clearing.

Hadn't she passed that way an hour or so ago? And weren't those the same three pine trees towering over a scrub oak bush that she'd thought looked like Shakespeare's three witches stirring their cauldron? Her stomach fell. She was going to die here. She'd die and her body would never be found.

Her knees gave way. She dropped to the ground and sobbed.

****

Early morning sunlight, damp earth, and the pinpricks of pine needles sticking into the flesh of her arms brought Frankie awake. The fallen needles and leaves she'd used as a blanket had offered little protection from the cold, and none against the mist of the late morning rain. She brushed off the soggy mat, sat up, and leaned back against the trunk of the pine tree under which she'd collapsed the night before.

She'd hoped it was all a bad dream. Hoped it would be somehow miraculously over upon wakening. But it was never going to end. She was going to—

No time for histrionics. Uncle Mike's voice again. *Get a grip.*

"But I don't know where I am," Frankie said to what she'd decided was her subconscious mind in survival mode.

Follow your instincts.

"Easy for you to say. You're already dead." Frankie stood and dusted the remaining pine needles and mud off her jacket and pants.

Every joint in her body ached. Her neck felt stiff from sleeping on the ground. Her knees wobbled like her old nanny's Christmas gelatin, and her tongue felt so swollen that it filled her mouth. She needed to find clean drinking water and someplace warm and dry. And she needed to find them sooner rather than later.

Everyone at work knew she would be away for two weeks. No one would look for her before then. Without anything that could be used as a weapon and lacking warm clothing or shelter, she could die of exposure long before two weeks passed. One misstep on the moist needle and leaf-strewn ground could end in an injury. Even a small cut could go septic and incapacitate her, making her easy prey to the carnivores that lived in the mountains.

Nausea again played with her gut. She drew the back of her hand across her runny nose, sniffled, and forced herself to take slow, deep breaths while she scanned the terrain.

What should she do next? Why couldn't she think, dammit? It was like her head was stuffed full of cotton balls and her brain's neurons had gone on strike.

The morning sun's position directly over her left shoulder meant she should be facing north. But wait— maybe it was south.

God, she was tired. And her heart was pounding like a trip-hammer. If she could just lie down and sleep. Just a few minutes of rest couldn't hurt, could it?

Fight, Frances. Get up. Come on, get a move on.

"Go away." Her voice was little more than a whisper. "Just a few minutes. Please, I need to—"

I said get up. Uncle Mike's tone had changed into drill instructor mode. *I'll not have any niece of mine acting like a malingering S-bird. Let's go.* The voice broke into a sing-song Navy Seal cadence, what she'd since learned was a cleaned-up version their uncle had made her and Tim echo during what he called their PT

Marches. *I don't know, but I've been told…*

She automatically responded in her raspy voice, "I don't know, but I've been told."

A frogman's money is good as gold.

"A frogman's money is good as gold." Frankie's voice grew louder as she answered the familiar chant.

Sound off.

"Sound off."

One, two, three, four. One, two, three-four.

"One, two, three, four. One, two, three-four."

By the time she sang out the last line, warmth had begun seeping through her mid-section. With Uncle Mike's voice calling out marching orders, she ran her trembling hands along the tree bark's deep striations, pulled herself into a standing position and stumbled toward what she hoped was civilization.

Chapter Three

Frankie was relieved when none of the regulars at the Eagle Nest café glanced up from either their breakfasts or laptops when she lurched through the door. Residents of a fishing and ski resort village, the locals were most likely used to the various sorts of humans who descended upon their town, tore up and down their mountains and left, leaving their trash and money behind.

But the older woman standing behind the counter did look up. She immediately came out from behind the bar she'd been wiping down and approached Frankie. Slender and tall, the woman moved with an athletic grace, although she appeared to be in her sixties. Her unusually black hair was cut short and spiked on top. The steel in her glance warned she could either be a good friend or an awesome enemy.

"How can I help?"

"Can I use your phone?" Frankie's voice trembled along with her body. She cleared her throat. "I lost my cell, and I need to call the police."

"There's one in my office. Follow me."

The two walked behind the counter, through a door and into the room beyond. An antique wooden desk faced the door, its hand-carved panels a deep walnut color. Atop the desk sat a black telephone reminiscent of those found in old Spencer Tracy movies. The wall behind the desk was festooned with framed medals and awards, along with a banner bearing the United States Marine Corps insignia. In one corner sat a wood-burning stove, its cast iron legs resting on a stone hearth. The stove's pot belly glowed orange, suffusing the otherwise dimly lit room with a yellow glow. Frankie stumbled toward the stove, holding her shaking hands toward the radiant warmth.

"You can barely stand." The older woman rolled a wooden chair out from behind the desk and pushed it toward Frankie. "Sit."

Frankie's knees buckled, and she dropped into the chair.

"I'll get you something hot to drink."

When the woman returned, she held a steaming mug. Frankie's icy fingers greedily reached for the warm, fragrant brew.

"Careful, it's hot."

Frankie lifted the mug to her lips and took a gulp. She winced at the bite of whiskey in the coffee, and sipped more slowly. The tension in her shoulders loosened up, and they sagged a bit.

"Better?" the woman said.

"Better, thanks."

"I'm Kate Stanger. I own this place. What's your name?"

"Frankie O'Neil." A loud noise from somewhere outside startled her. Her eyes darted around the room in search of an exit.

"Okay, Frankie, I need you to listen to me. Can you do that?"

Frankie turned and looked into Kate Stanger's face, barely registering the woman's slight start at the sight of her bi-colored eyes: one ice-blue, one amber-yellow. It was the way people had reacted to them for as long as she could remember. She shook her head, struggling to pull her focus back to what the woman was saying.

"Are you injured?"

"No. At least…no, I don't think so."

"Are you in danger?"

"I'm not sure." Frankie's body swayed, as if she were about to lose her balance and topple out of the chair. She was just so damned tired. "Please, can I use your phone now?"

"There's no police station here in Eagle Nest. We'll have to call the sheriff in Raton." Kate's face assumed an intent expression, and her voice radiated a comforting sympathy. "It'll take the law a while to get here. Meanwhile I'm going to call a doctor. You might be hurt without realizing it. But first we have to get you into some dry clothes." The older woman moved toward an armoire located against the wall opposite her desk. "I keep some things here in case we get snowed in."

Wire hangers click-clacked as Kate searched through whatever was in the closet. When she turned around, she held an armload of clothing. "These should work. Everything will be a bit long, but at least they're warm. When you feel like it, you can change in the restroom. It's just beyond the fridge and to the right."

Frankie accepted the clothes but made no move to leave the stove's warmth. "Thank you."

"I'll go find a bag for your things."

Kate had been gone only a minute or two before she returned with a clear plastic bag. "The law will need your clothes for forensics." She handed the bag to

Frankie, who accepted it and left the room.

When Frankie returned to the office, Kate's rolled-up blue jeans hung loosely at her waist. The knit tee shirt and plaid flannel jacket looked more like tunics than blouses, and the shoes were so large they could have doubled as snow skis. But the clothing was more precious than this year's Parisian couture: for the first time in nearly twenty-four hours, she was warm.

Almost ceremoniously, she placed the bag containing her bloodied clothing on the floor in front of the stove and sat down. She was still staring through the tiny glass square door at the dancing orange-red flames when Kate ushered a stooped white-haired man into the office.

"Is there any pain here?" the doctor asked as he poked, prodded and palpated Frankie's body with arthritic, gnarled hands. He held a stethoscope to her chest and asked her to cough. He pointed a tiny flashlight into her eyes and told her to follow his hand as he moved it from side to side.

Once he'd completed his examination, the doctor returned the instruments to his bag. His glance moved from Frankie to Kate. "Other than a few cuts and abrasions, I don't find any injuries. But she's dehydrated." He pointed to the bag of clothes. "The good news is none of that blood is hers. But the bad news is somewhere someone has been seriously injured."

As if on cue, the doctor and Kate simultaneously turned their heads toward Frankie. Kate's face appeared to be filled with concern. But, although it might have been her imagination, the doc's face radiated something akin to suspicion.

Feeling like an insect specimen on display in a science class, Frankie hunkered down in the chair, squeezed her eyes shut, and willed herself to awaken. But just as before, when she opened her eyes nothing had changed.

****

Larry Littlefield cleared his throat. A drop of sweat slalomed down his scrawny ribs, tickling the flesh in its race toward his beltline. He crossed and uncrossed his legs. Blue jeans molded against knobby knees that pushed out angular, geometric shapes from inside the fabric. He stroked his pockmarked face, stared at the tips of his fake ostrich-hide boots, and squirmed in the chair in front of the expensive mahogany desk behind which sat his employer, a man named Bellamy.

Mel Stubbs sat slouched in the chair next to Larry, his deceptively childlike face expressionless and his ever-present Broncos cap pulled down so low as to nearly cover his eyes. His legs splayed out in front of him, the heels of his brogan-shod feet rested on the floor. The toes of his boots canted outward, describing a vee. The bib of his once blue overalls bore chunks and dried splotches of vari-colored food. His hands lay in his lap, their dirt-rimmed nails chipped and yellowed. A web of scarred flesh held the pinkie finger of his right hand tightly at a ninety degree angle. Other than rubbing the misshapen digit with the fingers of his other hand, Mel sat still as stone.

"You smell," Bellamy said to Mel. "And your filthy boots are soiling our rug. How many times have we told you to clean yourself up before coming into our office?"

Mel remained unresponsive, giving no indication

that he heard his boss's words.

Bellamy turned toward Larry. "Can't you do something about him?"

"Yessir," Larry said. "I'll see that he showers."

"How many times have we told you to make sure he changes his clothes at least every other day?" Bellamy shuddered. "And buy him some new underwear this afternoon."

"Yessir."

Bellamy sat back in his chair. "Now, what do you have to report?"

"Mel and me found O'Neil. He went to his sister's house like you said he might. We parked a ways down the block and sat there for about ten minutes before he come out to his car and took out a little travel bag—"

"Came out. He came out to his car." Bellamy slapped his right hand on the desk top, the sound reverberating off the walls. "My God, how you torment the English language. Between you and your barely-human sidekick, our business is becoming a freak show."

Larry sniffed. "Yessir." Who but Bellamy would raise such a stink about him using a word wrong? What was it he'd read on the Internet about people like that? Anal retentive—that was it. And those words definitely fit Bellamy. The old guy's ass was probably so tight he couldn't even take a decent dump. An image of his boss's belly exploding from the build-up, showering his never-a-hair-out-of-place self with splashes of smelly green and brown crap brought a smile to Larry's face, an unwise smile he wiped off too late.

"Please share the reason for your sudden mirth." Bellamy's voice was calm and pitched low, but the face pointed toward Larry had turned dark red. "Did we say something funny?"

"No, sir. Just a touch of indigestion." Larry patted his stomach with his open palm and leaned forward. He propped his elbows on his knees and flicked an imaginary speck of dust from the brim of his oversized Stetson. "Next thing we knew, O'Neil put his travel bag into the sister's four-by-four and they drove off. I figured you'd want us to follow them."

Larry waited for the other man to show some sign he'd done the right thing. But no change of expression registered in the stare that pinned him to his chair. Had it been a laser, it would have burned a hole right between his eyes.

The taste of bile filled Larry's mouth and the beginnings of nausea toyed with his stomach. Hating the whine that crept into his voice, but unable to stop it, he continued. "They went to some pet kennel and took the interstate north. Just outside Eagle Nest, Mel got antsy and tried to shoot out their tires…"

Bellamy's eyelids lowered to half-mast. The words printed at the bottom of a replica of an ancient-world map shot through Larry's brain: *This be where monsters dwell.* Tightness prickled across his scalp, puckering it and starting up an ache in his head. A wuss, that's what he was. Wuss-man Larry, afraid of his own shadow. He swallowed hard and cleared his throat.

"You let Mel shoot at O'Neil with his sister in the car?" Like a schoolmarm assessing the truth of a misbehaving student's self-defense, Bellamy clasped his hands in front of his face and placed his steepled index fingers against his chin. He pursed his lips, an expectant look on his face.

"I told Mel not to shoot, I told him." Larry cleared his throat again. "But he gets all wound up sometimes and just loses it."

"Mel has the brain of an iguana. We never expect him to actually think." Bellamy poked an index finger toward Larry's face. "You're supposed to be the smart one. Did you even stop to think what might happen if you let Lizard Brain ride in a vehicle with a gun rack in the window?"

Larry glanced again at Mel. But the guy just sat there like one of those sculptures carved out of a tree trunk with a chainsaw. "It was all I could do to keep the truck on them bumpy dirt roads. No way I could've stopped him without losing sight of O'Neil."

"Enough excuses. It has become eminently clear why the two of you had to leave Amarillo in such a hurry. No self-respecting drug dealer would maintain such inept employees."

Larry studied his boots while he considered what to say next. He decided against mentioning Mel's shooting spree. And he sure as hell wouldn't say anything about the amount of blood they found in the jeep or the drag marks that played out over a rocky outcropping. No use in pissing off the boss any more than he already was. "They took off cross country and we lost them for a couple hours. We followed their tracks and found the Jeep a good ways off the road."

"So you captured O'Neil and the girl?" Bellamy looked up. A glint of something unnatural moved around under the smooth dark surface in his eyes.

At least, that seemed to be the best way to describe what was going on in the two holes someone had referred to as windows to the soul. Bellamy's *windows* were more like round hollows hacked and dynamited into the side of a smooth rock cliff. Bottomless holes that living things fell into and were never seen again.

"Well?" Bellamy smacked his hand on his desk again. "Do you have them?"

Larry shook his head. "They'd already left on foot by the time we got there. But we found the bags they left behind."

"And?"

"They were filled with the girl's things, men's clothes, and such. The rest of the Jeep was filled with food. O'Neil must've ditched your stuff before he got to his sister's house."

Bellamy took a deep breath and slowly released it. When he spoke, his voice sounded like a college professor trying to explain physics to a kindergartener. "We asked you to follow Tim in hopes he would lead you to our property, after which you would dispose of him in an apparent accident."

"Yessir." Larry nodded his head.

"But in your limitless wisdom you terrorized Tim and his sister and then lost them. Not only did you fail to bring us our property, but you have now involved the sister. If we have arrived at the wrong conclusion, please clarify."

We want this, we want that, kiss our ass—like some kind of frigging royalty. Larry took a deep breath. "Me and Mel…"

"Mel and I," Bellamy said through gritted teeth.

"Mel and I followed their trail until it petered out in the woods. Then we found their cabin. It had a plaque over the door with O'Neil written on it, so we waited for a while, thinking they might show up. But they never did. We couldn't get a signal for the cell, so we come…came on back to check in."

Bellamy walked over to a panoramically windowed wall that offered an unrestricted view of the sun-bathed Sandia Mountains. He stared through the glass while the muscles in his jaw alternately tightened and relaxed.

Although the old guy had to be in his sixties, his face remained nearly unlined. His immaculately trimmed Van Dyke goatee, a sleek mixture of black and gray, complemented his thick, snow-white hair. Standing at about six two, his slim build probably made him attractive to women—that and the self-confidence oozing from every pore. Yessiree, he'd most likely been a real cocksman once. Maybe still was, since the invention of that blue pill. One thing for sure, he'd probably never had to spend a weekend alone. And money? The pompous old prick must have piles of the stuff just laying around. Whenever he got bored, he probably rolled around on top of a huge pile of gold coins, like that Scrooge McDuck cartoon guy.

Bellamy turned from the window and faced the two seated men. "We don't like the way this is going. The only bright spot in this whole situation is that O'Neil hasn't yet gone to the authorities. If he had, all hell would have broken loose by now."

"So what's the plan?" Larry said.

"You mean beyond holding you responsible for any further trouble caused by this whole thing?" The look in the old man's eyes made Larry's insides turn to water.

"Yessir." Larry squirmed in his seat. What was that saying about never letting the other guy see you sweat? Sweat was the least of the Wuss-man's problems. He

31

clamped his rectum sphincter as tight as he could, the muscle contraction raising his body a good inch off the chair. Nosiree, it surely wouldn't do to crap his pants right here in front of the Boss.

"May we assume you still have your lock-picking tools?" Bellamy looked intently into Larry's face.

"Yessir. I keep in practice."

"Good. You and Mel go search the sister's house and O'Neil's car and apartment. We may yet be able to salvage this balls-up."

Bellamy walked over to stand in front of Larry, bent at the waist and placed one hand on each of the arms of the younger man's chair. He brought his eyes to within inches of Larry's face. "Find our things, or you'll have to start carrying parts of your face in a jar of that dreadful aftershave you insist on wearing." Bellamy's oddly cool breath hissed across his perfect teeth and stirred the tiny hairs in Larry's nose.

The younger man shuddered.

Bellamy evidently saw the movement because he chuckled. Completely devoid of cheerfulness, the sound reminded Larry of a dull knife scraping against bone.

Chapter Four

Colfax County Deputies Nick Rollins and Judy Pritney followed retired Marine Corps Colonel Kate Stanger into her office. A young woman sat at Kate's desk, her head bowed over a platter of the cafe's locally famous chicken fried steak, homemade mashed potatoes with cream gravy, and Cajun style coleslaw. A tiny waif of a thing, her toes barely reached the floor. With a nubby white blanket draped over her rounded shoulders, she looked like a child who'd got lost in the mall and was waiting for someone to find her. Shoulder-length auburn hair flecked with twigs and pine needles hung in damp ropes around the pale pixie-shaped face.

Kate, the new owner of the Eagle Nest Café, shot a series of meaningful looks at Nick—her way of telling him to be gentle with the young woman she'd apparently decided to champion. He nodded his head once in acknowledgment.

The tongue-prickling smell of food made its way from the kitchen into the office, where it mingled with the fragrance of the wood-burning stove Kate steadfastly refused to upgrade to gas or electric. But the homey ambiance didn't seem to register with the young woman.

Something about the small form tugged at Nick's heart. Perhaps it was the forlorn way she hugged herself, or the way she absently pushed back a thick curl that kept falling over her right eye. Or maybe it was the smudge of mud at her temple.

Nick slammed his mind into neutral. No one knew better than he did how deceptive appearances could be. By the look of the bloodied clothes in the bag Kate handed him, this angelic creature might have done something horrible to another human being—horrible and messy.

The hunched figure picked up the fork. Wielding it like a croupier's stick, she pushed the piles of food into different configurations, her movements slow and deliberate, as if requiring immense effort.

Kate put her hand on the seated woman's shoulder—lightly, as if afraid she would break something. "Frankie, this is Deputy Nick Rollins and his partner Deputy Pritney."

The young woman turned her face toward Nick, her strangely-colored eyes filled with the most intense despair he'd seen since his tour in Afghanistan. Hypnotic, ancient eyes in a child's face.

Kate spoke to Nick, her voice low. "Doc Williams just left. He says there's nothing physically wrong with her, but she's in shock." She shot another crusty look at him.

Nick nodded. Point taken.

He pulled a chair over to sit in front of the young woman. He rested his hands on his thighs and studied her face. "Can you tell us what happened, Miss O'Neil?"

Frankie stiffened and cleared her throat. At first, her words came haltingly, more mimed than spoken. But then, like pressurized reservoir water through a new eight-inch pipe, the events of the past thirty-six hours poured out while Pritney typed furiously on the laptop she'd brought.

"Would you recognize either of the men if you saw them again?" Nick said.

Frankie shook her head. "I only saw them in my rearview mirror. I just remember thinking there were two of them. One drove while the other one shot at us with a rifle."

"Just a sec." Pritney's voice sounded unusually loud and strident. "How can you be so sure all the shots were from the same weapon? And how did you know it was a rifle?"

Frankie looked at the female deputy. "My uncle taught Tim and me how to use and identify all kinds of weapons. A rifle sounds completely different than a handgun." She turned back toward Rollins. "Not an automatic, or even a semi-automatic. It was a single-shot rifle, the kind some hunters use. I'd say it was a Ruger 300."

Deputy Pritney's lips thinned. "You could tell all that just from the sound?"

Frankie shot a look of what appeared to be pity at Pritney and remained silent.

"Is there anyone you can think of who'd want to hurt either you or your brother?" Nick said.

"I've gone over and over that question in my mind. I don't know of anyone who would want me dead. And Tim's a doctor. He just wants...just wanted to help people."

"Was your brother alive when you pulled him from the vehicle?"

Frankie shook her head. "I don't...I wasn't sure. It

all happened so fast." Her voice caught and she cleared her throat. "But he had no pulse and he wasn't breathing. His head was…his face had been…" Frankie rubbed her eyes with the heels of both hands, as if trying to scrub away some image.

"So why didn't you leave him in the vehicle and go for help?" Pritney said.

"I figured whoever shot at us would come across the Jeep sooner or later. It just didn't occur to me to leave Tim behind for them to find."

Deputy Rollins nodded. He'd seen more than one Marine carry a dead buddy for miles, refusing to give him up until left with no other choice. "So you buried him and went for help."

"I couldn't leave him out in the open where the animals could get at him."

Nick took a business card out of his wallet. He studied the laptop screen in front of Deputy Pritney, wrote a case number on the back of the card, and handed the small square to Frankie. "I'll stay in touch over the course of the investigation. But feel free to call this number if you have any questions or remember anything."

Frankie dropped the card into the breast pocket of the borrowed shirt. She sat still, as if unsure what to do next.

Nick allowed his face to soften. "I know this is hard for you, but time is crucial. Can you tell me where you left your brother's body?"

"No. But I can take you there."

Pritney's head shot up from behind the laptop, and she squinted at Frankie. "I thought you were lost." Her voice oozed a level of sarcasm that surprised Nick but that Frankie seemed not to notice. "If you were lost, how can you remember where you left him?"

"Our uncle schooled us in woodcraft." Frankie turned her head toward the female deputy. "I kept track of the location."

Pritney cut her eyes sideways at Nick. Her lips pursed at whatever expression she saw registered on his face, and she turned back toward Frankie. "So you spent part of the night cuddling with a hibernating bear?"

This time Pritney's tone of voice did register, and Frankie cocked her head at the deputy. "I know that sounds weird, but that's what happened."

Nick looked at his partner. "Actually, there've been several bears spotted in residential areas this year. Because of the drought, they've come down out of the mountains looking for food. Some have lost their fear of humans and even interacted with them in bizarre ways."

Nick's face heated at the look Pritney shot back at him. And she had a point. For all he knew, Miss O'Neil was lying her ass off, making the story up as she went. He rubbed his hand along the thigh of his right leg, the hard, pea-sized knobs of scar tissue discernible through the fabric of his uniform trousers. It wouldn't be the first time he'd been conned by a female in distress.

"Okey dokey." Pritney lowered her head and jabbed her fingers on the laptop's keyboard, the subsequent clacking loud in the otherwise silent room. Once she'd finished typing, she snapped down the lid and stood.

Perplexed by his partner's behavior, Nick studied her face for a couple of seconds. "I'll take Miss O'Neil in the Rover, you follow in the squad car. I'll call it in on the way."

"You're the boss." Pritney grabbed up the laptop, her movement radiating more heat than the glowing potbelly stove.

****

Two hours later, Frankie sat inside Deputy Rollins' Range Rover a few feet from where she'd buried Tim. The area around the temporary grave had been cordoned off, and several people moved with purpose, fulfilling their roles in the well-oiled machine set up to deal with a suspicious death within the county's confines.

Frankie forced the memories of the past several hours into the dark recesses of her mind. She would bring them out into the light when things settled down. She'd go over every detail, relive every second, and allow herself to feel all of it. It would fill her, and she would grieve.

But not now. Not until she'd done everything she could for her brother. She swallowed the lump that kept creeping up her throat and turned her attention to the activity around Tim's grave. The county coroner bowed over Tim's body and performed the preliminary duties required of the Office of Medical Examiner. The buzz and hum of human investigative activities filled the forest and silenced the animals that made their homes there. The rich smell of over-turned forest soil mingled with the scent of moist pine needles wafting in through the deputy's open window.

Standing some distance from his vehicle, Nick spoke to a man carrying a silver clipboard. Black hair spilled out from under the deputy's tan hat. Tall and broad shouldered, he looked like someone who either worked out or did hard physical labor.

Rollins nodded his head at Clipboard and made his way back to the car. Frankie wondered at the cause of the deputy's slight limp as he slid into the driver's seat.

"We've secured this area and the area where you left your Jeep. We'll also comb the forest around your cabin. If there's anything there, we'll find it."

"What happens next?" Frankie searched the deputy's blue-gray eyes for answers to the dozens of questions swirling around in her head.

"The state crime lab folks from Santa Fe will process the scene, along with your vehicle. That means they'll take photos and look for anything that might help in the investigation."

"What about Tim?"

"The coroner's office will transport his body for autopsy. Once the medical examiner has done her job, there'll be an inquest. After that, the body should be released for burial."

Tears stung Frankie's eyes. She swiped them away with the back of her hand.

"It's never easy losing someone you love, especially like this. I've asked you some hard questions, and I'll have to ask more. I just want you to know I mean no disrespect."

Rollins left the car and returned to the gravesite. He and Clipboard talked for a bit before he pulled his ringing phone from a small scabbard attached to his belt and spoke into it. As he listened, he turned toward Frankie, a strange look on his face. He nodded a couple of times, murmured something, and broke the connection.

The unexpectedly comforting sound of the stream made its way through the open driver's window, bringing to Frankie's mind the melody of an old hymn from her childhood. The few words she could remember floated to the surface of her memory: something about angels walking by the bright, shining river of death. Not something that would be sung in a modern church, these lyrics had been wrung from someone's soul before the discovery of medicines made it easy to relegate death to the never-going-to-happen-to-me-or-mine sphere. She hummed the haunting melody.

The deputy's return to the Rover yanked her back to the present. He stooped over and peered at her through the window, a strained look on his face. "You're sure it was only you and your brother in your Jeep?"

"Yes." Frankie felt her face register surprise. "Why?"

"And neither of you returned fire at the other men?"

A chill ran up Frankie's spine. "No. Neither of us brought a weapon. What's going on?"

"I'm afraid I'm going to have to ask you to come back to the station with me, Miss O'Neil. I just got a call from the officers who secured the area around your cabin. They've found a man's body a few feet from the back door. Can you tell me about that?"

"I don't... Maybe one of the men who killed my brother turned on the other and shot him."

Rollins' lips thinned. "Footprints in the muddy driveway at your cabin indicate two people stepped out of a vehicle, wandered around a bit, and then got back in. Because of the rain there's no way to know exactly when those prints were made. But what we do know is someone shot a man just outside your cabin and left him there to bleed to death."

****

Frankie spent several hours at the police station in Raton answering questions about Tim's shooting. Again and again she went over the sequence of events. The questioning officer's voice grew more and more strident each time she denied any knowledge of the dead man found near the cabin. His eyes bored holes into hers as he studied her every facial expression, every muscle twitch and eye blink. The tone of his voice never softened, even after another officer came into the room to tell him the dead man had been identified as a hunter from Idaho who'd been reported missing by relatives in Taos the day before Tim's death. That, along with the Coroner's preliminary report, indicated the man had been suffering from exposure several hours before Frankie and her brother left Albuquerque. His death was looking more and more like a hunting accident. Someone made a call to the pet boarding establishment, which supported Frankie's claim regarding the timeline.

"Interview terminated at fifteen hundred hours," the questioner said. Eyes narrowed to slits, he ordered Frankie not to leave the state. Insinuating that she was being allowed to go home only because no weapon or other evidence against her had been found, he held the door open. His body positioned so that she had to turn sideways to avoid rubbing against him, his eyes followed her through the door. She fled into the hall, where deputy Rollins stood from a chair where he'd apparently been waiting.

"Do you have a way home?"

Frankie shook her head. "No." She had no way home, no one waiting, and no living family. Other than her old nanny Alma, not one living person loved or even cared what happened to her. The lyrics of a golden oldie scraped across her memory like nails on a blackboard, something about one being the loneliest of all numbers.

"I have to go to Albuquerque for training tomorrow," the deputy was saying. "But I was thinking of going in this afternoon to visit friends. I'll take you home, if you like."

"Thanks." Frankie wanted to scream into his face to go eat pig balls and die—he and his suspicious police friends. She wanted to yell that she'd rather hitch a ride with the first friendly trucker who stopped. But exhaustion and a continuing sense of unreality held her back. She just wanted to go home, even if it meant riding with the enemy and sleeping on the floor of her empty house.

Deputy Rollins pushed a music CD into the player in his vehicle as Frankie buckled up. Music from the seventies and eighties poured into the otherwise dead airspace. Rollins tried several times to open up polite conversation, but Frankie didn't respond. Instead, she sat with her body pressed up against the passenger door, her spine so rigid she quickly worked up a headache.

In some circles her behavior would have been considered impolite. In others it could be defined as dripping with attitude. Either of those was fine by her. Her little brother had been shot before her eyes, and she'd basically been accused of murdering a man she didn't even know for some reason she couldn't fathom. So yeah, she was feeling pretty pushed out of shape right about then.

The officer who interrogated her, although he'd called it an interview, had left no doubt as to what he thought of her story. He and his protect-and-serve buddies would undoubtedly be expending lots of energy in digging up evidence against her, trying to find some connection between her and the dead hunter. So, securing an attorney would probably be a wise move. But taking into account the state of her finances, she wondered at her chances of finding one willing to work for homemade strawberry or raspberry jam.

Like harbingers of things to come, words about staying alive floated from the CD player and into the charged air. Frankie swallowed hard against what felt like giant hands kneading and twisting her stomach.

Chapter Five

Larry's stomach tightened as he dialed Bellamy's number. A body would think that after a couple of years working for the old guy Larry could at least talk to him on the phone without feeling the need to hurl his beans. Maybe his innards were trying to tell him something his head hadn't quite figured out.

Bellamy picked up after the second ring. "Ah, Larry. You have good news, yes?"

"Mel and me rifled through O'Neil's place. We didn't find anything there, so we went on over to the sister's house. She's got the place locked up tighter'n a drum. Besides an alarm, there's deadbolts on the front and back doors. We figured you wouldn't want us to risk breaking in and being seen."

"What about Tim's car? Were you able to manage a look at that?"

"We didn't see anything inside O'Neil's car." Larry added a silent *screw you* at the sarcasm in his boss's voice. "We were about to pop the trunk when some old blister came out of the house next door and yelled what were we doing, so we took off. We could go back later tonight when everyone's in bed."

"We'll chat about that later. We received an interesting call this morning from our songbird. It seems O'Neil is dead."

Larry's stomach lurched at the thought that

Bellamy knew he'd withheld important information. He gulped then cleared his throat. "That's good, right? At least now he can't make trouble."

"That's all you have to say for yourself? What other details did you leave out of your report?"

"I didn't know O'Neil was dead, I figured he was just hurt. But him being dead takes care of our problem, right?"

"That remains to be seen. The Colfax County Sheriff has issued an all-points bulletin for two men in a green pickup, along with a press release asking for any witnesses. It seems another man was shot as well, a hunter whose timing and choice of hunting grounds turned out to be a terminal mistake."

Larry swallowed hard, the sound embarrassingly audible. "What'll me and Mel do?"

"We will give you instructions, and you will follow them to the letter. Mel has hidden the pickup at the farm. We'll get it repainted when things have died down a bit. You take the old Camaro we keep in the barn. Drive it into town, get it serviced and fill it up. Mel will drive it."

"Yessir."

"Is that ancient Mercedes you stole from your ex-boss still running?"

"Yeah, it runs good. I mostly just drive it around town."

"Are your tags up to date?"

"Yessir, I've been real careful about that ever since you fixed the title and all."

"Excellent. We wouldn't want you to attract the attention of the local gendarme."

"The what?"

"The law." Bellamy snorted into the phone. Like the airbrakes on an eighteen wheeler, the puff of air blasted into Larry's ear. "How have you managed to survive this long with such a miniscule brain?"

What kind of messed up pleasure did Bellamy get out of making fun of Larry's lack of education? Just because he'd dropped out of school didn't mean he didn't know stuff. He wanted to remind his boss that several of the ideas used to streamline the operations at Bellamy's chicken farm had been his. And that the farm's website design had been all Larry's doing. He wanted to yell that into his boss's ear, but thought better of it. Far be it from him to deprive Bellamy of one of his favorite pastimes. Besides, he made it a practice never to buck anyone who could handle sharp instruments the way the old man did.

And then, of course, there was Bellamy's *collection.*

One of the first things the boss had done after hiring Larry and Mel was to take them to his basement and show them his pride and joy. He'd laughed and said there were people who'd give an arm and a leg to own the things he'd spent the past twenty years accumulating.

A feeling washed over Larry—a feeling his ma used to say meant a goose was walking over his grave. He clamped his jaws together so tight his neck started to ache.

"You will watch the sister," Bellamy was saying. "She is not to see you or suspect she is being followed. It is within the realm of possibility that she might yet find the items O'Neil took."

"What should I do if she does turn something up?"

"In that event you are to notify us immediately. Oh, and make sure Mel doesn't pull any more stupid stunts. If something suspicious happens to the sister, the law will investigate everyone associated with both of them. We don't want to have to deal with that kind of heat."

Beads of perspiration popped out on Larry's forehead and upper lip and an all too familiar feeling started up a hum along his nerves—the same feeling that made him leave Amarillo without even packing up his belongings. He hadn't understood the reason for it at the time, but later he'd learned he escaped only minutes ahead of his ex-boss's two shooters. And now here was that feeling again.

Bellamy smacked his hand on his desk, the sound loud in Larry's ear. "Well? Moan. Grunt. Make some sound to indicate you understand."

"Yessir, I got it."

"And another thing, find out if O'Neil rented a freezer locker, or any storage unit with electricity, for that matter. If he did, we only have about one month before the owner is legally allowed to break into it and auction off the contents. At that point, the proverbial *poo* will hit the fan. And you know what that means."

"Yessir." It meant every man for himself.

Chapter Six

Tim's body was released for burial the next week. The funeral was held in the church where Frankie served as music director and organist. Her boss, Pastor Dan, offered a lovely eulogy, and her choir sang an exquisite anthem to the filled-to-capacity gathering. Although heartbroken, it comforted her to see how many people her brother's life had touched.

Once home from the cemetery, Frankie pulled a recorded pipe organ concert out of her collection and slid it into the player. She walked to the new leather sofa in her living room, kicked off her black patent leather heels and sat, her legs drawn up underneath her. With her head rested on the back of the sofa, she closed her eyes and allowed the majestic sound of Widor's "Toccata" to pour over her as the dammed up grief for her brother broke loose.

She had just picked up a pile of soggy tissues and headed toward a waste basket when the sound of an all-too-familiar, disembodied voice made her hand freeze in midair.

Please help me…

Frankie cocked her head to one side, listening.

Please…

The tissues slid from Frankie's suddenly-numb fingers. She braced herself against the wall to keep her knees from buckling. "Stop it. Go away," she said to the empty room.

Please help me. Don't let her…

"I said go away." Frankie's voice rose to near-screech level, so distorted she barely recognized it as her own.

Like a goldfish dropped onto the floor, she opened her mouth wide, sucking great gulps of air into her lungs. She stumbled to a table in the entryway next to the front door, grabbed up her purse and pulled her phone from the leather holster attached to the side of the bag. Barely able to control her trembling fingers, she punched a pre-set speed-dial. The phone was picked up at the other end after two rings.

"The offices of Doctors Angela and Peter Demaris, Raynell Lavender speaking. How may I help you?"

"This is Frankie O'Neil. I have an appointment with Doctor Angela Demaris next week, but I was wondering if you could work me in sooner…maybe sometime tomorrow?"

"Is this an emergency?" The young-sounding female receptionist's voice, undoubtedly modulated to soothe the savage beast, flowed with her version of gentle understanding—something for which she'd probably earned high marks in Receptionist Training 101. But for some reason Frankie couldn't fathom, rather than calming her, the sound scraped along her already raw nerve endings.

"I guess that depends on your definition of the word. But I would like to see her as soon as possible."

The phone first went dead, then pulsed with Muzak while the receptionist checked the doctor's schedule. Her eyes drawn to the snotty tissues on the floor, Frankie chewed on her thumbnail. She winced when her teeth tore a sliver of nail too close to the quick and sucked at the resulting drop of red.

The sight jerked her memory to the vision of Tim's blood pouring from his marred face. To the thick redness pooling on the floorboard at his feet, and to her clothes drenched in it.

"Hello, Miss O'Neil?"

"I'm still here."

"You're in luck. Doctor Demaris has had a cancellation for three tomorrow afternoon."

"Perfect. I'll be there." Frankie hung up and hugged herself.

What would the therapist say when she told her about hearing voices? Would the expression on her face change from the standard I'd-like-to-help warmth into the wide-eyed, yikes-you're-crazy stare?

Frankie stood in her entryway and cried. She had no one with whom to share her fears. No one to just be there for her. She had only herself to depend on. And now even that was beginning to look shaky.

Words like *crazy*, *cracked*, and *wack-o* floated through her mind.

"Dammit," she said to the cosmos. "Dammit, dammit, dammit."

Chapter Seven

Frankie awakened early the next morning. The sun poured through her half-open venetian blinds and lit her room with a cheeriness she recognized but didn't feel.

Still in her pajamas, she padded to the kitchen and made a pot of her own special blend of chai tea. As she sipped from a steaming cup of the fragrant, spicy brew, she stepped over to the large pantry she'd had installed, pulled open the wooden accordion doors and slid her eyes over the rows of items stored there.

Cans of asparagus, green beans, peas, and turnip greens sat next to yellow wax beans and corn. Sweet potatoes and carrots sat alongside cans of miscellaneous fish and meats. Bags of dried beans, peas and rice lay next to the cans, and four five-gallon bottles of water stood on the pantry floor amid cases of packaged soup mix and marinara sauce.

She adjusted the cans so that the labels faced outward and placed the most recent purchases at the back of each row, checking the expiration dates as she went. She felt relieved to find that nothing would need replacing for the next several months.

Fruit—that's what was missing.

She added the word to her shopping list and wrote *twenty dollars* next to it.

Finances would be tight this month. She twisted her lips in a wry smile. Okay, so she'd pay the minimum on her Visa instead of the two hundred dollars she'd promised herself. Problem solved.

At least she'd had enough savings to cover the cost of Tim's funeral. The young mortician, a scion of the owner operator, had been kind. His voice had been pitched low in well-rehearsed, comforting-the-bereaved mode as he showed her the photos and itemized expenditures of the funeral packages available. Frankie had nearly swallowed her tongue at the prices before settling on a modest but lovely blue polyester-lined casket in spite of the guilt trip the young man laid on her.

"This will be your brother's final resting place. Of course you'll want to do right by him."

"Actually," Frankie had responded, "this will merely be his body's resting place. My brother is no longer here. And if he were, he'd be yelling at me to have him cremated and use the savings to help someone in need."

An image had blown through Frankie's mind of the casket maker's employees sifting through the landfill, collecting plastic milk and water jugs to melt down and mold into their obscenely over-priced wares. The memory of the crestfallen look on the young man's face brought a grim smile to her face.

After another sip of tea, she touched each can exactly three times before doing the same with the packages, bags, and bottles. Then she moved to the hall closet and performed the same ritual with the food stored there. As usual, the process calmed her, soothed her.

Back in the living room, she stood staring through the picture window at Tim's old Volvo. The vehicle's once-shiny, emerald green paint had oxidized to a dull matte finish. The interior had the unmistakable smell of an old beater, and the odometer read two hundred thousand miles. But she'd keep it. Tim's nearly palpable presence was a comfort to her as she sat in his driver's seat. The good news was the engine still ran so smoothly as to be nearly silent.

She'd decide what to do with her Jeep once it had been cleaned up and repaired. One thing was certain— she could never again drive the vehicle in which her brother died. The image of its interior horrifically baptized in his life's blood would haunt her dreams for the rest of her life.

The hungry whine of her stomach pulled her attention back to the present. She returned to the kitchen and filled a plate from the truckload of food brought by the members of the church where she served as choir director. A breakfast of ham and sweet potatoes was nutritionally sound, wasn't it? Couldn't be any worse than cold pizza. Reflecting that she should probably have something green, she spooned lime gelatin into a cup.

When the microwave dinged its all-done bell, she noticed for the first time the blinking light on the landline sitting next to it. Like the warning beacon before an approaching train, the phone's built-in answering machine blinked six times. Six messages.

Frankie had initially kept the outdated phone because it belonged to her Uncle Mike. But after a solar flare jacked up her android's reception, she decided to maintain the landline's service. She pressed the replay button.

The machine's pseudo-human voice announced the

dates and times of each message, the first of which had been left nearly one week earlier. All the messages were from the same young male. And although the first message was spoken in matter-of-fact tones, each successive message grew in intensity and decibel level, until the final one, which dropped off to more of a pleading whimper.

"Miss O'Neil, this is Greg at...at The Regal Scratching Post. Could you please come and get your cat? Um...could you do that, like, right now?"

Collette. She'd completely forgotten about that damned cat.

Frankie wolfed down her breakfast, ran to her room and dressed, grabbed Tim's car keys and headed for the door.

****

As Frankie entered the Regal Scratching Post's front door, a young man walked from behind the counter and approached her. He wore khaki pants and a green Henley style tee shirt with the establishment logo appliquéd on the left side of his chest. Embroidered in neon yellow, the name Greg had been stitched on the right. The young man sported brightly-colored cartoon character bandages on his face, arms, and hands.

Frankie introduced herself.

"Thank goodness you've come." Greg rubbed his index finger over the bandage on his chin, his eyes so wide the whites showed all around the brown irises.

"I'm sorry, I've had a death in the family. I only just got your messages a few minutes ago."

"It's a good thing you came today." Greg moved close to Frankie, his voice low and conspiratorial. "Mom Blatney was going to take your cat to the pound this afternoon. And they only keep animals there for a few days before putting them down."

"Mom Blatney?"

Greg nodded. "The owner. She makes us all call her Mom." He wrinkled his nose as if he'd just caught a whiff of something disgusting. He leaned in closer and lowered his voice even more. "Personally, I don't even want to think of anyone getting close enough to actually make her a mom, if you know what I mean."

Unsure of how to respond, Frankie said, "Ah."

After motioning for her to wait in the foyer, Greg disappeared through a metal door. In a couple of minutes, an older woman—apparently the infamous Mom Blatney—walked back through the same door. With the light of battle shining in her eyes, the woman approached.

Somewhere in her mid-sixties, Mom Blatney resembled a grandma from the 1950s. Silver hair in tightly permed rosettes rested above gray, doe eyes. Her mid-calf-length dress—a veritable meadow of floral print fabric pulled tightly over what appeared to be two thick sofa cushions jammed together and fastened to her chest—hovered above black slip-on clogs.

The woman's voice, however, took Frankie by surprise. The *basso profundo* rasp reminded her of the sound her garbage disposal once made when she dropped a teaspoon into its grinder-maw. The attendant effluvium of stale cigarette smoke suggested the cause.

"I deeply regret that we cannot continue boarding your creature." Mom Blatney then embarked on an extended diatribe highlighting the dangers of spoiling one's pets.

Frankie fought back the instinctive sympathetic

urge to clear her own throat during the woman's phlegm-rattling rant.

"It's popular for pet owners to treat their animals like little people wearing fur coats." Like an air-impact drill removing lug nuts in a machine shop, Blatney's barking voice resounded off every hard surface in the office. "That's nonsense. It's neither good for the pet, nor its caregivers. Our animal friends not only need to be disciplined, they expect it."

Suitably chastised, even if only by proxy, Frankie studied the tops of her shoes.

"Greg will take you to Collette." Blatney sniffed and peered down her lumpy nose at Frankie. "None of my staff is willing to approach your animal. You'll have to gather her yourself."

Greg materialized from somewhere and escorted her into the back of the building. Alternate hissing, meowing, growling and purring filled the air. Someone had sprayed air freshener, but the fragrances of vanilla and lilac had long since given up their heroic battle with the *essence du* boarded pet urine and feces-soaked litter boxes. Frankie's stomach tightened.

Greg unclasped the door to Collette's kitty-condo and quickly stepped back out of attack range. Unsure of what to expect, Frankie approached the cage, holding the open pet carrier in front of her like a warrior's shield.

A gaggle of Pet Pals stood silently by in high anticipation. But in an act of anticlimactic insouciance, Collette first shot withering glances around the room then went passively from cage to carrier.

Frankie smiled inwardly at the stark disappointment on the faces of the encircled staff. She latched the carrier's door, and made her way back to the front desk.

Mentally calculating how many months it would take her to pay off the ludicrously high fee, she plopped down her Visa. She breathed a sigh of relief when it wasn't rejected for being maxed out, hoisted the pet carrier and made for the exit.

As the door shushed closed behind Frankie and the conspicuously docile Collette, Mom Blatney hurled her voice at them like the Biblical stones out of David's slingshot. "Consider taking our Perfect Pet Parenting class. It would do you both some good."

Once back at her vehicle, Frankie lifted the carrier onto the back seat and peered in at the scowling kitty face staring back at her. "Perfect Pet Parent? Please. A Perfect Pet class…now that's an idea."

Collette shifted inside the confined space, showing her backside to the world. Most likely the kitty equivalent of giving someone the finger.

Frankie chuckled. "Brat. Wait 'til your daddy gets back."

She'd just climbed into the driver's seat and buckled up when a flash of light caught at the periphery of her vision. She instinctively turned her head toward the source—an ancient Chevy sitting a few spaces away. Sunlight reflected off the other car's windshield, making it impossible to see the driver's face, but Frankie was certain she'd seen the vehicle a couple of times that day, once driving down her street and again at a gas station.

Coincidences did happen. That's why someone made up the word. But even as she argued with herself, the tiny hairs on the back of her neck stirred.

Chapter Eight

Dr. Angela Demaris was Frankie's fourth therapist since her divorce. She'd dropped her first therapist after he sat staring at her breasts and dubbed her recurring nightmares unresolved sexual fantasies. She dropped the second when his habit of picking invisible lint off his trousers suggested her story bored him to near catatonia. And she dropped the third therapist when, after seeing her only once, he diagnosed her with a mental disorder and wanted to start her on powerful, potentially lethal medication.

She'd found Angela's office by closing her eyes and randomly placing her index finger on a listing in the yellow pages. Having passed Frankie's tests for empathy, intelligence, sense of humor, and compassion, Angela seemed to be the best choice yet.

During the first few sessions, Frankie would be expected to metaphorically spill her guts onto Angela's geometrically patterned rug to bring the therapist up to speed on her issues. Since the health insurance her church job provided would cover only a few sessions, the knowledge that time was limited prompted her to talk as fast as she could. Once the insurance ran out, she'd be on her own, and there was no way she could personally afford the over three hundred dollars per hour Dr. Demaris charged.

"When did you begin to hear voices?" Angela's

voice was deep, somewhat husky. She leaned forward in her chair and her kind eyes studied Frankie's face.

"I first started hearing them shortly after my divorce three years ago."

"And how have you coped with your divorce?"

You keep doing that come-here-go-away thing. What's that about? Either you want me in your life or you don't. At least I have buddies, guys I can hang with. But you? You don't have one single close friend. Stephen's last words rang in Frankie's head. The words he'd flung over his shoulder as he walked out the front door of their apartment.

She responded to Angela's question with a shrug. "Okay, I guess. It took several months for me to realize my marriage was actually over. I always thought Stephen and I would get back together, that we were just going through a rough patch." She snorted. "Boy, was I ever wrong."

"Oh?"

"For the first few weeks we stayed in touch. But the phone calls grew further and further apart. Then about six months ago I caught sight of him with another woman in a health food store. They were pushing a stroller and looked happy as clams." She took a deep breath and blew it out through pursed lips as the scene rushed back with the intensity of a Wagnerian opera.

She'd ducked back out the door, but not quickly enough to keep the sight from searing its image into her brain. Like the phantom shadow burned into a laptop screen when a static image is left too long, the picture of that happy little family popped into her head when she lest expected it—the fond smiles, Stephen's protective arm around the woman's waist, and the cooing, gurgling human that was his tiny, pink-faced replica. The snapshot mocked her, accused her.

"Tell me about your marriage. Was it happy?"

"Happy is not a word I'd use to describe it."

"Unhappy?"

"Not at first. Stephen was a Bad Boy…That seems to be the kind of guy I'm attracted to." Frankie shrugged, cast her eyes upward, and searched her memory. "Let's see, there was Paul Scranberry in grade school who later drove a limo for a drug lord, David Crandosh in middle school who was later indicted for white collar fraud, and Allen Tukes in high school who was an anarchist. Not sure what became of him."

"How did Stephen fit your definition of Bad Boy?"

"Pretty much how you'd guess. He loved to party and drink, spent more time with his drinking buddies than he did with me. More than once he smelled like perfume when he came to pick me up for a date. But he was so possessive of me, so jealous. I thought he must love me madly. I grew up in a sheltered environment, never knew anything about the kind of life he lived. It seemed so full of adventure and excitement, so…" Frankie waved her hand in the air. "So anything-but-boring. Of course I couldn't wait to marry him."

"And you chose to keep your maiden name?"

"Yes. I perform four to six pipe organ concerts a year; it's my professional name."

"Ah." Angela nodded. "Whose idea was it to break up?"

"Stephen's, would you believe?" Frankie snorted again.

"How did you feel about that?"

"I was crushed. I mean, isn't it usually the woman

60

who wants out?" Frankie shook her head and looked at the floor. "He told me I was afraid to jump in with both feet, that I always held something back. He said he knew I never really loved him."

"And did you love him?"

"I must have. I mean...I think so. I've missed him, missed having someone." Frankie's face screwed up into a tight wad of flesh. She probably looked like one of those hand-carved, dried-apple-heads she'd seen during a trip through the Ozarks. Dried up. That was going to be her future—a dried up old woman. She sniffed. "But relationships always bring problems, don't they? All relationships. You let yourself love someone, and they move away. Or stop loving you. Or they die." She shook her head, a couple of tight little jerks. "I decided a long time ago that it's better not to get sucked in too deep. Life's easier without having to wait for the freight train you know is just waiting to run you over. It's like...I mean, why just stand there waiting for the bullet that'll tear out your heart? Seems like a no-brainer to me."

Angela sighed. "So you avoid the pain of loss by keeping everyone at arm's length. How has that worked for you so far?"

Frankie blew a puff of air through her stiff lips. "I'm getting by."

Angela's face softened, as did her voice. "You've gone through a divorce, you've lost the uncle who raised you, and you've seen your brother killed before your eyes. In spite of your efforts, in a fairly short time you've sustained a great deal of what you're trying so hard to avoid. No one could suffer that much loss and remain unscathed."

"Oh, I'm definitely feeling pretty scathed." Frankie snorted. She forced her lips upward at the corners, but the rest of her face felt like a slab of concrete.

"Humor can be a great coping mechanism. But if you continue to work with me, you'll have to face your losses head on. No holds barred and no exceptions. Are you up for that?"

"I'm willing to do whatever it takes."

Angela nodded. "Glad to hear you say that. And I'll do my best to help." She smiled again. "Have you been in any relationships since your divorce?"

"Not really." Frankie picked at her thumbnail. "Unless having tea with my elderly neighbor every couple of weeks counts."

"You have a great sense of humor. But just so you know, whenever you deflect a question by tossing out a meaningless response, I'm going to call you on it." Angela smiled to soften her words. "Let me be more specific: have you been involved romantically with anyone since your divorce?"

"I haven't...no one else has... No."

"So what do you hope to get out of our sessions?"

Frankie shifted her eyes toward the room's single window and focused on the deep burgundy leaves of a Japanese maple and the blue, cloudless sky beyond it. "I just want to have a normal life. I can't remember ever feeling normal."

"Having what you think of as a normal life and feeling normal are two different prongs of the same fork. Describe your version of a normal life."

Frankie turned her eyes back toward the therapist. She lifted her hands in front of her, palms outward, as if trying to stop a charging bull. "I guess the first thing I want is for the voice to stop." She grew thoughtful. "And I'm tired of always having a knot in my stomach."

"People carry their emotions in different parts of their bodies. Some develop stiff necks and shoulders, and some carry their fear and anxiety in their stomachs. But therapy is a little like lining up dominoes. You push one over, and the rest will follow."

"Okay, what's the first domino?"

"Let's begin with the voice. Do you recognize it?"

Frankie shook her head. "When I'm stressed I hear my uncle telling me what to do. But this child's voice is different. Sometimes it seems familiar, sometimes not."

"And when do you hear the child's voice? What are you doing when it's most likely to speak to you?"

"It sometimes comes in a dream, but it can happen anywhere. It's even popped up while I'm in the middle of choir practice."

"And what kinds of things does it say?"

"She usually cries and begs for help. Sometimes it's like she's talking to someone else, and I just overhear it."

"She?"

"Yes." Frankie took a deep breath in through her nose and slowly let it out through her lips. "I don't know why… It just seems like it's a little girl's voice."

"And what does she want you to help with?"

"She never actually says. She just cries and pleads." Frankie sucked in another gulp of air.

"Can you tell me what's going on with your breathing right now?"

"I sometimes hyperventilate. Have done since I was a kid."

"Do you need to take a break?"

Frankie shook her head. "I think I need to keep going."

"Okay." Angela's smile was gentle. "Does this child ever ask you to hurt yourself or someone else?"

"No. But it breaks my heart that she's so scared."

"You're wringing your hands. Can you tell me about that?"

"I guess I'm dreading what you're going to say."

"What do you fear I'm going to say?"

"I don't know. I…I guess I'm afraid you'll tell me I'm losing my mind. My last therapist told me I was borderline schizophrenic."

"Oh? And how did you feel about that?"

"At first I was pissed. It might be denial, but I don't agree. I mean, do mentally ill people recognize they have a problem?"

"It's been my experience that they often do."

"But schizophrenia? I mean, wouldn't I be doing things like wearing aluminum pyramid hats, or living on the streets?"

"Not necessarily. That diagnosis covers a pretty broad spectrum of issues. Although, sadly, some people suffering from that disorder do wind up on the street due to lack of resources, I have schizophrenic clients who do quite well once we get the right medication going." The therapist cocked her head. "But let's get back to the voice. Tell me what you feel when you hear it."

Frankie clasped her suddenly-clammy hands together under her chin and forced her breathing to slow down. "Terror. Sometimes it's so strong I feel like I can't breathe."

Angela leaned forward in her chair, her face intent on Frankie's. "How long does the terror last?"

"Until I tell her to stop and go away."

"Does that work?"

"At first it did, but lately not so much."

"And that feels like…" Angela left the question open for Frankie's response.

"It feels like she knows she's running out of time."

"Before what?"

"I don't know." Frankie opened her mouth wide and pulled in a lungful of air. "But whatever it is, I have a feeling I'm not going to like it."

Chapter Nine

In a chamber atop a morgue attached to an Albuquerque hospital two rubber-apron clad cutters sat on stools at their stainless steel work station tables. It was the cutters' job to harvest ligaments, tendons, and other tissue from the continuing stream of human remains donated to the hospital's Willed Body program. Once excised, the flesh would be packaged and transported to a nearby facility for cleaning.

Various body parts lay on the table in front of one cutter. Two arms and a leg rested side by side along one edge of the table, mutely awaiting their turn under the knife. The cutter's blade skillfully flashed over a partially skinned head from which the eyeballs had already been harvested.

On the other table lay a complete human cadaver, as yet untouched. The second cutter retrieved a long-bladed butcher knife from a pile of instruments of various sizes and shapes with which he expertly removed the corpse's arm at the shoulder joint. He whistled a tuneless melody as he moved around the table to do the same with the other arm.

At some point, one of the cutters would retrieve the leftover bones to which bits of flesh still adhered. He would wire a metal tag etched with specimen data to each bone and put it into a plastic bin for transport down the hall to the Colony.

In the Colony area, the cutter would place the bones on a gray paper tray then cover the whole thing with moist paper towels. He would then introduce the bones to a colony of dermestid beetles. In less than a week, the flesh-eating insects would have completely cleaned the soft tissue from the bones, which would then be treated and sold to medical schools, research facilities, and medical practitioners for use in replacement surgeries.

The whistling cutter, Hector Cordero, glanced at his watch. Time for his lunch. His mouth watered at the thought of the handheld burrito his wife packed for him: pinto beans, *carne adovada*, *queso*, and red chile, all wrapped in a homemade tortilla made of *masa*.

Hector sighed. At least he would try to enjoy his lunch. It was growing more and more difficult for him to enjoy anything these days. Ever since that *cabrón* Bellamy and his enforcer came to Hector's modest home, his life had grown steadily less comfortable.

The empty-eyed Bellamy was smooth, even courteous as he made his demands. But the other one, the one Hector referred to as *El Dedo* because of his disfigured little finger—that one had the unmistakable look of one to whom violence came easily.

Before giving in to Bellamy's demands, Hector had spent hours searching for a way out of his deal with the devil. He'd considered quitting his job at the hospital and finding other work. But his wages were better than any he'd had since coming to this country. And the health care benefits covered his little daughter Anna's steep hospital and medical bills.

Born and raised in the streets of Juarez, Hector had known some very bad men. But the way El Dedo had stared at his nine-year-old baby Anna made the hair on Hector's neck stir and his insides turn to stone.

That look had ensured Hector's compliance.

And now he was in too deep. If the law found out about his role in this ugly business, Hector would go to prison, leaving his family unprotected.

A man of abiding and optimistic faith, Hector prayed every morning and every night to the Blessed Virgin for intercession. But even as he prayed, he kept his eyes open for the opportunity to quit his dance with the devil. He didn't doubt for one minute that Our Lady would present such an opportunity when the time was right.

Hector stuffed the last bite of burrito into his mouth. He licked the red chiles' liquid fire off his fingers, washed his hands, and went back to work.

****

Her morning can-counting ritual completed, Frankie retrieved the business card Nick Rollins had given her. She punched the number into her phone. A woman answered on the fifth ring and identified herself as the dispatch operator for the Colfax County Sheriff's Department.

"This is Frankie O'Neil. May I speak to Deputy Nick Rollins please?"

"He's in the field. But if you'll leave your number and a message, I'll see that he gets it. He's good about returning calls."

"Would you please tell him to call me?" Frankie repeated the number in case the deputy had misplaced it.

"Wait a second, Deputy Pritney just came in. Would you like to speak to her?"

"I think I should speak to Deputy Rollins. He's the one who's been working with me."

"Deputy Pritney and Deputy Rollins work cases together. Hold on, I'll get her for you."

After a couple of beats, Pritney's voice came over the line. "Hello, Miss O'Neil. How can I help you?"

"I was just wondering if there's anything new in the investigation of my brother's death."

"It's ongoing." Pritney's voice was cool, the words crisp. "Have you remembered something?"

What the hell was the attitude about? Frankie could almost sense the statuesque, raven-haired woman rolling her eyes at the phone. "No, I haven't. But Deputy Rollins told me I could call for updates."

"Okey dokey. I'll let Nick know you called." Pritney's voice lingered on her partner's first name, the implied message clear regarding their relationship. "One of us'll be in touch if anything important comes to light. Bye now." The deputy hung up with a dismissive click.

Other than Pritney's physical appearance and suspicious demeanor, Frankie barely remembered her from their sole encounter at Kate's. Had she committed some kind of chain-of-command *faux pas* by telling the operator she preferred to speak with Deputy Rollins?

She pulled a couple of cans of sugar-free fruit cocktail, pears, and peach slices from the market shelf and slipped them into her shopping cart. She reached for a can of cherry pie filling just as her cell phone rang. She tapped her ear bud and answered.

"Hello, Miss O'Neil," Nick Rollins said. "Dispatch said you called."

"Yes. Deputy Pritney said there's been no progress

in the investigation?"

Frankie placed her items onto the conveyor belt at the checkout. The canned fruit was more expensive than she'd realized. She'd have to cut something else from her budget this month. Damn.

A young man she assumed to be a market employee motioned that he would carry the shopping bags to her car. She absently nodded agreement.

"We've had no response to the all points," Rollins was saying. "We questioned the locals, but no one admits to seeing or hearing anything out of the ordinary. We haven't found a weapon or any other evidence that might help find the men you said followed you."

"The men I said followed us?" Frankie's voice rose in pitch. Why did everything that came out of the deputy's mouth irritate her?

Seemingly unaware of the sudden tension in Frankie's voice, the young man placed the bags in the back seat of Tim's car. He closed the door, smiled, and raised his hand to his forehead in a mock salute. But instead of returning to the market, he walked to an old banged-up Mercedes parked several spaces away and got in.

"We found footprints around your cabin, so we know at least two people other than the dead hunter spent some time wandering around there—"

"Right." Cutting off what she knew Rollins was about to say, Frankie's voice shot from her mouth as if fired from a howitzer. "Like I said…they were waiting for us."

"Miss O'Neil, it's hunting season, and your cabin sits right up against federally held land. That's a popular hunting area."

"I don't believe this. Are you really trying to convince me my brother's death was just some hunting accident, like that other poor man? These guys followed us all the way from Albuquerque. They shot at us and then stood around our cabin waiting for us to show up. Does that sound like an accident?"

"Look, we should talk about this in person. I could either make a trip in to town or we could meet somewhere."

Frankie forced herself to take a deep breath so she wouldn't shout her next words into the deputy's ear. "I'll be in Eagle Nest tomorrow to return Kate's clothes."

"I'll be in that area as well, maybe we could meet at the café."

"Fine. I'll see you at noon." Frankie tapped the ear bud off and climbed into Tim's car, where she sat staring through the windshield. Was it possible she'd been wrong? Could Tim's death really have been an accident?

One of Frankie's psychology professors had said that memories are malleable and fluid things, designed to help in the struggle for survival rather than for absolute verity. As subjective products of the mind, memories can metamorphose over time, depending upon need and the chemicals firing in the brain of the one doing the remembering. Was her memory of Tim's death an artifact of her brain functioning in panic stricken, self-preservation mode? Could her mind have manufactured the voices at the cabin? Had she spent several terror-filled hours running through the forest like a mad woman for no reason?

Running through the forest like a mad woman—the words pounded through her head.

What was happening to her? Only a few days ago she'd been looking forward to starting a new life in her new home. And now her life had turned into something out of a horror movie.

With shaking hands and trembling fingers, she started the car.

****

Larry watched Frankie pull out of the market parking lot. He tugged his phone free from his pocket, punched in a number and held the phone against his ear.

"Hullo?" Mel said at the other end of the line.

"Where are you?"

"On my way back to the farm."

"Why have you been following me?"

"I wasn't following *you*." Mel's emphasis on the last word caught Larry's attention.

"Really? Then if you're not following me, who are you following? Because I keep seeing you everywhere I go."

"I figured I could help you keep track of the sister." Mel let go with one of the twisted, little-girl giggles Larry hated. "When you brought the Chevy back to the farm you seemed pretty tense. You know, like you were kind of, I don't know…it got me to worrying, that's all."

Larry grunted. "Right. You don't need to worry about me. You ought to be worrying about what we're going to do if O'Neil's sister finds Bellamy's shit."

"What can she do? She won't know what to do with it even if she does find it."

"See, now that's the kind of thinking that could put

us away for the rest of our lives. All she has to do is show that stuff to the law. They'll connect the dots from there."

Unbroken static on the line indicated Mel was considering Larry's words.

"And don't think Bellamy will jump in to help us," Larry added. "The law won't mess with him. He's got piles of money, as well as friends in high places."

"You know something funny? I don't even remember pulling the trigger."

"I know." Larry blew out a long breath. "I don't hold it against you. It's just the way your brain's wired. But don't worry. I'll take care of things just like I always do." Larry broke the connection.

Mel's inability to control his impulses was a growing problem. He'd nearly got them both killed by skimming money from their boss in Amarillo, and he'd always been quick tempered. Quick on the attack. But lately he'd been doing crap that didn't make sense. Stupid crap, for no reason.

And now it all came down to that O'Neil bitch. Larry had plans for his life. And he had good ideas, ideas that were going to make him rich. She could destroy it all in five minutes. Yessiree, Miss Frankie O'Neil was the real problem here.

Larry started his car and drove out of the parking lot.

Chapter Ten

Once home from the market, Frankie dodged an ambush by a grumbling Collette and pulled groceries from her bags. Finding no space in her pantry, she stashed the canned fruit in her hall closet beside a fifty pound bag of cat food. She scooted the wire hangers to the far left of the closet for another few feet of space.

"At this rate, I'll have to add on a room," she said to Collette.

The cat answered with a drawn out yowl.

"Right. Enough idle chatter. Food coming up."

While Frankie scooped food into the cat's dish, her mind went over her strange conversations with deputies Pritney and Rollins. Where Pritney had brushed her off, Rollins had sounded concerned—like he was taking her seriously. That was at least worth something.

Even though she'd gone through her can counting ritual for the day, she felt compelled to repeat it. With guilt and self-censoring thoughts leapfrogging through her mind, she touched each can, package and box three times. She added a few more times for good measure, until the tightness in her neck loosened and the agitation singing along her nerves calmed a bit.

She put the kettle on, pulled a tin of tea from her pantry, and got a mug from the cupboard. The answering machine's blinking light caught her attention. One blink.

She pressed the playback button and listened to the recorded voice of her boss Pastor Dan reiterating kind words of sympathy and suggesting she take more time off if needed.

She called the church office and expressed her gratitude for her boss's offer, then called various choir members and instrumentalists to ensure the music would be covered for the next two Sunday services. Having one less thing to worry about, she heaved a sigh of relief.

Frankie walked to the mailbox beside her driveway and pulled out today's offerings. She sauntered back to the house, rifling through flyers and sales junk to find one piece of actual mail—a letter from Collette's owner. She tore open the envelope.

Short and direct, the letter said her friend had met and married his soul mate while passing through Jackson Hole. He was in love; life was short; blah, blah, blah. The words at the bottom of the page, however, got Frankie's undivided attention: *The cat is my gift to you. Enjoy.*

"Oh no you don't." Frankie punched a number into her phone. But after one ring, a recorded voice announced she had reached a non-working number.

"Great." She glared up at Collette, who was perched in her favorite spot on top of the new six-foot high bookcase in the den. "We need to come to an understanding, at least until I can find you a new home."

The cat returned Frankie's gaze. Their eyes locked, and a struggle of wills ensued. Frankie was first to blink. "Don't let that go to your head." The memory of Mom Blatney's scolding words hung in the air. "I make the rules. My house, my rules."

Collette licked her lipless chops, stretched, yawned and closed her eyes. The gentle rumble of kitty snoring filled the room.

****

The next morning Frankie made a list of things she had to do to finalize her brother's affairs. A self-professed minimalist, Tim had lived alone. And unlike so many people Frankie knew, Tim had shown no interest in acquiring what he called *stuff*. He didn't own any of the latest electronic toys, even if he could have afforded them—which he couldn't. At least not yet. Instead, he'd purchased a used laptop out of sheer necessity while in medical school, and only recently broken down and bought a prepaid cell phone. As a result, the to-do list was heartrendingly short.

In the absence of a credit history at the time her brother moved into his apartment, Frankie had cosigned his lease agreement. She retrieved her copy of the document from her files and jotted down the number for his landlord.

"I'm glad to hear from you," the landlord said. "I was going to call you this afternoon. Sorry about Tim. He was a good tenant, always paid his rent on time." The man cleared his throat. "When do you think you could come get his things?"

"I guess I didn't realize there was a rush."

"Technically, there's not. Tim's paid up through the end of this month. I told the police as much when they came and searched the place a few days ago. But I have a potential renter who wants to look it over this weekend."

"Of course you do." Frankie struggled to keep her

voice steady. "But as you say, Tim was paid up through the end of the month."

"Sorry." The landlord cleared his throat again. "But life goes on. I would have called Tim's brother, but I don't have a number for him."

"Tim's brother?" Frankie sat bolt upright in the chair.

"Yeah, he showed up a day or so, you know, after the police searched the apartment…said he needed to take a shower and pick out some clothes for Tim's funeral. I let him and his friend in. They seemed like nice guys."

"I'm Tim's only living relative. I don't know who you let into the apartment, but neither of them was a family member."

"Umm." The landlord stammered something unintelligible. "Oh man, I'm sorry about that. You want I should go check the place out to make sure nothing's missing?"

"No, I'll be right over."

The landlord mumbled something again.

"Excuse me?"

"I said so you'll clean out the apartment this afternoon?"

"As I said, I'll be over in twenty minutes." Frankie took a deep breath and let it out slowly. "And please don't let anyone else in before I get there."

She grabbed her bag and Tim's key ring, and headed for the door. Like snow flurries, new questions swirled in her mind, her focus so intense she didn't remember the drive to Tim's apartment.

The investigating officers from Albuquerque Police Department, working with Deputy Rollins as a jurisdictional courtesy, had informed Frankie she could clear her brother's things out of his apartment before his funeral. But she'd kept putting it off.

Unlike in movies where the deceased's will was immediately read to a gathering of sharp-faced heirs, she'd let several days slip by, unwilling to consign Tim's life to the past tense. And now here she stood, rooted to the floor in front of his door, trying to dig up the courage to go through it.

Frankie understood why people chose to leave untouched a deceased or divorced-but-still-loved-one's stuff. She'd left the few things Stephen didn't take with him where they lay for several weeks after he moved out. Things that would have no meaning to another soul—like his stained coffee cup. Even the washcloth he'd used during his last shower seemed almost sacred.

But it was the remnants of his smell that proved to be the toughest thing to deal with. His shower gel fragrance clung to the walls of their shared bathroom, lying in wait to ambush her long after he'd left. That and the slowly dissipating smell of aftershave he'd spilled on the carpet had prompted her to move into a place of her own.

She unlocked the door to Tim's apartment. Although she'd steeled herself against the rush of emotion she knew would come with stepping into her brother's space, she was totally unprepared for the scene that greeted her.

Tim's living room looked as if some deranged poltergeist had found its way into the apartment and invited all his mean little friends to come play. A dismantled chair and pile of sofa stuffing lay just inside the door. Clothes, papers, and books lay scattered everywhere. Pictures had been taken from the walls, their backs removed and tossed aside. Tim's golf bag lay on the floor, half in and half out of the hall closet. Golf balls had poured from the bag's slashed sides and rolled across the floor.

Frankie stepped on a portion of torn newspaper, realizing too late that a golf ball had come to rest beneath it. She spent the next several seconds doing a frantic tango to regain her balance, nearly twisting her ankle in the process.

The scene in the kitchen was of the same natural disaster motif. Torn cereal boxes had been emptied onto the floor. Cabinet doors hung open, their contents scattered onto the counter. A glass jar of spaghetti sauce lay broken on the floor, the dried tomato pulp resembling thick, coagulated blood.

Senseless—did anyone really think something valuable would be hidden inside a jar of spaghetti sauce?

Three fuzzy, blue-gray orbs sat in a bowl in the center of the tiny dinette. The smell of rotted fruit permeated the gnat-filled air. The stench, combined with the unending buzz of various species and sub-species of winged insects, filled Frankie's senses. Her stomach tightened. She swallowed hard, pulled her phone from its holster and speed dialed emergency. Then she retraced her steps and stood just inside the front door to wait for the police.

The responding officer photographed Tim's apartment and dusted for fingerprints. Frankie gave her statement while he typed into a laptop, just as deputy Pritney had done at Kate's café in Eagle Nest.

"This obviously happened days ago," the officer

said. "Is there anyone who can verify whether or not anything is missing?"

Frankie shook her head. "No. My brother lived alone and I've only been here one other time."

"Judging by the valuables sitting in plain sight, this doesn't look like a random break in. It looks like someone either held a grudge against your brother or was searching for something specific."

"I don't know if you are aware of it, but Tim was murdered a few weeks ago. The landlord told me two guys talked him into letting them into the apartment just after the police searched the place."

"We'll check with the neighbors and the landlord to see if anyone saw anything. Hopefully, someone can give us a description of the guys." The officer studied the doorjamb. "No sign of forced entry. Who else had a key?"

"Other than Tim and the landlord, I don't know of anyone."

The officer wrapped up the interview. Though the expression on his face told Frankie not to hold her breath for results, his words assured her someone would look into the break in. He gathered his things and left while Frankie began the task of cleaning up.

Among the books and papers scattered on Tim's desk, she found a notebook with the logo *Flatte and Flatte Financial Services* embossed in white letters on its dark blue, nylon cover. She sat cross legged on the floor, opened the notebook, and thumbed through the papers in it. The corner of a business envelope caught her eye. She opened it and withdrew a letter several pages in length, written in Tim's neat cursive.

Dated a couple of months earlier, the letter

recounted memories from their childhood. Frankie alternately laughed and cried at her brother's descriptions of their shared antics. At the bottom of the final page, beneath his signature and in a different colored ink, Tim had added a final paragraph:

By now you've read my journal and know what kind of mess I got myself into. I know you'll do the right thing with the funds and information I'm leaving. I pray you'll forgive me. I thought at the time I was doing a good thing.

Journal? Funds? Forgive him for what?

A sense of urgency sent Frankie through the living room and kitchen again. But failing to find a notebook, binder, or anything Tim might have used as a journal there, she moved on to his bedroom.

The act of stepping into her dead brother's personal space was almost more than she could bear. Wave after wave of fresh grief washed over her as she went through Tim's closet and chest of drawers. She put useable clothing into a plastic bag for donation, while anything too worn went into a trash bag. She made several trips to her car with important papers and other things she wanted to keep.

Tim's twin mattress had been dragged from the bed and cut open. Clumps of its stuffing lay all around, as if a tiny mattress factory had exploded in the small space.

On the floor, just under the edge of the bed frame, lay Tim's laptop. Briefly wondering why the police hadn't taken it during the initial search, she put it and its power cord into the carrying case she'd found in the top of the closet.

She'd just emptied the refrigerator of two cans of

beer and one bottle of salad dressing when a couple of men from the charity showed up. Frankie explained what had happened and asked them to look around for anything useable.

The men thanked her and rummaged through the apartment. They left as the landlord showed up—a short man who appeared to be somewhere in his late fifties.

"Have the police talked to you yet?" Frankie said.

"Yeah, two of them came to see me a while ago."

"Do you know anything about all of this?" Frankie moved her hand in an arch.

"All's I know is what I told the police. A couple of guys came by asking me to let them in the apartment. One said he was Tim's brother. He said his buddy had picked him up at the airport and brought him here rather than to a motel or to your place."

"To my place?"

"Yeah. He said his sister had moved into a new place and didn't have any furniture yet."

Frankie's breath caught in her throat. Who besides Tim had known that? Maybe he'd mentioned it to someone at work. She searched her memory for anyone she might have told, but came up blank. Stephen had been right—she didn't have anyone to tell.

"Did you describe the guys to the police?"

The landlord nodded his head furiously. "I told them everything I could remember."

"Was there anything remarkable about them, anything that caught your eye?"

"Not much. Like I told the cops, the one that did all the talking had a kind of pockmarked face, like his skin used to be bad. And the shorter one had a smooth, baby face. They seemed like nice guys."

"So you've said." Frankie held her arms rigid at her sides, her hands clenched into fists. "And on the strength of their word you let them into Tim's apartment."

The landlord held his hands up palms outward, as if to ward off a blow. "I'm sorry, okay? I'll return Tim's cleaning deposit to you. I'll cover the cost of having the carpets cleaned and all this junk hauled off."

"Yes, you will." Frankie put the apartment key into the landlord's open palm, slipped the strap of Tim's laptop case over her shoulder, turned on her heel and left.

While still a few steps from her car, her attention was caught by the roar of a vehicle gunning its motor somewhere nearby. Tires squealed, and Frankie turned in time to see an old, dark blue Chevy Camaro headed toward her. Although the driver wore a baseball cap pulled low over his eyes, her impression was of a young man. He turned his head away from her as he sped away.

Could be a coincidence. But unless more than one resident of Albuquerque owned a vehicle of the exact model, make, and color, it had been the same car she'd seen several times over the past few days.

Maybe the driver was a plainclothes detective who'd been ordered to keep track of her in case she decided to leave town. Or maybe the Raton sheriff's office had requested the Albuquerque police watch her in hopes she'd lead them to a den of thieves and cutthroats. But would a detective wear a baseball cap? Or drive a twenty year-old Chevy?

Okay, not the police. Perhaps a con man who'd

found out she lived alone and was intent on scamming her…or a pervert trying to suss out where she lived. Whatever it was, nothing about it felt good.

Maybe she should call the police. Frankie shook her head and snorted. She could just imagine how that scenario would play out:

Police: Do you know the driver of the vehicle?

Frankie: No.

Police: When did you first notice you were being followed?

Frankie: A couple of days ago.

Police: Has the driver threatened you in any way, either physically or verbally?

Frankie: No.

Police: Has he made any effort to speak to you or contact you in any way?

Frankie: No.

Police: Do you know why anyone would want to follow you?

Frankie: No.

An extended silence would be followed by something along the line of: Right. If you'll give me your name and address, we'll add you to our list of local nut jobs…

No, the police would be no help at this point. But something wasn't right. The knot in Frankie's gut told her so. And Uncle Mike had driven into her head the importance of never ignoring her gut.

Chapter Eleven

Something was going on in Larry's insides. Not his actual innards, like gizzard and guts, but the stuff inside people that made them write poetry or sing a love song. Something in him was shifting, changing. Sappy words like *love* and *soul mate* seemed to be growing into solid things—they weren't just words any more.

His face grew warm. That kind of hog's wallow was typical of the Wuss-man. And it was all because of that O'Neil woman. She was working her way under his skin, making him think things he'd never thought before. Warm things. Soft things. Weak things.

He got dizzy just thinking about the intimacies they shared. The way her hair fell over one eye, the sound of her humming while she worked in the yard, and her heart-pounding silhouette when she slipped into and out of her clothes. He found himself thinking about her constantly. Fantasizing about her.

During the daytime he watched her through binoculars from the living room window of the vacant house across the street. The lenses brought Frankie's image so close it seemed he could reach out and touch her, could almost smell her.

At night, dressed in black and wearing a dark ski mask, he parked a block down the street and walked to her house. He'd climb a huge old cottonwood tree a few feet from her bedroom window, where he'd sit, hunkered down among the thick lower branches.

Once certain Frankie was asleep, he'd drop out of the tree, his fall cushioned by the bark mulch at the tree's base, and return to his apartment for a frantic whiz, a dump, and a short sleep. He would set his alarm for five-thirty and be back in position in the empty house before she woke up.

Watching her wander around her house at night was one of his favorite things to do. He loved seeing her prepare for bed. She sometimes forgot to close her venetian blinds and the sheer bedroom curtains were unable to completely blot out her form. It was at those times his imagination would run wild.

He kept telling himself not to let his guard down and do something stupid. But he'd begun to crave the feeling that gripped his stomach as he sneaked around. He savored the way his pulse sped up at the risk of being seen by a nosey neighbor and reported to the police. Adrenaline made every sense pinpoint sharp. It made his heart beat like crazy and his thinking clear as glass.

He'd not survived this long by ignoring the *ping* his gut sometimes sent his brain. At the age of sixteen it told him to get away from his sombitch of a stepfather; it had warned him to leave Amarillo; and now it was warning him to get the hell away from Bellamy.

And it was definitely telling him to get away from Psycho Mel. The guy had proven over and over he couldn't be trusted not to do something stupid. And there was no place in Larry's plan for stupid.

But there was no way he could just up and leave his Beauty. He'd have to be smart. Smart and wily. Because he'd not be allowed to just walk away, especially since he'd witnessed firsthand Bellamy's unemployment and severance policies.

He reviewed the details of his plan. If need be, he could always make minor adjustments. Yessiree, with a little luck everything would work out just fine.

But then, of course, he didn't really believe in luck.

****

"Update?" Bellamy leaned back in his office chair, his mouth tightening at the resultant squeak.

"Miss O'Neil is apparently unwilling to let this all go away," the voice at the other end of the line said.

"Details?"

"She calls several times a day, asking questions and venting her anger. She seems to have found some papers her brother left behind."

"What kind of papers?

"Nothing specific. Just notes."

"That's it?"

"So far. She apparently has no clue about what her brother was involved in."

"Good. We're going to be too busy tomorrow to speak to you, but we will expect an update the day after. And by the way, if you ever again leave a message on our office answering machine you will force us to do something uncharacteristically dramatic."

"I thought you'd want to know her movements."

"That's the trouble, you did not think at all. What if someone else had listened to the message? We cannot afford one iota of suspicion at this point. Is that understood?"

"Yessir."

"We'll give your regards to your grandmama. It seemed for a bit that she was going to need medical attention, but perhaps that can be put on hold."

"If anything happens to her—"

"Now, now. No reason for alarm, at least not yet. It's all up to you." Bellamy broke the connection, cutting off whatever the other person was saying. He glanced at his wristwatch and stood. It was time to check on his Pretties.

Bellamy's drive home was made in a state of eagerness. This was the highlight of his day—a part of his schedule he fiercely protected.

He pushed the automatic garage door opener clipped to the visor above his head. Excitement sizzled through his body as the door silently opened.

As was his custom, once inside the kitchen he made himself a tall gin and tonic. To prolong the exquisite torture of anticipation, he took exactly two leisurely sips then headed toward the basement and the part of his collection he thought best to keep away from prying eyes.

Nothing in his life gave him more joy than being in the presence of his specimens—all human, though many of them appeared to be anything but. He'd seen some fairly extensive collections in museums of natural science around the world, and although he'd been overbid for the testicles of one of the last castrati—still preserved in their original wine-filled pottery jar—to his knowledge, no other individual had amassed a collection comparable to his.

The ice clinking merrily in his drink, he ambled over to the object that had started his collection: a foot with seven toes. He pulled a handkerchief from his pocket and polished the clear, vacuum-sealed glass dome, pleased to note hardly any deterioration in the mummified flesh beneath.

"Beautiful, absolutely beautiful." He smiled and nodded, as if the thing under the dome was whispering the secrets of the universe to him. "We're so glad you like the latest addition. No, we're not done. We've bid on a torso with six arms. Marvelous, don't you agree? A four-armed fetus was just auctioned, but a six-armed adult is a record." He raised his glass in a toast toward the dome. "Cheers."

In near-worshipful silence, Bellamy walked among the bits and pieces the rest of the world would view as monstrosities. No matter where he was or in what activity he was engaged, his Pretties were never far from his mind. But this was more than a collection—it was an extension of him. Not because of any malformation of his own person, but because of the rarity of his carefully selected pieces.

An image of Frankie O'Neil sprang into his mind. She of the tiny hands and feet. She of the striking eyes. Rare eyes, glowing at him from the picture frame in which O'Neil had kept her photo.

How best to preserve those eyes—one sky-blue, the other amber-yellow? Formaldehyde? No, that didn't prevent decay, it only slowed it. And alcohol would alter the cell structure such that bits of flesh would loosen and peel away, destroying the face's loveliness. No, no…that would be unacceptable.

Cryonics was the answer—a complex procedure ending in the head's being submerged in liquid nitrogen and maintained at absolute zero. He'd have to create an insulated, clear glass repository attached to an electric motor capable of switching to battery power in the event of an electrical outage, but that was easily done.

He'd be the proud owner of the only known example of that rare condition called heterochromia iridium. It would be the crowning glory of his collection.

Bellamy threw his head back and drained his glass before heading up the stairs. Whistling a melody from one of his favorite arias, Bellamy locked the basement door and headed for the kitchen, where he put together a chef salad. Then he pulled a dinner roll from a white enamel breadbox atop the gray granite kitchen counter, and poured a glass of dry white wine. He carried everything to his dining table and started to eat.

Of course, he'd have to devise a plan for dealing with Miss O'Neil. An accident would work. Or perhaps a grief-stricken suicide? The possibilities were endless.

Bellamy rubbed his hands together gleefully. What fun.

Chapter Twelve

"She plays the piano in the dark," Larry said into his phone. "She makes up pretty stuff like I've never heard before."

Mel's snort shot across the connection and burrowed into Larry's ear like a boll weevil looking for a home. "Are you getting soft on her? I thought you said she's our main problem. Besides, she's way too old for you."

"She can't be more'n thirty-five or so."

"That's still nearly old enough to be your ma."

"What's your point?"

"I'll bet you're getting excited right now just talking about her. I'll bet you watch her undress and stuff."

"It's not like that. She's—"

"Hey, you don't have to explain nothing to me. I'll bet you haven't had a woman in over a year. Seems like you'd want to find someone willing to share instead of mooning over some uppity slash that wouldn't look twice at you."

"At least the women I've dated have all been conscious and willing."

"Aw, man. You promised never to bring that up. Besides, it was just the once."

"Yeah, yeah. What do you want anyway?"

"Bellamy's pissed. He says he's been trying to

reach you, but you aren't answering your phone."

"Tell him O'Neil's sister hasn't done anything suspicious."

"You'd better tell him yourself. He said for you to call him right now."

Larry broke the connection and keyed in his employer's number while his stomach cranked bile up his throat.

"Ahh, the Prodigal deigns to call in." Bellamy's voice hissed through the ether. "What's the story?"

Larry repeated what he'd told Mel.

"Our songbird indicates the investigation into O'Neil's death has stalled due to lack of leads. Right now the only potential threat seems to be from the sister herself."

"I'm telling you, she doesn't know anything, and she doesn't have the stuff."

"She may know more than she realizes, or she may indeed not know anything at all. But she's digging into O'Neil's affairs, and there is always the possibility she'll stumble upon our property."

"She's never out of my sight. I'll know if she finds anything."

Bellamy's *tsk-tsk* sounded loud in Larry's ear. "You aren't by any chance developing a dangerous fondness for our little Miss O'Neil, are you?"

"No sir." Larry's face heated up and he swallowed hard. "It's just that I've been watching her real close, and I'd know if she found anything."

"That's good to know. However, we have decided upon a different course of action. Your watchful presence at her house will no longer be necessary."

"But how'll we know—"

"Go to the farm and stay there with Mel. We'll be in touch."

"What's the plan?"

"Not to worry, this no longer concerns you." Bellamy broke the connection.

Larry's stomach clenched into a ball. If whatever happened next had nothing to do with him, it most likely had something to do with Mel. And that concerned Larry a great deal. A window in his memory opened. Sights, sounds and smells came into sharp focus as he remembered a scene at Bellamy's chicken farm, just outside the city.

He'd needed help at the loading dock and gone to find Mel. He found him in the barn, stuffing chunks of meat into the chicken feed grinder. Mel's hands and arms were covered in red, his face speckled with red dots. The machine was vomiting out pulverized pink, white, and gray stuff into a tin bucket, the air heavy with a coppery smell Larry knew all too well.

For the next several days, local news reports focused on a missing local woman, her photo and pleas from family members splashed across the television and newspaper. A woman who'd worked for Bellamy.

At least Larry'd had the sense to hide the rifle Mel used on O'Neil and that hunter. His ace in the hole. If push came to shove, he'd give it to the police and cop a plea.

Frankie's silhouette suddenly appeared against her sheer curtains, the sight pushing away every other thought. Something old as life itself stirred in Larry's midsection, and an almost physical pain drew a groan from his lips.

"What would you do if you knew the chances I

take just to be close to you?" he said to Frankie's image. "Would you let me love you if you knew?"

****

It was late by the time Frankie got home from Tim's apartment. Too tired to eat, she made her way to her in-home office, where she had a computer and digitized keyboard, along with the software to interface them.

For the next several hours she wrote music dedicated to Tim. It would become her theme song, and she'd play it at the beginning of all her concerts.

She emailed the music to herself and closed down the computer before showering and slipping into her pajamas. Humming Tim's song, she sat on the edge of her bed and brushed her hair.

A furtive movement slid along the edge of her peripheral vision. She jerked her head toward the window, her pulse instantly skyrocketing. As in every horror movie she'd ever seen, she half expected a misshapen face to peer back at her from the other side of the glass. But no face appeared. Nothing except her wild eyed reflection stared back at her from the black rectangle made semi-opaque by sheer curtains.

A sense of dread ran tentacles across her scalp. She jerked the blinds closed, her hands shaking and clumsy. Whoever demolished Tim's apartment not only knew he had a sister, but knew personal details about her. It seemed ludicrous to think they wouldn't know where she lived.

She thought of Stephen and his little family—of that special softness in his eyes, now focused on his woman and child. And she remembered how safe she'd always felt with him. He may have been trouble, but at least he'd been her trouble. And he'd have known what to do about a peeping tom.

Frankie slid into her bed. She turned off her bedside lamp and pulled her comforter up to her chin. She shivered in spite of its downy warmth.

*****

At the sight of Frankie moving toward the window, Larry scurried back into the shadows. His heart pounded and his head felt light. His body hummed with excitement.

He prided himself on being a self-educated man. Before he started watching Beauty, he'd spent nearly every evening online, asking his laptop questions on every topic from medicine to philosophy. He'd read everything he could find about the subconscious mind, and learned that people got into relationships, ate certain foods, and even read specific books without really knowing why.

That meant Frankie might sense his presence at some level. She might have avoided confronting him because she actually welcomed him. Maybe it made her feel safe to know he watched over her. And maybe she knew that when the time was right he'd come for her.

He smiled into the darkness.

Chapter Thirteen

Once on the road to Eagle Nest, Frankie loaded the CD player with her favorite organ concerts and allowed her mind to float on the waves of sound. Even as she watched for any sign she was being followed, the virtuosity of the contemporary artists poured over her and the miles flew by.

A couple of hours later, she pulled in to the Eagle Nest Café parking lot. She parked next to Nick's patrol vehicle, retrieved the bag containing Kate's clothes, and went inside. The smells of coffee, baking bread and various spices welcomed her.

Kate was wiping the already spotless counter when Frankie walked through the door. The older woman smiled, dropped her cleaning cloth somewhere under the counter, and walked toward her with outstretched arms.

Slender and athletic, Kate was all whipcord and boot leather. Where she'd obviously once been pretty, she'd matured into a sun-wrinkled and handsome woman.

"I can't thank you enough for your help." Frankie held the clothes toward Kate.

Kate accepted the bag and gave the younger woman a big hug. "I'm glad you're okay. Sit, sit. I'll get menus and the necessary *accoutrements*."

Nick Rollins sat at a table near a window. As

Frankie walked toward him, he removed his hat and stood, an old fashioned courtesy rarely seen nowadays. She clamped her lips down on a budding smile as unwelcomed warmth began to spread through her midsection.

"Thanks for meeting me." She took the seat across the table.

Deputy Rollins' welcoming smile lit up his handsome face. Frankie's lips stiffened at the way her treasonous body reacted to the deputy. She gritted her teeth and reminded herself that sooner or later all relationships suck, that people die, or they just stop loving the ones they vowed never to leave.

"This was good timing," Rollins said. "I often come here for meals. Do you think we could have lunch before we get down to business?"

Kate returned with silverware, napkins and menus. Frankie decided on the Parris Island Cobb salad, while the deputy ordered the Semper Fi sirloin burger.

Once their food arrived, the two fell to eating. Rollins talked about his service in the Marine Corps, and Frankie surprised herself by telling him about the extraordinary years she and Tim spent being raised by their Uncle Mike and his housekeeper, her nanny Alma.

As Frankie spoke, the deputy's eyes never left her face. The gentleness of his demeanor set off a warning claxon in her head, and she fought down the urge to bolt for the door. What was happening to her? She was acting like a virgin about to be sacrificed to a volcano god. As if assuring herself of its location, she glanced toward the exit.

"I've never met anyone raised by a Special Forces operative," Rollins was saying. "Your uncle sounds like quite a man."

"He was tough, that's for sure. But he had a soft heart. We never doubted he loved us."

"And every summer he put the two of you through his own brand of survival training. That must have been interesting."

Frankie breathed a puff of air out through her nose. "I guess that's one way of putting it. Uncle Mike was not what you'd call overly affectionate. When we needed hugging, it was Alma we went to."

"It must have been tough to lose him. My grandma is my only living relative, and I'd hate to lose her."

Frankie nodded her head and again slid her eyes toward the exit.

The deputy's face reddened. "That's the fourth time you've looked at the door. You look like a prisoner searching for an escape." Frankie started to protest, but Rollins held up his hand. "No explanation necessary. I didn't mean to interrogate you." He smiled ruefully. "It's an old habit."

"It's just that we were never allowed to talk about the past. Uncle Mike used to say it's the here and now that matters." Frankie scooted her chair back and put her napkin on the table next to her plate. "Look, I need to get going. Any news about the investigation?"

Deputy Rollins made a move to rise from his chair. "I wish I had more to tell you. We'll follow any leads that come to light, but at this point we've hit a brick wall."

"Hit a brick wall as in everything's at a standstill, or hit a brick wall as in something we'll either go around or climb over?"

Nick took a deep breath. "People watch crime

investigation shows on television and think that's the way things work. But we have limited manpower and equipment. I'm not making excuses, just telling you what to expect." The expression on his face pled for understanding.

"Okaaaay. Disclaimer duly noted. It's possible I'm a bit thick, but what does that actually mean when it comes to Tim's murder?"

"Look, there are only two of us working this whole county. That's an area of several hundred square miles apiece. There will not be a group of highly trained, well-equipped crime and forensic specialists focused solely on this case." The deputy sighed.

Heat flared up from the soles of Frankie's feet and into her face. She glared into the deputy's eyes. "I see. So what you're saying is that I should just move along?"

Rollins blinked as if he'd been slapped. "No. I'm trying to bring you up to speed. I've spoken to every storefront operator in Eagle Nest, Angel Fire and Red River. We've found no less than six green pickups, but none with tires that match the impressions."

"Then you haven't found the right pickup." The muscles in Frankie's jaw and neck tightened. "What's the bottom line, Deputy Rollins?"

"We're still looking."

"And what about my Jeep?"

"After forensics is done with it you can pick it up in Santa Fe. It looked like someone went through your luggage, probably looking for valuables. We dusted for prints, but got nothing." He looked closely at Frankie. "I thought you said you were only planning to stay at the cabin a couple of days."

"That's right."

"Then how do you explain the fact that your Jeep was completely filled with canned and packaged food?"

Frankie avoided the deputy's eyes. "I…I try to keep the cabin well provisioned in case we make a spur of the moment trip, or in case we get snowed in. Hard weather came early this year."

Good God, was that the best explanation she could drum up? Everything she said made her look more and more suspicious—even to herself.

Rollins nodded his head as if to say he was trying to understand, but the perplexed look remained in his eyes.

"What do we do now?"

"Look Miss O'Neil, I appreciate how you feel. But there is no 'we.'"

"Then I guess that leaves only me."

The deputy cocked his head to one side and squinted. He shook his head a couple of times. "You've heard of something called 'obstruction of justice'?"

Frankie held her hands up palms out. "I'm not obstructing anything. I'm just a concerned citizen." She lowered her hands, stood, and glared down at the deputy, her arms ramrod straight at her sides. "But it is good to know you'll wait a few more days before tossing my brother's file on top of the rest of your cold cases."

Rollins reached into his shirt pocket and pulled out a business card identical to the one he'd given Frankie at their first meeting. He pulled a pen from the same pocket and scribbled on the back of the card.

"I'm giving you my personal cell phone number. In the event you remember something, call and I'll drop whatever I'm doing." He held the card toward Frankie. "And please don't try to do anything on your own. Think about it—if someone was willing to shoot your brother in front of you, they wouldn't hesitate to shoot you."

And they know who you are, Uncle Mike's voice intoned.

"Now you tell me," Frankie said out loud.

Rollins looked surprised. "It's just logic."

"Sorry, I was talking…I mean…" Her face aflame, Frankie yanked the card from the deputy's fingers and stuffed it into her handbag. She squared her shoulders and strode toward the cash register.

Deputy Rollins' chair scraped on the hard wood floor behind her, but she didn't look back.

Chapter Fourteen

"Right on time," Bellamy said into the phone. "That's more like it. Anything new to report?"

"Not really," the voice at the other end said.

Bellamy held the phone between his shoulder and ear, freeing up his hands to straighten the papers on his desk. "Are you asking us to believe that absolutely nothing has happened in the past forty-eight hours worth reporting? We may have to re-evaluate our cost-benefit ratio with regard to your employment."

There was a pause as the person on the other end of the line apparently considered how to answer. "She's not happy about the whole thing. But in my opinion she'll eventually accept it as an accident."

"Is there something you're not telling us?"

Another pause. "What do you mean?"

"You wouldn't be ill-advised enough to leave out any vital information would you?"

"Of course not."

"That's good. It wouldn't be wise."

"I may be lots of things, but stupid I'm not."

"We sincerely hope that's true. Stay in touch. If she finds something or becomes suspicious, we may have to change our strategy."

"What does that mean?"

"It means exactly what you think it means."

"You said you didn't have anything to do with

what happened to O'Neil, so why would you need to hurt his sister?"

"Just covering our assets, so to speak. However, you're in no position to question either our motives or our actions. Check in tomorrow at the usual time."

"I might not be able to do that. I'm going to be busier than usual."

"Please do not waste our time with your saber rattling. Our agreement has been sealed, or have you forgotten how deeply involved you are in all of this? Must we remind you of the multitude of accidents or illnesses that can befall the elderly? We would hate for your grandmama to suffer an inconvenience."

"You son of a bitch."

"We can be." Bellamy chuckled. "But only if you do not do as you are told."

****

It was late by the time Larry arrived at the chicken farm. The dark squares that were the bunkhouse windows meant Mel had gone to bed. A halogen bulb mounted on a nearby telephone pole threw the buildings into stark relief, lending an eerie feeling to the place.

Larry pulled his vehicle up to the locked, galvanized metal gates. Leaving the engine running, he got out, walked to the gate, twisted his key in the padlock, and pushed against the oblong frame. When the gate was open just enough for him to drive through, he returned to his car and turned off its lights. He drove a few feet into the compound, cut the engine and allowed the car to coast to a stop. Every motion slow and deliberate, Larry again stepped out of the car. After resting the door against its frame to avoid any telltale click, he started toward the bunkhouse.

The smells associated with thousands of chickens living, eating, crapping, dying and moldering assaulted his nose. Just as a pizza parlor employee can grow to despise the smell and taste of anything Italian, he'd developed a dislike for all things poultry. He fought against the impulse to gag.

Almost as bad as the smells, were the sounds. The noises the chickens made in their jammed-up spaces were pitiful. It was like they were pleading for someone to let them out into the sunlight and open air. But it was their eyes that bothered Larry most of all, their frightened, beady little eyes darting around, searching for a way out. He'd often wondered if they somehow understood what was going to happen to them.

His face grew warm. Who cared what the chickens felt, anyway? Yessiree, Wuss-man Larry was in full wuss mode tonight.

The bunkhouse consisted of two rooms: a large living room cum sleeping room, and a tiny bathroom with a shower barely large enough for a single person. In the absence of closets, either for clothing or storage, he and Mel had driven nails into the walls from which they hung their work clothes.

Daily activities at the farm always followed the same format. A handful of workers arrived at Bellamy's only legitimate business around five every morning and left at two in the afternoon. Two or three workers fed the chickens, and cleaned and packed eggs for delivery to local customers. One employee oversaw the feeding and care of the baby chicks in the nursery. Two employees killed, cleaned and packaged the hapless older hens that no longer laid eggs regularly and put them on ice for delivery to a locally owned fried chicken establishment. Any chickens that died overnight were thrown on top of several inches of chicken dung and covered with more dung. In a couple of weeks, the birds would become part of the rich compost sold to local nurseries.

Larry stepped to the bunkhouse door. He slowly turned the key in the lock until he heard the mechanism click then opened the door just enough to glide through. He left the door slightly ajar to ease his silent departure.

Light from the outside lamppost along with half-hearted moonlight sifted through the filthy windows. The combination generated just enough visibility for Larry to navigate the room where he'd lived for the first year he worked for Bellamy.

The snoring lump that was Mel lay on his cot. Larry moved over to the empty bed where he slept when required to stay on the farm, and pulled his clothes from the nails he'd driven into the wall beside it. Between periodic furtive glances toward Mel, he draped the things over his arm, grabbed his work boots and headed for the door.

But a familiar sound froze Larry's hand in midair as he reached for the doorknob—a mewling whine that told him Mel was dreaming again. The attendant thrashing, groaning and whimpering never ceased to freak Larry out, even though he knew of Mel's recurring nightmare. Was, in fact, part of it.

Right after they'd dropped out of high school in Amarillo, Mel had talked Larry into burglarizing a home during the funeral of the wealthy owner. They shinnied over a seven-foot brick wall surrounding the house and climbed through an open window. The two boys filled their pillowcases with jewelry and other small valuables, and then climbed back through the same window.

Once outside, Larry tied the top of his pillowcase in a knot. He threw the bundle over the wall, and climbed over after it. But Mel had filled his pillowcase too full to tie. He was trying to figure out how to get it over the wall without losing any of his treasure, when the deep barks and growls of an approaching guard dog sent him into a panic.

Mel squeaked in fear and frantically threw his pillowcase over the wall, raining plundered stuff onto the ground on both sides. He scrambled to haul himself over as well, but the dog was faster.

His head and shoulders disappeared as the dog must have clamped its jaws around the targeted foot and yanked down. For the next several seconds, growls mingled with Mel's screams and the sounds of thrashing bodies.

Frozen in place, Larry vacillated between feelings of self-preservation and the impulse to help. If the grounds keeper hadn't arrived when he did, the dog would have killed Mel.

The surgeons took several hours to repair Mel's throat and gnawed fingers. The throat wounds left a crisscross pattern of puckered scars that lightened with passing time. But the pinkie finger on Mel's right hand healed wrong. Permanently bent at a ninety degree angle, a pale, fibrous web of skin held the digit tightly in place. The web reminded Larry of a tiny, albino bat's wing.

After doing time in the juvenile detention center, the two had shared a lopsided bond. Mel followed Larry around like a gosling follows its mother, and a guilt-ridden Larry allowed it. Until lately, the relationship had been tolerable.

Experience told Larry he had about a minute before Mel jerked awake, sat up and turned on the bedside lamp. So he did what he'd done before getting his own place: he put his things down by the door, tiptoed over to Mel and shook him by the shoulders.

"Go back to sleep. It's just a dream, man."

Mel never even opened his eyes. He grunted, turned over and fell asleep again almost instantly.

Larry waited until Mel's breathing slowed and deepened into a persistent snore. Like a wraith, he moved back through the bunkhouse. He picked up his belongings, slowly pulled the door open, and stepped into the night.

He backed out the gate and drove up the road a distance before turning on his lights, wracking his brain for any detail he might have overlooked. Though there were a couple more issues to resolve, he felt his plan was good.

Smiling in anticipation, he drove to Frankie's house.

****

Mel came awake slowly. He threw back the blanket, sat up, and put his bare feet onto the floor. He stretched, chuffing as the circulation in his muscles and joints kicked in. Not yet fully awake, he moved his eyes around the bunkhouse. His gaze passed over the room a couple of times before spotting what had been niggling at him.

He reached for the phone recharging on the nightstand, pursed his lips in what Larry called his blowfish face, and speed dialed his buddy. When Larry didn't answer, he broke the connection and tried again. This time Larry's phone went straight to voice mail.

"Hey it's me," Mel said after the beep. "What's up? Your stuff's gone from the bunkhouse and I haven't seen you since you brought the car back. Call me."

Mulling over what Larry's prolonged absence might mean, Mel went to the bathroom, relieved himself, and got dressed in his work coveralls. He picked up his work boots and sat back down on the edge of his bed. From inside one boot he withdrew two soiled and sweat-stiffened socks, which he slid onto feet so dirty they looked like rusted blocks of iron.

With the soles of his boots alternately either sticking to the linoleum floor or crunching on and pulverizing something, he headed toward the coffee pot. He punched the button to start the brew, and tried Larry's phone again. This time when Larry didn't answer, Mel was ready with what he wanted to say.

"What the hell's going on with you? Ever since you started watching that O'Neil bitch you've been different. You'd better call me or I'm going to tell Bellamy you've taken up with her."

No sooner did he end the call than he had second thoughts about his message. What if it wound up doing the opposite of what he'd intended? What if it just pissed Larry off?

Poor judgment—that was Mel's problem. At least that's what his grandma used to say. She said he was born without whatever it was that made people think before they did things. And she ought to know, since she was the one who raised him.

Grandma had sure enough taught him the ways of

the world—he owed her that. If she told him once, she'd told him a thousand times that the world was made up of two kinds of people: those who got hurt, and those who did the hurting. It was the way of things, pure and simple.

He ran his fingers over a lumpy patch of small circular scars on his right forearm as the memory of Grandma's final life lesson slid into his mind. He'd since dubbed the day as Judgment Day—even had the date tattooed on his left ass-cheek.

As usual on lesson day, Grandma had held the red, smoking tip of her cigarette against Mel's arm and waited for him to scream. But this time he hadn't uttered a sound. This time he just stared right back into her eyes without even so much as a blink. Her eyes had opened into huge round saucers, and her jaw dropped as he plucked the burning thing from her fingers and ground it out against her wrinkled, brown-spotted cheek.

But he especially enjoyed remembering the sounds she'd made as he wrapped his hands around her boney neck and squeezed. Squeaky, gagging sounds that made him feel like he could do anything he wanted. Like he could rule the world. He'd never known a person's eyes could bug out so far—except in cartoons, or like one of those rubber doll things with eyes that shot out when you squeezed it.

Even though her face was dark purple by the time he finally threw her against the wall, he guessed she must have survived, because the police hadn't come looking for him.

Mel knew he wasn't real bright. But Larry sure was. He was smart as a whip. And he was the only one in the world who'd ever treated Mel okay—who'd ever seemed to understand him.

Oh, Larry had ragged on him good and proper when he smashed everything in O'Neil's place just for the hell of it. And he'd sure enough been pissed when Mel shot that hunter guy he'd thought was Tim. But he got over it, just like he always got over Mel's mistakes.

Larry even forgave him for getting even with the dog that chewed on him. He didn't speak to Mel for several days after that, except to say the dog didn't mean it personal, that he just did what he was trained to do. But he'd finally come around.

And now all Larry could think about was that O'Neil woman. Her with that thick, shiny hair and tiny feet. She wasn't hardly big enough to be full grown. But Larry was in heat with a capital H, and it was like the years of their friendship never happened. It was like Larry said before that witchy woman put a spell on him: she was the real problem.

The seeds of a familiar black emotion started up in Mel's stomach. It shot roots throughout his solar plexus, the pulse of it threatening to choke him.

Chapter Fifteen

Frankie called the office of Tim's attorney, the name and number of whom she'd found inside the front cover of the Trust notebook. She spoke to an assistant and set up an appointment for later that afternoon to go over details regarding her brother's will. Maybe the attorney would have some answers as to what had been troubling Tim.

The drive to Flatte's office took her through Nob Hill, past downtown, and into Old Town Albuquerque. As if traveling backwards in a time machine, she drove past upscale modernized storefronts and condos, dry cleaners and automotive shops, and into the hundred-year-old square of adobe shops and eateries.

The air in the square was redolent with the aromas of baked breads and tortillas fresh off the griddle. She inhaled the subtle bouquet of beef, chicken and pork simmered in red or green chile. Though she'd already eaten, her mouth watered as the fragrances pricked at her tongue.

A hand-carved wooden sign, crafted to match the building's adobe architecture, announced the offices of Flatte and Flatte, Attorneys at Law. The well maintained xeriscaped grounds boasted a variety of moss rock and indigenous plants geared toward water conservation. A small sign positioned next to a paved driveway discreetly invited visitors to park in the rear.

She did as the sign suggested, then made her way through the front door and to the front desk. She identified herself to the young receptionist, who in turn pointed to several heavy, carved wood chairs grouped around a glass-topped coffee table, and disappeared down a hallway. Frankie took a seat.

Whoever decorated the waiting area must have been the director of a museum or mausoleum in a former life. Heavy, dark wood furnishings sat beneath a collection of original watercolor and oil paintings, their weighty, Baroque frames suspended from silk ropes. An overabundance of native pottery and sculptures rested in glassed-in enclosures atop woven wool rugs. The coffee table boasted a huge silk flower arrangement, so tall and wide Frankie had to crane her neck to see around it. Heavy-handed use of cinnamon aerosol thickened the atmosphere. No whispered offer of aid to the litigious public here—the décor virtually screamed old school credibility and worthiness. By the time the receptionist returned, lethargy had set in and Frankie was in near-snooze mode.

"Miss O'Neil?" The young woman spoke in hushed tones through barely parted lips, as if she'd received her receptionist training from the same undertakers' university as the decorator. She motioned for Frankie to accompany her through an arched doorway and into a spacious office.

A man in his mid to late forties stood from behind an antique oak desk, pushed back his custom fitted, ergonomically perfect chair, extended his hand, and moved toward Frankie.

The man stood at somewhere around six foot-three. His carefully styled, sandy-colored hair flourished above a broad forehead. An artful and precisely symmetrical salting of gray adorned the sides. His tan face offered a sun splashed backdrop against which to display his unnaturally colored eyes, something between lapis and violet. And his face bore a carefully calibrated smile of pure plastic.

The attorney's office attire consisted of lizard skin cowboy boots, designer jeans, and a yellow Polo shirt. He wore a turquoise and silver bolo tie, the style and rich patina of which proclaimed it to be from the 1950s, give or take. A brown tweed jacket, complete with twin leather elbow patches, had been carefully folded over the arm of an overstuffed leather chair in one corner.

"Good afternoon Miss O'Neil, I'm Jeremy Flatte."

Frankie shook the proffered hand, and the attorney waved her toward a wood Mission style chair strategically placed in front of his desk. He reclaimed his seat.

"What intriguing choice of eye color." Flatte placed his elbows on the desk and leaned forward, positioning his manicured hands to best display his diamond-studded horseshoe ring. "But doesn't it mess with your head to see the world through one blue and one yellow contact?"

"I don't wear contacts. It's all DNA. Just weird genetics."

"I see." The attorney's smirk said he wasn't going to fall for that story. "Well, they certainly make for an interesting look."

Frankie's eyes slid upward from Flatte's face to the framed certificates and licenses arranged on the wall behind his desk. That the attorney had earned a doctorate in Jurisprudence from Pepperdine University answered her unspoken question as to why Tim would have hired him. But how had he paid the man's undoubtedly astronomical bills?

"For the most part, Tim left everything he owned to you, with the exception of a couple of small bequests. If you have any questions, I'm at your disposal." The attorney paused, an inquisitive look on his face.

Frankie glanced around the office. "I'm concerned about your fees. Tim only recently graduated from medical school and his student loans are enormous. I'm pretty sure whatever funds are in his bank account will not be enough to continue covering your services."

The attorney rubbed the palms of his hands together. "I don't know anything about Tim's level of debt, but all my fees have been paid in full. My records indicate he always paid within a week of receiving my invoices."

Frankie's eyebrows rose as if by their own volition. "Sorry?" Her voice cracked like a twelve-year-old boy fighting puberty.

The attorney's eyebrows defined a quid pro quo arch at Frankie's surprise. "I said my fees have been paid. You'll want to get copies of your brother's bank records for a full picture of his finances."

Flatte bared his teeth again in what he seemed to think of as a rapport-building smile. He opened a drawer in his desk, pulled out a file about a quarter of an inch thick, and pushed it across the desk. He spent the next several minutes explaining the nature of Tim's will and of Frankie's role as executrix.

"I hope I'm not out of line, but I'm curious about something. Did your brother strike you as being worried about anything?"

"What makes you ask?"

"He seemed uneasy the whole time he was in my office. I don't know how else to describe it, other than to say he acted like a man trying to put his house in order. It's almost as if he knew something was going to happen to him. Then when I read about his, um, his accident, it just seemed kind of ironic."

When Frankie didn't respond immediately, Flatte glanced at his diamond-encrusted watch, pushed his chair back and stood. "Sorry, but I have another appointment." He walked to his office door, opened it, and looked expectantly toward Frankie.

"What do I—"

"Call after you've looked over Tim's financial records. I'm sure you'll have a better picture of things by then."

Frankie did a slow walk back to her vehicle. She'd hoped the attorney might have been able to at least give her a hint regarding what had been going on with her brother. Instead, she was coming away with even more questions.

She spent the rest of the day at her church office, where she made some calls and did some paperwork then stuck her head into Pastor Dan's office to give him an update on her situation.

"This is the first vacation you've taken in three years," Pastor Dan said. "You've got a few days still coming. As long as music for the services is covered, do what you have to do."

After thanking her boss, she tossed a goodbye at the church secretary and headed for the parking lot.

As she neared her car, a flash of blue caught at the

corner of her eye. She whipped her head around in time to see the Camaro speeding directly at her. With only a split second in which to react, she threw herself onto the hood of her vehicle. Frantically, she curled her fingers over the metal lip behind which lay the windshield wipers and held on tight against the impact she felt certain was to come.

But none did. The driver gunned the engine and sped past, barely missing Frankie's flailing legs. He pulled out of the parking lot and burned rubber into the street.

But this time he'd made a mistake. This time Frankie had clearly seen his face.

She slid off the hood to land legs planted wide, her weight on the balls of her feet in fighting posture. Heat pulsed in her blood and pain shot up both arms as her fingernails ground into her palms. She stared at the rear of the receding vehicle, her eyes straining to read the license number that was all but obliterated by mud. Whoever this guy was, he was no longer satisfied with merely following her.

Forewarned is forearmed. As if on cue, Uncle Mike's voice sounded in her ear.

"So speaketh the dead sage." Frankie instantly regretted her tone, even if it was only aimed at the aural memory of her uncle. "Sorry, but if you're going to keep hanging around, at least make yourself useful and warn me *before* something bad happens."

Instead of heading home, she drove to a hardware store. She purchased two lengths of steel pipe that would fit into metal brackets at the sides of her front and back doors, thereby rendering them nearly impervious to break in, two high intensity motion activated lights, a motion activated digitized recording of a large barking dog, a police issue taser gun, and three king sized containers of Man Down pepper spray.

While standing at the checkout counter, she pulled the packaging off one can of pepper spray and put it into her purse. She carried her purchases to the Volvo, opened a second package of pepper spray and put it into her glove compartment.

Once home, Frankie spent a couple of hours installing the Katy bars and setting up the motion activated barking dog. She'd have to wait until the next day to install the spot lights, but at least she'd made progress. And forewarned was definitely forearmed.

"Bring it, ass wipe."

Now if she could gin up the confidence those words implied.

Chapter Sixteen

Next day Frankie installed the spotlights. She attached one to the header above her front door, the other above her back door. If she'd done everything correctly, they'd light up the whole freaking block anytime someone came within a hundred feet of her place.

After she set up the barking dog sound machine, she set it off several times until she was pleased with the volume. Even though she knew it was only a recording, the deep-throated *woof* interspersed with growls made her upper lip break out in a reassuring cold sweat.

Happy with her handiwork, she worked in her herb patch until the sun went down. The smell of sage and basil wafted into the air as she pruned the plants. Warmth from the compost she'd nurtured into dark, rich soil sent waves of earthy fragrance into the air as she turned it with a pitchfork.

The newly planted perennials would, hopefully, erupt after a winter during which they'd sink long, healthy roots. In the spring, she'd sow seeds for the annuals.

She slapped her gloved hands together to dislodge the dirt in which she loved to dig and headed into her house. She'd just engaged the barking dog and was in the process of slipping the Katy bar into its brackets when her conscious mind registered something her subconscious had been screaming from the time she walked in.

She threw the bar onto the floor, grabbed her purse off the kitchen table, yanked the door open and ran back outside. As advertised, the barking dog machine kicked into high gear the instant the back door opened. Her eyes darting around the yard, she fumbled in her purse for her phone.

"Someone's in my house," she said to the emergency operator. Holding the phone so tightly her hand began to cramp, she made her way around the house, let herself out the side gate, and walked to the front. Her eyes surveyed the dark street for any sign of movement, she stepped onto her driveway. Her front spotlight flashed on, momentarily blinding her in its intensity. At that point, she'd have been unable to see anyone, even if he'd been standing on her foot.

The female voice asked some questions and told Frankie to stay on the line, offering assurance that someone would be there soon. Within a few minutes, a police cruiser pulled up, its red, white, and blue lights flashing like Fourth of July fireworks. A couple of neighborhood doors opened just wide enough for the occupants to watch the goings on.

"You've had a break in?" the young officer said.

Frankie nodded and pointed to her house. "I live there. Someone must have come in while I was working in the back yard."

"Did you see the intruder? Can you describe him?"

"No, but I did smell him."

"You smelled someone?" The officer's voice sounded puzzled, but he maintained a carefully neutral expression on his face.

Frankie blushed. "I…I don't wear perfume. I'm allergic, so my nose is sensitive to fragrances. I smelled men's cologne."

"I see." The officer slowly nodded his head while studying her face. "Okay. Please stay right here." He unsnapped the strap on his sidearm and turned toward the front door.

"You can't get in that way." Frankie pointed her index finger and made a circular motion with her hand. "You'll have to use the back door. Um…the front's locked."

Double-bolted and barred. All but sealed with pine pitch. Tim's playful voice teased.

"Not funny," Frankie muttered.

"Pardon me?" the officer said.

"I was just saying it was funny that whoever got in knew to avoid the spotlights."

In a few minutes the officer returned with assurances the house was empty as well as odor free. "At least it was empty except for a cat that nearly got itself shot. Scared the bejeezus out of me. Jumped right on top of my head."

"Sorry. I should have warned you about Collette."

The officer nodded. "And the huge dog I never saw."

"It's not a real dog." Frankie pasted what she hoped was a guileless smile on her face. "It's a digitized recording, supposed to be a deterrent."

"I see." The officer nodded his head as if what Frankie said made perfect sense. But she had a feeling he could hardly wait to get back to the station and tell his pals about the ditzy woman and her Alcatraz cum apocalypse prepper security.

"Did you open a bedroom window after you went back inside?"

"No. Why?"

"The window screen is still in place but the window is open. No way to know if someone used it to gain entrance because of the xeric rocks under it."

"I guess I forgot to close it." Frankie avoided the policeman's eyes.

All that high powered security she'd put in place, and she blithely leaves her window wide open. A side window—the only spot that wouldn't light up like the sun in the face of an intruder.

A door slammed somewhere down the street. Frankie jerked at the sound, her hands flying to her face.

"The lights are not a bad idea." The officer spoke in a gentle voice. "But you may get complaints from your neighbors, especially the nearest ones." He suggested she accompany him through the house to determine if anything was missing, had been moved, or if anything had been left behind that didn't belong. The two headed toward the back yard.

Once inside the house, Frankie turned off the dog. With the officer walking ahead, they made their way through the house while Collette eyeballed them threateningly from atop her usual perch.

Nothing out of place. Nothing missing. In spite of herself, Frankie felt a bit disappointed. If something had been taken, she'd not look like such a looney toon.

Another thought blossomed like a mushroom cloud. Maybe her illness had metastasized and her sick brain was no longer satisfied with merely sending out voices. Maybe it had decided to throw olfactory hallucinations into the mix. She chewed on her thumbnail.

"We'll check with the neighbors," the officer was saying. "Maybe someone saw something." Pretending not to see the deadbolts and the Katy bar as Frankie unblocked the front door, the officer handed her the usual business card with a case number on it and left.

As soon as the patrol car was out of sight Frankie nearly ran to her pantry. She pulled open the doors and touched each of the cans, boxes, and bags of food three times. She ran through the ritual again and again, until her panic began to subside. Then she added an extra time for good measure.

Once her breathing returned to near normal, she went to her bedroom and flung herself onto her bed. She grabbed up the canister of pepper spray kept on the nightstand, placed her thumb lightly on its pressure trigger, and clasped it to her bosom. For several minutes she lay staring up at the ceiling.

What if she wasn't in the process of losing her mind, what if she'd already lost it? What if her body was actually sitting in some institution rocking mindlessly back and forth while her alive-and-well uncle Mike and brother Tim shook their heads and said how sad that Frankie had gone completely mad?

Tears ran down the sides of her face and onto the satin pillowcase.

****

Larry listened to Frankie cry from the shadows outside her bedroom window. He wanted to go to her, to hold her and stroke her hair.

"Don't cry, Beauty," he whispered. "Everything's

going to be okay."

He lifted his treasure to his nose and breathed deeply of its lavender fragrance. At the right time, he would return the blue satin hair ribbon he'd just taken from her bureau. He'd offer it to her, and she would look at him with eyes full of gratitude.

Chapter Seventeen

Frankie sat in a forest green leather chair across from Dr. Demaris. The therapist, sitting with her long slender legs crossed at the ankles, pushed the red button on a small digital recorder on the coffee table, folded her unexpectedly strong, square-shaped hands in her lap and looked into Frankie's face.

"Tell me about the name you've given the voice. Have you ever known anyone named Jenny?"

Frankie shook her head. "I don't think so. It just seemed like a good name for her."

"How would you feel about asking her to tell you what she wants?"

"You mean ask her to talk to me?"

"That seems a good place to begin."

"No offense, but that sounds whacked out. I mean, the whole reason I'm here is to make her go away. Besides, she doesn't really exist, right? She's a product of my imagination."

"No offense taken." Angela smiled. "But our imagination stems from our subconscious. And your subconscious is trying to get your attention by using a child's voice. A child in obvious distress."

"You're saying Jenny's voice is me talking to myself?"

"Pretty much." Angela dragged an empty chair over and placed it in front of Frankie. "Pretend Jenny is sitting in this chair. What would you like to ask her?"

Frankie looked into her therapist's eyes. "I'd want to ask her—"

Angela held up her hand. "Don't ask me, ask her."

Frankie turned her head toward the chair and tried to envision a seated child. "Who are you and what do you want from me?"

At the therapist's instruction, Frankie then sat in the empty chair and pretended to be Jenny. But after a couple of minutes she shook her head. "How can I answer my own questions? I'm sorry, I'm just not getting anything other than what I've already told you."

"It's okay. We'll try something else next time." Angela crossed to the door and held it open. "Your assignment is to get into a dialogue with Jenny. Ask her what she wants from you. Write down whatever she says and bring it to your next appointment."

Feeling like she'd failed an important exam, Frankie left the office.

****

Next morning Frankie awoke out of a troubled sleep. Although she'd heard it was possible to consciously control what takes place in one's dreams, she'd never been able to achieve that state of lucid dreaming. Instead, she awoke in sweat-soaked pajamas with the feeling that things were spinning out of control.

"What do you want from me?" she said into the dawn-lit room.

No answer.

"So you're only going to torment me when you feel like it, is that it?"

Silence.

"I hereby give Jenny permission to tell me what's going on." The volume of Frankie's voice had risen a couple of notches and the familiar tightness in her neck was kicking up.

"Then bite me." She stepped out of bed and headed for the kitchen pantry. After reviewing her food stores, she slipped into her jogging outfit and slid her socked feet into her gel heeled walking shoes.

The walks relaxed her, and today her thoughts suggested it was time to go through Uncle Mike's papers. Other than his will, she'd been emotionally unable to handle seeing his notes and private papers. And she'd already put it off too long. Besides, maybe touching his papers would help her feel closer to him. At least it would take her mind off Tim's murder and her inability to find his killers. And maybe a break was just what she needed.

She headed for the door, opened it and stuck her head out. As if it were an oscillating fan perched atop her neck, her head swiveled back and forth as her eyes strained for a glimpse of the Chevy. But the guy had apparently been smart enough to stay indoors on this chilly morning.

Relieved, Frankie stepped through the door, pulled it closed behind her, and engaged the deadbolt. She stuck the house key in her pocket along with a canister of pepper spray and headed toward the street.

The icy air teased its way through the fabric of her knit mittens. Its frigid fingers searched for a way under the headband protecting her ears, while the moisture from her breath curled up around her cheeks and disappeared over her head.

The neighborhood dogs remained quiet in

recognition of the small human who passed through their domain each morning. She waved at her neighbor Lola, a sweet elderly woman who'd brought food when Tim died.

Deep in thought, Frankie barely glanced at the vaguely familiar young jogger who approached her from the opposite direction. He nodded at her, his slightly pockmarked face smiling and friendly. She absently nodded back.

At the end of her walk, she pulled her house key from her zippered pocket, unlocked the thick wood front door and stepped into the entryway. Collette, true to form, hurtled out of the semi-darkness, caromed off her right thigh and disappeared again into the unlit hallway.

"Okay," she said to the cat's retreating backside, "you've made your point."

She opened a bag of gourmet dry cat food, measured one third cup into the cat's food dish, and set it on the floor in front of the feline. Collette threw a withering look of reproof over her shoulder, the look as articulate as any words as to how she felt about the small portion.

"Don't pull that look at me. The vet says you need to lose some weight. No one's going to adopt a fat kitty."

After she'd showered and dressed, Frankie put the teapot on. She selected a jar of chocolate mint tea from her stash of homemade teas, dropped a teaspoonful into the infuser of her porcelain teapot, and poured not-quite-boiling water over it. She steeped the tea for exactly three minutes, filled her insulated travel mug with the brew and headed for the garage.

For the next three hours she went through the two drawer metal filing cabinet containing Uncle Mike's important papers. She made two piles: one to keep and one to trash.

Schooled in the art of making do on very few resources, Uncle Mike had never thrown anything away. The discovery of an electric bill from twenty-five years ago stiffened Frankie's resolve to go through her own papers and throw out anything over three years old.

In the second drawer she spotted a manila folder with the words *Documents - in case of need* written in her uncle's nearly illegible scribble. She opened the folder and pulled out a pile of legal papers, some of them brittle and yellowed with age.

At the top of the stack she found an original death certificate for someone named Jonathan Christopher Stanton dated thirty-two years ago. Behind that were two birth certificates, one for a female named Colleen Frances Stanton, and another for a baby boy named Peter Timothy Stanton. The father for both was listed as Jonathan Stanton, the mother a Kelby Jean Stanton. Both births took place at Llano Estacado Memorial Hospital in Plainview, Texas.

Although Uncle Mike had never come right out and said so, he'd led Frankie and Tim to believe they were born in Albuquerque. Why would he lie about that?

Adoption papers behind the birth certificates indicated Michael James O'Neil in Hale County Texas had adopted a girl three years old and a boy age eight months. At the bottom of the final page were the signatures of her mother, Uncle Mike, Uncle Mike's attorney, and a judge. Each signature was followed by a date.

The image of her young, terminally ill mother signing away her two small children brought tears to Frankie's eyes. It must have been tough to know she would not live to see her children grow up. Heartbreaking to know that they were so young they would not even remember her within a few years.

Like an elastic string yanks a paddleball backward against its wooden paddle, her eyes jerked back to the date at the bottom of the document. Assuming it was not a typographical error, the paper had been signed over a year after Uncle Mike said their mother had died. He'd lied about that as well.

Bits and pieces of memory, meaningless when taken singly, began to coalesce. Things like Uncle Mike's anger when Frankie or Tim asked questions about the circumstances surrounding their mother's death. He'd adamantly refused to talk about their parents at all. She'd always chalked the anger up to her uncle's inability to deal with the loss of his sister.

Careful not to damage the documents, she replaced them in the manila folder. She pulled her phone from the pocket of her poncho and punched in a number.

"*Buenos días*, Nana Alma," she said. "Any chance you'd let me buy you lunch tomorrow? I'd like to talk to you about some things."

"Of course, *mi'jita*. It's been too long."

Chapter Eighteen

For the better part of two hours the next morning Frankie went through her ritual. The process was beginning to eat up way too much time, and once she started back to work she'd have to make some adjustments. But for now she needed the sense of security that came with looking over her provisions. And hadn't she read somewhere that it was a good thing to have a stockpile of non-perishables in case of an emergency?

She remembered a television documentary about people who never threw anything away. Their houses became so filled with trash and filth that many of them were declared health and fire hazards. A couple of them were even slated to be torn down.

But Frankie only collected food, not random garbage. And she kept her stash neatly organized. She wasn't like those people on television, was she?

She pulled a plastic box from her hall closet, set it on the kitchen table, and pulled off the lid. She lifted out the check books she'd taken from the junk drawer in Tim's kitchen.

As Flatte suggested, she scanned the carbon copies of the few checks her brother had written over the past two years. Most of them were for rent on Tim's apartment. She'd have to get account details from his bank, but he'd made notations of debit card purchases and an occasional cash ATM withdrawal. None were ever more than a couple of hundred dollars. He'd apparently used online banking to pay his utility, cell phone, and other bills. The checking account balance, currently less than twenty dollars, hadn't reached more than five thousand dollars.

Frankie went over the register again, but found no record of the funds Tim had mentioned in his letter. And she didn't find any payments to Jeremy Flatte. At first she'd thought he might have used plastic to pay his bills, but no credit cards had been found in his wallet, and no bills had come in the mail.

Feeling like a student unable to understand a simple math concept that had been repeated over and over for her benefit, she headed for her closet to select an outfit for her lunch with her old nanny. Maybe Alma could clear up the questions about the documents she'd found. And maybe she knew what really happened to her mother.

****

As Frankie pulled into Alma's driveway the old woman came out to greet her. Of substantial yet rock solid weight, Alma's strides were strong and her body nimble, even though she must be nearing eighty. Her thick, silver hair was pulled back into a tight bun at the nape of her neck. Her walnut colored face creased in a smile as she enveloped Frankie in a bear hug and half dragged her toward the house.

"Did you think I would allow you to spend your money on food when I can still cook?" Alma pushed the front door open. "Come inside, I've made some of your favorites."

The *chiles rellenos, enchilada* and *refritos* meal

131

accompanied by warm, buttered, homemade flour tortillas was as flavorful and marvelous as any Frankie could remember. The two women chatted amiably as they ate, and Frankie basked in the love of the only mother figure she'd ever known.

After lunch, the two washed and put away the dishes before Alma pulled out the stainless steel, stove-top percolator she'd used since Frankie was a kid.

"Go make yourself comfortable in the living room. I'll bring you a cup." Alma began measuring coffee grounds into the percolator's basket.

Frankie wandered around the living room, looking at the family photos displayed on the walls. Spread out like a geological timeline, the earliest photos started at one corner, ending with the later ones at the other. Memories tugged at her heart as her eyes slid over the photos of a young Uncle Mike, an adorable smiling infant Tim, and her own image, her teenaged mouth filled with shining metal braces.

Why did otherwise intelligent people insist on displaying pictorial proof that life was terminal, proof that we will inevitably lose the ones we love? What masochism drove humans to memorialize the havoc wreaked on each other by time? To lovingly capture its inescapable march as baby teeth erupted and disappeared, as first love burst onto the scene and left heartbreak in its wake, and finally as wrinkles appeared, eyelids drooped, chins sagged.

But worst of all were the changes to the eyes. The sparkling, joyful, in-the-moment gaze of the toddler became the insecure, self-conscious sideways glance of the teen, which then dimmed into the life-hardened, the desperate, the lonely stare of…

Tears pricked at Frankie's eyes, and she wiped them away with the back of her hand. That was the trouble with photos—they kept you bound to the past. Kept you from focusing on now.

"Do you still take your coffee black," Alma called out from the kitchen, "or have you taken to drinking that artificially flavored swill?"

"Still black and strong enough to float a new quarter," Frankie yelled back. She turned away from the photos and walked to the sofa.

Alma returned with two thick ceramic mugs. Ribbons of steam curled upward from each cup, wafting the marvelous fragrance of freshly-brewed coffee into the room. She handed a mug to Frankie and sat down on the sofa next to her.

"What's troubling you, *mi'jita*?"

Frankie's face heated up.

Alma chuckled. "No need for embarrassment. I'm happy you called and I'm very glad to see you. But I know you too well not to know when something's up. What is it?"

Frankie described the papers she'd found. "Do you know anything about our adoption?"

Alma's gaze dropped to the mug she cradled in her hands. "I know your uncle loved you and Timmy as if you were his own. I know he always did what he thought best for both of you. What more do you need to know?"

"I need to know how our mother could have signed the papers over a year after Uncle Mike said she died. I need to know why Uncle Mike basically changed our names. I need to know who I really am."

"Then I'm afraid you'll be disappointed at what I

133

can tell you. Your uncle hired me at the same time he brought you and Timmy home." Alma's eyes shifted to the right, just above Frankie's head. "I never saw these papers you describe."

"Nana, did Uncle Mike ever tell you our parents' real names?"

"If he did, I don't remember it. No, he never spoke of family history. You know how he felt about that."

"Only too well."

Alma patted Frankie's shoulder and looked into her eyes. "Then perhaps you should leave the past alone."

"That sounds fine in theory. The problem is the past won't leave me alone."

"And how is that?"

"I'm afraid I may be losing my mind." Frankie looked into her old nanny's eyes, her own filling with unshed tears. "I'm hearing things."

She was surprised to see Alma smile. "Things?"

"Voices."

"Ah. Voices of your dead relatives?"

Frankie's astonished look must have been comical, because Alma laughed. "I'm sorry, *mi'jita*." She laid her hand on the younger woman's arm. "I know it's not funny to you. I'm just so glad you're finally opening yourself to be who you're meant to be."

"Who I'm…" Frankie shook her head as if trying to dislodge a huge spider web from the corners of her mind. "What are you saying?"

"I'm saying you hear voices because you're fae, Child. Fae, like your Irish ancestors."

"Fae? What does that mean?"

"It means you were born in the caul. Your mother's water never broke. You were delivered while still in the amniotic sac, a sure sign of the gift."

"But what has that got to do with my hearing voices?"

"The gift shows itself differently in every one who receives it. With your uncle it was the ability to understand what other people were thinking. That's what made him an extraordinary operative. As for you, you've been given the ability to hear and talk to your Irish ancestors."

Frankie searched Alma's face for any sign that she might be joking. But her old nanny just sat there, her face beaming in innocent delight.

"So being fae made Uncle Mike a hero while it makes me look like a lunatic? Not sure how I feel about that."

Alma chuckled. "I know very little about these things. Only what your uncle told me when you began to show signs of having the gift. He was so afraid you'd misunderstand it, but was more afraid of how the world would deal with you."

"And Tim?"

Alma pursed her lips and sighed. "Timmy was a wonderful young man. Smart, generous, kind. But he wasn't fae." She smiled, a far-away look in her eyes. "I remember coming into your room when you were small, and there you were in your Wonder Woman pajamas, standing in the center of your room, laughing and chatting away with someone I could neither see, nor hear. As you got older, the other kids probably made fun of you. For whatever reason, you pushed it away until it eventually grew silent."

"I don't remember any of that."

Alma patted Frankie's hand. "Now that you've

opened your heart to the gift, it will come when the time is right." She stood and picked up the empty mugs. "Can I get you more coffee?"

"No thanks, I'd better get going. I still have several errands to run."

After goodbye hugs and promises to call more often, Frankie walked to her car.

She was no nearer the truth about her past now than before, but she had learned a couple of things. Not only was her old nanny growing senile—all that talk of some kind of fae thing—but Frankie was convinced Uncle Mike had told her a family secret. A secret of such magnitude that Alma wouldn't speak of it, even years after his death.

Your past helps make you who you are. But your job is to learn from it, not allow it to define you.

As if a cold draught had blown across her scalp, Frankie's hair moved and she shivered. Because although she didn't understand how she knew it, this voice wasn't Uncle Mike's, Tim's, or Jenny's—it was Grandmother O'Neil's. And she'd died long before Frankie was born.

Chapter Nineteen

Once she'd completed the legal paperwork to donate her Jeep to a new mission sponsored by her church, Frankie called the young pastor and explained her intentions. He offered copious thanks and said he could be there within the hour to pick it up.

To pass the time, she made hot tea and sat at her dining table. She pulled Tim's laptop toward her and turned it on.

The screen lit and the monitor wallpaper blinked on to reveal a photo of Uncle Mike with his arms resting on the shoulders of a teenaged Tim and Frankie. The photo should have brought a smile at memories of happier times. Instead, it seared her heart with grief.

Other than the dock running along the bottom of the screen, no icons appeared on Tim's computer screen. She clicked through various windows and drop-down menus before clicking on the Documents icon. Among dozens of files, she spotted one labeled *Journal*.

The tempo of her pulse kicked up a notch as she opened the file and scanned Tim's daily entries, the first dated nearly two years ago. Written in a tone of excitement, the first pages included interesting bits of arcane medical anecdotes and stories about people with whom he worked.

At first, Tim's words reflected his joy and gratitude at being allowed to fulfill his dream of becoming an anesthetist. But they soon grew morose, questioning, and filled with doubts about his vocational choice.

It broke Frankie's heart that her brother had kept all his pain inside—that he hadn't felt he could come to her with his concerns.

At the end of the word processed pages Tim had attached a five-column spreadsheet. The leftmost column consisted of thirty-two names. Next to each one Tim had typed in things like *ft amp* and *kid rem*. Possible abbreviations for medical procedures? Foot amputation? Kidney removal? Dates filled the third column, and the fourth listed dollar amounts. The mostly-blank fifth column contained a few dates, the most recent only days before Tim's death.

She could understand why her conscientious brother might keep a record of his patients. But surely he'd performed medical services for more than thirty-two people over his two-year residency.

And the costs he'd listed, if that's what they were, had to be wrong. There was no way a kidney removal would be billed at only three thousand dollars. And where, outside a slaughter house, could a foot amputation be done for only one thousand dollars? And what were the dates in the fifth column, follow-up visits? If so, why were there only five?

Frankie shut off the laptop. Time for a trip to the hospital to pick up Tim's personal things and have a chat with Mina Landowski, a nurse who'd sent flowers to the funeral. Maybe she could shed some light on what had been going on in Tim's life that made him, as Flatte said, behave as if he needed to get his house in order.

She checked the locks on her windows, set the

Katy bar on the back door, turned on the barking dog, and grabbed her purse and jacket. After ensuring she'd put a canister of pepper spray in her purse, she locked the front door and headed for her car.

She drove to the hospital, parked in the visitors' lot, and made her way to the main entrance. The double glass doors opened when she stepped onto the black rubber pressure pad in front of them, then shushed closed behind her. As if it had been lying in wait, the smell common to hospitals everywhere enveloped her, and she wrinkled her nose.

How was it that Tim could joyfully show up every day to a place that smelled of antiseptic, cleaning solution, despair and human suffering? Hospitals were populated by people who fell into one of three categories: those trying to get well, those trying to die, and those whose job it was to help everyone achieve their goals. Call her vapid, insensitive, or just plain chicken, but she'd never felt the remotest desire to face down the Grim Reaper day in and day out. Still, she'd been supremely proud of Tim's commitment to do just that.

A pink-smocked matron sat behind the information desk immediately inside the front door. As Frankie approached, the cotton-fluff-haired woman looked up from her paperwork and smiled. Frankie identified herself and asked directions to the surgical floor.

"I'm so sorry for your loss," the woman said, "Doctor O'Neil was already gone when I began working here, but I've heard so much about him. He must have been a wonderful man."

Frankie smiled. "Thank you." She took a step closer to the counter. "I've come for my brother's things. Can you direct me to his office?"

"I can do better than that." The woman pointed to a row of chairs along a wall to her right. "Have a seat while I make a call."

After settling into a brown, vinyl covered chair, Frankie selected a dog-eared health magazine from a pile on a low table in front of the seats, and thumbed through it. She'd just finished reading a paragraph touting the virtues of psyllium fiber, when an elevator bell dinged somewhere. She looked up as a man walked out of the hall behind the information desk. He came toward Frankie, his right hand extended.

"Good morning Miss O'Neil. Doctor Reynold Bellamy at your service. We cannot tell you how very sorry we were to hear about Tim's accident."

Frankie shook the proffered hand. "Thank you. I apologize that it's taken me so long to get around to this, but I'd like to pick up whatever personal items my brother may have left here."

"Of course." The doctor stared into her eyes like a hunting dog on point. "After Tim's passing, we had a staff member clean out his desk and locker and put his things in a storeroom."

"I was also hoping to speak with Mina Landowski, if she's available."

"Mina Landowski?" Dr. Bellamy pursed his lips as an unfathomable look flitted across his face. He instantly replaced it with a smile. "We believe Mina is working today. If you would be so kind, please come with us." Bellamy turned and headed down the hall.

The doctor's gait reminded Frankie of the goose stepping soldiers she'd seen on Uncle Mike's collection of old war news reels. And Bellamy's habit of referring to himself in the first person plural seemed a strange affectation. If his goal was to distance himself from the rest of humanity, he'd certainly achieved that.

Dr. Bellamy opened a door bearing a brass nameplate etched with his name and title. He motioned for Frankie to go into his office, closed the door behind them, and pointed toward two chairs in front of his desk. "Please, make yourself comfortable."

Frankie sat while the doctor walked to his desk, picked up his phone and punched in a number. While waiting for someone to pick up, he absent-mindedly straightened papers on his already immaculate desktop.

Bellamy's office was a study in what Frankie thought might be characterized as medical-eclectic. A mass-produced poster of a pastoral scene hung beside huge colorful prints of dissected bodies, one male and one female, complete with labeled parts. Predictably, one wall was fronted by a bookcase filled with thick medical tomes such as *Gray's Anatomy* and the latest iteration of the *Physician's Desk Reference*. A lighted display case along the opposite wall held various oddly shaped bones, jars of pickled growths, and what appeared to be a calcified lung. Frankie shuddered at lumps of what she suspected were petrified vital organs. One large jar of yellowish liquid held a light gray human brain, its lobes, fissures and folds smooth but for a dark yellow growth on one side the size of a golf ball. On the wall behind the desk, in a tight, perfectly symmetrical grouping, hung the doctor's medical pedigree beside a photo of him in pristine surgical garb.

But what most intrigued Frankie was the human skeleton that stood suspended from a metal frame in one corner. Tim once commented that a complete skeleton made of plastic resin would cost less than a real human skull. He said whole skeletons, especially those from some third world countries, were often of sketchy origins so now most doctors contented themselves with the man-made replicas. But instead of the stark white typical of the facsimiles Tim had used in school, Bellamy's life-sized marionette bore a shiny, deep ochre patina. Frankie shivered.

Dr. Bellamy lowered the receiver to a position just under his chin. "I see you've met Barbara." He showed his teeth as a bizarre chuckle escaped through his nearly closed lips. "A disgruntled employee." He winked. "Just kidding, of course."

A hinky feeling hit Frankie a glancing blow between her shoulder blades. She took a deep breath, told herself to stop imagining things, and smiled back at the doctor.

"Please feel free to browse this small portion of my collection of medical oddities. All are unique, and some are quite rare." Bellamy re-positioned the phone and spoke into it, "Ah, good. Doctor O'Neil's sister is here. Would you please ask Mina to bring the box containing his personal effects to our office? Thank you."

The doctor hung up the phone and turned back to Frankie. "Would you care for coffee or water? Juice perhaps?"

"No, thank you." No way her stomach could keep anything down in these surroundings.

Bellamy gave a slight shrug. "As you wish." He sat down behind his desk, winced at the resulting loud squeak, and again pasted the rictus smile on his face. "It is so nice to meet you in person, Miss O'Neil. We had the very great privilege of hearing you in concert at the

Cathedral in Santa Fe last fall. We especially enjoyed your interpretation of the Bach Toccata and Fugue."

"Thank you. Bach's one of my favorites."

"Just out of curiosity, your hands are so small, and many of the passages so intricate, how do you—?"

Both Frankie and Bellamy turned their heads as a petite blonde stepped into the office. She placed a cardboard box on top of the doctor's desk, and turned to look at Frankie.

"Miss O'Neil, this is Mina Landowski, our head nurse."

A brilliant smile lit up the nurse's face. "It's so good to meet you. You look a lot like your brother. Except for your eye color. I mean…"

"No need to apologize. I've considered wearing a contact lens in one eye so they'd match, but I could never decide which color to go with."

Dressed in the standard nurse's uniform of white slacks and vee-necked pullover, Mina wore her thick blonde hair swept back and held in place with two large starburst-shaped barrettes made of a silvery metal.

Frankie must have been staring, because Mina raised her hand to touch one barrette. "My parents brought these back from one of their many trips abroad. I probably wear them too much, but they're the only things I've found heavy enough to control this mop."

Frankie smiled. "I think they're beautiful."

Bellamy cleared his throat. "Well, as lovely as this little tête-à-tête has been, our presence is required elsewhere." He turned to Frankie. "Please feel free to call in the event we may be of further assistance."

The doctor walked to his door, opened it and stood to one side. The unspoken message for the two women to clear out hung in the air. Frankie picked up the box of Tim's things and followed Mina out of the office. Bellamy barely gave the women time to move through the door before closing it firmly behind them.

"How well did you know Tim?" Frankie said as she and the nurse walked toward the exit.

"Pretty well, we often worked together in the operating room. He was the best anesthetist I've ever worked with. That's why I was so shocked when Dr. Bellamy let him go."

Frankie checked her forward movement and turned toward the nurse. "Tim was fired?"

"Yes. In fact, it wasn't long before he died. He and Doctor Bellamy got into an argument, and Bellamy fired him on the spot."

"What was it about?"

"I was on rounds, so I didn't hear the fight. But the rumor mill had it that Tim looked like he was going to throw a punch at Doctor Bellamy."

"That's unlike him. Any idea why?"

"Most likely he didn't agree with something Doctor Bellamy did in surgery. That kind of thing happened a lot. They yelled at each other for a while, and then Doctor Bellamy told Tim to leave. He wasn't even allowed to get his stuff—security escorted him off the grounds right then and there."

"Wonder why Doctor Bellamy didn't say anything about firing Tim? He acted as if Tim worked right up until his death."

"No idea," Mina said. "Maybe he just didn't want to have to deal with any questions you might have about it."

When the two reached the exit, Mina stopped. "I'm

still on my shift, but I'd like to talk to you when we have more time. Maybe we could get together for coffee?" She pulled a marker from a side pocket and jotted two phone numbers on the box lid. "Landline and cell numbers. This week I'm working the three to eleven shift, so call me any time between eight in the morning and two in the afternoon." Mina pursed her lips. "Maybe it would be a good idea for us to talk."

Chapter Twenty

As soon as the two women disappeared down the hall, Dr. Bellamy opened his desk drawer and pulled out a burner phone. He punched in a number, put the phone against his ear, and drummed the top of his desk with the fingers of his free hand. When someone at the other end answered, he sat forward in his chair.

"Did we miss your call, or have you made the mistake of blowing us off?"

"I've been tied up. And I told you not to call me on my car phone, it's too easy to trace." Though muffled, the voice sounded loud, as if the phone was resting against the speaker's lips.

"Your cell is off," Bellamy said.

"I forgot to turn it on."

"Your memory lapses are becoming problematic. But if anyone checks, we're chatting about your grandmother."

There was no response from the other end.

"Pardon our chuckle. We can wax witty, don't you think?"

"What do you want?"

"We need information, and we need it now. The sister is snooping, and we're getting nervous."

"What kind of snooping?"

"She and the head nurse just left our office in deep conversation."

"Does your nurse know anything?"

"We don't think she has a clue as to the true nature of our business."

"Then why in God's name are you calling me?"

"We need to know what Miss O'Neil is telling the police."

"She's not one of their favorite people right now. She calls every other day, bugging the police both in Albuquerque and Colfax County. And last night she called the police out to her place on some trumped up break-in false alarm."

"What was that about?"

"Who knows? But she's looking more and more like an attention-grubbing neurotic."

"That could work in our favor," Bellamy said. "If the police came to believe she is *non compos mentis*, she could be written off as a nut. That would support the idea that Tim was actually killed in a tragic hunting accident and help settle this poo storm."

"It might."

"What would happen if further evidence came to light indicating Miss O'Neil is indeed mentally vacationing in another reality from time to time?"

"It would have to be pretty convincing. But at this point, both Colfax County and APD would like to get this off the books, one way or another."

"What would it take to convince them she's lost it?"

"I'd have to think about it." Pause. "What's your point?"

"Time to pay the piper," Bellamy said.

"You want me to set her up?"

"How nice to work with such a quick study."

147

"What do you want me to do?"

"You've proven to be quite creative in the past, you figure it out."

"When?"

"Within the next twenty-four hours would be fine. Of course, you'll take the usual precautions, so nothing might be traced back to us."

"Or to myself."

"A laudable sense of self preservation. Keep us informed."

****

Frankie's phone rang just as she pulled into her therapist's drive. She tapped the ear bud, allowing Nick Rollins' smooth voice to slide into her ear.

"I just got your message," Rollins said. "Have you remembered something?"

"No, but I've found Tim's journal."

"Anything that sheds light on his death?"

"Not directly, no. But when I went to the hospital to pick up his things, I found out he was fired just a couple of days before his murder."

"Miss O'Neil, it sounds like your brother was going through a rough patch. But unfortunately, every day thousands of people lose their jobs and millions are chronically depressed."

"But not all of those people get shot and their apartments demolished."

"True," Rollins surprised Frankie by saying.

"So tell me why no one is trying to find the men who killed him?"

"It's not that no one is trying. In fact, I looked over the report on the break-in at his apartment. No fingerprints were found, so whoever it was knew enough to wear gloves. I believe the break-in is related to your brother's shooting, but so far we just haven't been able to find anything that would get us off the dime."

"Maybe that's because you haven't looked in the right places."

The line went silent for several beats before the deputy answered. "If you're holding something back that has to do with this investigation, I'd encourage you to rethink that."

"I'll tell you what I think, I think if anyone's going to find my brother's murderers, it'll have to be me." Frankie tapped her ear bud, cutting off the deputy's protests.

Immediately, Uncle Mike's voice rang in her head: *Careful Frances, careful not to overload your hummingbird butt with your alligator mouth.*

"Mind your own business." Frankie got out of her car, careful to lock it behind her and headed into Angela's office, where she sat waiting for her appointed time.

In a few minutes, a depressed-looking fellow exited the inner office. He mumbled a greeting in Frankie's general direction and seemed to be relieved to make it to the outer door.

Angela smiled from the doorway to her office and motioned her in. Frankie took her usual seat—what she called the *hot seat*—still warm from the body that had just vacated it. Angela handed Frankie a chilled bottle of water, clicked on the recorder, and sat back in her chair.

"How has your week gone?" the therapist said.

"Jenny hasn't spoken to me since our last session,

but my nightmares have started up again."

"Nightmares? Tell me about them."

"Most of them are variations of the same dream I've had since I was a kid." Frankie clenched her hands together, kneading her fingers. "I'm in a dark place, I hear a baby crying, I'm worried about the baby, but I'm stuck in the darkness and can't find my way out. I try to yell, but when I open my mouth no sound comes out."

"People often dream of being unable to speak when they feel something is out of their control in their waking lives, when they feel they have no voice. Is there something going on with you that feels like that?"

"My whole life feels like that." Frankie told Angela about finding the adoption papers, about learning that her uncle and nanny had lied to her, and about discovering that Tim had become involved in something for which he felt ashamed. "What good are my dreams if I can't understand what they're saying?"

"That's why you're here. It takes a lot of mental energy to repress memories, so the psyche starts sending out little snippets to get the ball moving. If you choose to swallow it rather than allow it to come out, own it, and let it go, you can be assured it will erupt in some other form. I deal with clients every day who suffer from all sorts of obsessive-compulsive behaviors rooted in their inability to let go of something from their past."

"Obsessive-compulsive behaviors?" The words erupted from Frankie's mouth, scouring her tongue like a nettle as they escaped into the still office air.

An inquisitive look flitted across Angela's face. "Yes, behaviors people feel forced to perform. Eating disorders, rituals like hand-washing, hoarding, things like that."

"Ah." Frankie picked at the chair's fabric upholstery. For an instant she considered telling Angela about her food stockpile, but decided against it. There were too many other things she needed to get a handle on first. And too little time in which to do it. Besides, what she did couldn't actually be called hoarding, could it?

"Your assignment for next week is to get a book for journaling, if you haven't already. Keep it with a pen by your bed. Every morning as soon as you wake up write down anything you can remember about your dreams. Pay special attention to any feelings associated with them. Bring the journal with you next time."

Frankie shifted her eyes to the pattern in the rug. "I might not be able to make it for a couple of weeks."

"I see." Angela leaned forward and patted the top of Frankie's hand. "What you're feeling is typical. Your impulse is to avoid emotional pain. It's your call, but if we stop digging now, things will only get worse."

"Okay." Frankie ran the fingers of her right hand through her hair, pushing a wandering lock behind her ear. "I'll see you next week."

Chapter Twenty-One

The typically sunny Albuquerque sky was filled with clouds the density and blackness of burning rubber when Frankie woke. Per Angela's assignment, she sat up in bed, pulled her blank-paged notebook onto her lap, grabbed her pen, and jotted down her memories from the night before. Although she couldn't remember specific dream images, the attendant feelings hummed in her head. She jotted down the date and time, and added the words *panicked*, *afraid*, and *unable to speak or breathe*. Almost of its own accord, her pen added *hungry*. Not much to go on, but it was a start.

She jumped out of bed. After a brief mental skirmish, during which the word *obsessive* rang in her head like a gong, she counted her cans before slipping on her jogging outfit and heading for the front door.

While putting on her mittens and headband, her eyes slid to the wooden bowl and the single key remaining on Tim's key ring: most likely the key to a safe deposit box. As to why she'd done nothing about it before today she had no answer. But the tingle at the base of her neck told her she should take care of that as soon as she got back from her walk.

The Chevy never far from her thoughts, she took a long look out the front window before moving to the front door. Nothing moved on her block, and no non-neighborhood vehicles idled nearby. She patted the pepper spray in her pocket and headed out into the cold.

****

When Frankie arrived at the bank a female employee scrutinized her identification along with the proof of Tim's death. The woman led the way back through a steel gate and into a concrete vault. She inserted her key into the double lock of one of the large safe deposit boxes running along the bottom of the wall, and motioned for Frankie to do the same with Tim's key.

After a brief struggle to pull the box out of its crypt, the employee hefted the box onto the table in a viewing booth. She puffed "whew," and discreetly went back to her work station.

In a state of high expectation, Frankie pulled the lid off the box. She didn't know what she'd expected, but what greeted her was a layer of old Star Wars figurines, most of them still in their original packaging.

"It's so like you to leave you trust papers laying around for anyone to find while filling your safe deposit box with old toys," she muttered.

Don't knock it, Tim's voice rang in her head. *Never know when you'll need a cool toy.*

Frankie sighed. "Anyone else have something to say?"

Silence.

"No? Okay then."

She removed the figurines and placed them on the table, exposing a large manila folder underneath. A label affixed to the front proclaimed the contents to be the original medical records of someone named Esther Emory.

With the feeling that she'd seen that name

somewhere before, she lifted out the folder and put it into her tote bag for later review.

The next layer consisted of several small, clear plastic bags. A label at the top of each bag indicated its contents originated from a company named Gaylord Gold Investments. The company's address and phone number were printed just below its name.

She selected a bag, opened it, and pulled out a paper with the words *Certificate of Provenance* printed across the top. Something fell from a fold in the paper, and clacked onto the tile floor. She bent to retrieve the clear plastic, box-encased gold coin that winked up at her.

Hands trembling, she pulled out several more bags. Each one contained a provenance and tiny plastic box in which lay a gold coin dated from the mid to late 1800s. Frankie put her hands onto the table to steady herself.

"What did you do, Little Brother, rob Fort Knox?"

On a notepad she pulled from her tote bag, she wrote down the name and contact information of the company printed on the label. She returned the certificate to the opened bag, resealed it, and put all the bags back into the safe deposit box.

Feeling as if she'd stepped into a scene from the old Twilight Zone television series, she summoned the employee to help carry the box back to its slot, slung the tote bag strap over her shoulder and left the bank.

She'd found no paper trail, nothing in Tim's effects to indicate a purchase of the magnitude reflected by the cache of coins. So how had he paid for them?

It was always possible he'd been holding the coins for someone else. But wouldn't that person have come forward to claim them by now?

Another possibility reared its head. What if Tim had accepted the coins as payment for medical services, rather than the checks on which he'd be required to pay taxes? Was that why he'd been so ashamed? Had he been involved in income tax fraud?

Frankie returned to her car, each step mocking her memories of Tim. It was becoming more and more obvious that she hadn't really known her brother at all.

Once home, she pulled out the contact information from the gold coins. She sat in the chair next to her landline, dialed the number for Gaylord Gold Investments, and punched in several numbers in response to a recorded menu before a human voice came on the line. The representative regretted that she would be unable to give out any specific details regarding Tim's account without a written request accompanied by corresponding legal documentation. She then detailed the fairly complicated process necessary to receive a printout of Tim's transactions. Frankie jotted down the instructions, thanked the employee and hung up.

What had happened to the sweet, loving kid she grew up with? What became of the third-grader who punched Mark Lackey in the nose for teasing his sister, to the teenager who warned her Tom Brazel had taken a bet to ask her to the prom, or to the young doctor driven by the desire to help those less fortunate?

She sat at her dining room table, pulled the manila envelope from her tote bag, removed a thick sheaf of paper, and scanned the pages.

At the time of the last entry, Esther Emory was eighty and suffering from heart disease. No family members were listed. Due to the elderly woman's indigent status, Medicare or Medicaid covered most of her hospital bills. Cottonwood Medical Center and Hospital Foundation, a local non-profit, assumed responsibility for the remaining portion.

Esther had been a resident of the Chaparral Convalescent and Assisted Living Center attached to the hospital. According to the records, Dr. Bellamy put her on blood thinners and cholesterol medication to manage her heart disease. The last entry was dated about eighteen months ago.

On a clean sheet in her notepad Frankie jotted down the questions she'd ask Flatte. What was her responsibility with regard to the gold coins? Could Flatte access Tim's account at Gaylord Gold Investments? And what should she do with Esther Emory's medical records?

She pulled her phone from its holster, punched in Flatte's number, and asked to speak to the attorney. The assistant said he was out, but assured Frankie she'd tell him about her call.

While waiting, she retrieved the cardboard box of things she'd brought from Tim's office. She pulled the lid off and picked up the items one at a time: a paperweight holding a once-living scorpion frozen inside a bubble of clear resin; the Mont Blanc pen set she'd given Tim upon his graduation from medical school, and on which she was sadly still making payments; a silver-framed photo of the both of them at his graduation from medical school, a small booklet for addresses and phone numbers—most pages of which were empty, and a fingernail clipper.

Idly, she leafed through the address book. She

chuckled to see her address and phone number under *S*, presumably for Sis.

She put the booklet down onto the table, and it fell open to the C section. The only entry, someone named Hector Cordero, was followed by a local phone number. Beneath Hector's name was scribbled a time and date followed by an exclamation mark.

Whoever this man was, Tim had scheduled an appointment with him the day of his death. And it had been only an hour before he showed up on her doorstep.

Frankie keyed Hector's phone number into her cell. Voice mail kicked in after the fourth ring, and a man's voice with a heavy Mexican accent cordially invited her to leave her name and number for a return call.

"Hector, my name is Frankie O'Neil. I'm not sure if you're the Hector who came to my brother's funeral, but I would really like to talk to you. Please call me when you get the chance." She repeated her phone number twice before breaking the connection.

On impulse, she called the number Mina Landowski had scribbled on the box lid.

"Lunch sounds great," Mina said in response to Frankie's invitation. "I don't have to be at the hospital until three this afternoon. Twelve noon at the Turquoise Trail café on Silver Street sounds perfect."

For the next couple of hours Frankie pored over Tim's journal, his bank statements, and his trust folder. She couldn't shake the feeling that the answers were right there in front of her, but nothing announced itself. The tickle at the base of her brain still niggled away as she left for her meeting with Mina.

****

Frankie arrived at the café early. She stepped to the

counter, ordered a Thai beef salad, and carried the plastic table tent with her order number engraved on it to a booth near the door. She sipped mango iced tea and mulled over how much she wanted to tell Mina.

Should she tell the nurse about finding Esther Emory's medical records? She should probably return the records at some point, but to whom? To the hospital? To Esther Emory's family, assuming any could be found? Or should she just destroy them?

Mina entered, waved at Frankie and walked to the counter. She placed her order, then dropped her plastic tent on the table and slid onto the booth's orange vinyl-covered bench.

"Either you're early, or I'm late," Mina said.

Frankie smiled. "I'm early. I'm behaviorally incapable of being late for lunch. Pavlov had nothing on my uncle."

The nurse laughed. "Sounds like the guys who raised us might have something in common."

"Thanks for suggesting lunch. It will be nice to talk to someone who knew my brother."

Mina's smile faded. "No need to thank me. I've been meaning to talk to you ever since Doctor O'Neil's accident."

"It wasn't an accident." Frankie lowered her voice and described the events around Tim's death. She was surprised to find the pain of his loss soften a bit as she spoke.

"Oh God, and he was killed right in front of you? I can't imagine anything so horrible." Mina patted Frankie's hand, a gesture of sympathy that nearly made her dissolve into tears.

"The police want to call it a hunting accident, but I

know better. I just don't know who did it, or why."

"But who would want to hurt Tim? Everyone liked him—everyone except Doctor Bellamy, that is."

Frankie scooted forward in her seat. She rested her forearms on the table and absently ran the fingertips of her right hand up and down the outside of her tea glass, describing parallel vertical lines in the condensation. "What do you know about Tim and Doctor Bellamy's working relationship?"

"As you may have noticed, Doctor Bellamy is just a tad arrogant." Mina shook her head a couple of times, her lips compressed. "Tim was building a reputation as a superb anesthetist, and I think it enraged Doctor Bellamy. The man is a narcissistic ego maniac. No one is allowed to outshine him. Certainly no one he would perceive as being an underling. And that would include the rest of humanity."

Frankie did a quick mental run-through of Tim's journal. "I never heard my brother say anything negative about the people he worked with."

"That's because he was a kind, gentle soul. But something relatively no one outside the hospital knows is that Doctor Bellamy is a hack. On more than one occasion I've seen him make some pretty awful surgical mistakes. I decided to leave long before Tim died. In fact, I'm sending out another batch of resumes today."

Frankie pushed the manila folder containing Tim's spreadsheet across the table. "Would you do me a favor? Would you look at this and tell me what you think?"

Mina picked up the envelope. "What is it?"

"It's a copy of something I found on Tim's laptop."

The nurse pulled the pages out of the envelope and

scanned them. A frown creased her smooth features. "Do you know what this is?"

"I assume it's patient medical information."

"You say Tim had this on his laptop?" Mina looked thoughtful.

Frankie nodded. "I considered deleting the spreadsheet and forgetting about it, but I couldn't. It was obviously important to Tim."

"What are you going to do with it?"

"I hoped you might be able to help me with that."

"Me?" Mina's carefully penciled eyebrows again rose into arches over her eyes.

"I didn't know where else to start. It occurred to me that you could look over the names to see if any of these people stayed in the hospital recently. Maybe you helped care for them."

Mina again studied the sheets then raised her head. "I do remember some of these."

"And what about the dates…any idea what they refer to?"

"The first column seems to be dates of various surgeries, some of which I remember. And I believe the last column refers to a patient's death. But some of this is not right." Mina looked up. "This is an exact copy?"

"Yes. Straight off Tim's laptop."

The nurse frowned. "There are a couple of things I'm not sure about…"

"What?" Frankie prompted when Mina lapsed into a prolonged silence. "What are you not sure about?"

"Do you mind if I keep this? I'd like to check out a couple of things."

"Please do. Anything you can tell me would be greatly appreciated."

The two women finished lunch. Frankie tried several times to steer the conversation back to whatever it was about the spreadsheet that had caught Mina's attention, but the nurse steadfastly refused any further comment.

"Give me a day or so," Mina said. "I'll call you either after my shift tonight, or first thing tomorrow."

The women said their goodbyes, and Frankie headed to her car, uneasiness skittering across every nerve in her body.

"Uncle Mike, if you're really there, tell me what was it about Tim's spreadsheet that upset Mina so much."

Silence.

"Just as I thought—a figment of my imagination."

Her eyes darting back and forth between her rearview mirror and the road, she drove home via a different route than the one she'd come.

For several minutes after arriving home, she sat in her parked car and reviewed her conversation with Mina. She pulled her house key from her purse, exited the car, and walked toward her front door. Distracted by thoughts of what information she might get from the nurse, she didn't look at her porch until she was standing on it. Then her breath caught in her throat.

A dead dove lay on her welcome mat, its head at a right angle to its body. Pearl gray feathers barely ruffled, the dull black eyes stared at nothing. On the smooth concrete next to the mat someone had printed *YOUR TURN* in white children's sidewalk chalk.

The tiny hairs on Frankie's forearms moved and a slight nausea sluiced around in her stomach. Her fingers fumbled with the key as she unlocked her door. She hurled her body through the door and slammed it behind her. She shot home the deadbolt, pulled her phone out of her purse and called the police. Leaning against the door for support, she commanded herself to breathe.

By the time an officer arrived, she had managed to calm down a bit. Her ears picked up the sound of a car pulling into the driveway, and she opened the door a millisecond before the doorbell rang. It was the same officer who'd caught her break-in call.

Frankie took a deep breath. "I've received a death threat."

The officer looked closely at her face. "I see." He sighed.

"It's a note. It's written on my porch, right there, in chalk, a little to the right of the dead bird."

"Dead bird?" The officer stepped back and scanned the area.

Frankie opened her screen, stepped out, and pointed to the perfectly clean concrete. "Someone put a dead dove right there."

The officer's face devoid of expression, he widened his search to include the yard. But the bird was nowhere to be found.

Frankie fought to control her voice. "I'm telling you, it was right there."

The officer studied her face. "Do you still see it?"

Gorge rose in Frankie's throat, and her face warmed. "No, I don't. But why would I make up such a thing?"

"I'm not saying you're making things up." Like a teacher talking to an offending student, the officer held his index finger in the air. "And I'm going to let this slide. But just so you know: calling for help under false pretenses is an actionable offense."

"I'll remember that." Frankie clenched her hands into tight balls. "And I won't bother you again."

The police officer returned to his cruiser. He spoke into his car phone and sat for several minutes making notes.

What words would he use in his matter-of-public-record report? *Crazy* or *cracked* would work.

Maybe the whole being-followed thing had been her imagination after all. Or maybe her brain had turned into a big, thick, steaming bowl of oatmeal. But there was no way she'd misread the intentions on the face of the guy driving the Chevy. And although she had no explanation for their disappearance, her imagination had not manufactured the dead bird and note.

Frankie leaned her forehead against the cool wooden door frame, her thoughts turning to the guy in the old Chevy. She'd almost welcome his appearance right then. In her current frame of mind she'd make mincemeat of him and feed him to her cat.

She was getting tired of jumping at every noise, of acid shooting up her throat at unexpected shadows. She was sick of feeling like a marionette made to dance to someone else's banjo.

To co-opt Angela's words, it was time to thump a domino. And at this point, any domino would do.

Chapter Twenty-Two

Larry's lips thinned as he listened to the threatening message Mel had left on his phone. Things were happening too fast, and he wasn't ready. One thing he knew for sure, Mel didn't make idle threats. That meant he'd have to speed up his timetable.

He jabbed Mel's number onto the keypad with such force that pain shot up his index finger. Mel answered on the first ring.

"Leave her alone, she doesn't know anything." Tiny flecks of spittle flew from Larry's lips and onto the phone.

Mel snorted. "Yeah, that's what you keep saying. But how am I supposed to know anything about that, seeing as how I haven't seen you in such a long time?"

"I'm busy checking things out and taking care of business. You can tell Bellamy that."

"I'll tell Bellamy you've lost it unless you come on back to the farm. I'll tell him that you've made a deal with the police."

"I'll be back after I find what we've been looking for."

"Bellamy told you to stop watching her. So, why are you still—?"

"Because I don't agree with Bellamy. I guess he's afraid if she finds out someone's watching her she'll tell the police and they'll start up the investigation again. But I think watching her is the best way to find the stuff O'Neil took. That stuff is our only hope. If we find it, Bellamy will pay us enough so we'll never have to work again. We can go someplace nice. Someplace with palm trees and pretty, willing women."

"Okay. But what're you going to do about her? You know…if she does find the stuff?"

"I'll worry about that when the time comes. One thing for sure, if the police get it they'll dig into every corner of Bellamy's business. Then they'll come for you and me. It's us that'll do time for killing O'Neil and that hunter. You can bet Bellamy won't spend a day inside for that."

"What'll we do?"

"I'm working on it." Larry felt like one of those circus guys who somehow managed to get fifty plates spinning on sticks all at once. If even one plate hit the ground though, all bets were off as to what his future would be.

"All right," Mel said. "But when're you coming back? Things don't feel right, you being gone and all."

"Like I said before, tell Bellamy I'm busy running down a couple of leads."

"And then you'll come back?"

"Yep," Larry said, like a man telling his mistress he was going to leave his wife. "Then I'll come back."

****

In the sheriff's office in Raton, New Mexico, Nick placed a cardboard box on top of his desk. On the side of the box were written in black permanent marker the words *O'Neil, Tim,* followed by a case number. The deputy lifted the lid off and peered down at the collection of what anyone else would see as garbage.

One at a time, he pulled out the bagged and labeled pieces of potential evidence from the shooting.

The coroner had said Tim's wound was a through-and-through, and the resulting search for the bullet had been intense. But the forest covered thousands of acres, and that crucial piece of evidence remained elusive. The bullet from the dead hunter had been retrieved, but without the one that killed O'Neil to match it, there was no way to know if the same weapon had been used on both men.

"Come on, talk to me." Nick pulled a thick manila folder from a black wire, louvered holder on his desk, opened the folder and reviewed his notes on O'Neil's death. He re-read every field note and scribbled marginal notation, all of which he'd read so many times he could quote them from memory.

Frankie had said two men tailgated her and Tim from the time they left Albuquerque. And she seemed fairly certain Tim knew them because of his reaction when she asked about a green pickup. If that was the case, someone at the hospital where he worked might know something. Or one of his neighbors might have seen something. And she was right about one thing, although it did happen, anyone who hunted knew it was illegal to fire a weapon from a vehicle. Especially from a moving vehicle.

That left three possible explanations: either the O'Neils had been partners in some scheme that made them both targets, but the shooter missed Frankie; or Tim had been the target all along; or Frankie had been the real target. But unless Frankie was a consummate actress, and Nick reluctantly had to admit to that possibility, she had no idea as to why someone would shoot Tim. He'd bet a year's wages she didn't manufacture the look that flared in her eyes when he told her the investigation had stalled due to lack of evidence. Anger, and not an inkling of fear for her own safety. No sign of guilt, or any other indication that she knew the reason behind her brother's murder.

He read through the statements made by O'Neil's friends, neighbors, and co-workers. All of them expressed surprise at Dr. O'Neil's death. All of them appeared to have held Tim in high esteem. No one could think of anyone who would want to hurt the good doctor, et cetera, et cetera.

The statement given by a nurse named Landowski piqued his curiosity. He read with interest how she skirted some of the questions put to her by the interviewing officer, as well as her oblique references to an antipathy between doctors Bellamy and O'Neil. He reached for the desk phone and punched in a number. After several rings, a voice answered.

"Hey, Ted," Nick said. "How're tricks in the Albuquerque Police Department?"

"Nothing new, old buddy. Just the usual mayhem, political squabbling and bureaucratic BS you'd find anywhere else in this great country. No different than when we were MPs in the Corps. What's happening in your neck of the woods?"

"You remember the O'Neil shooting? I've been going over the statements you guys took. By the way, thanks for keeping me in the loop on that."

"No problem. Anything useful?"

"Not much to go on. But I was wondering if your guys did any follow up. Hoping maybe someone added something to their earlier statement, that kind of thing."

"I sent you copies of everything we have in the file. You want to ride into town, shoot up the place, and drag answers from the populace?"

Nick chuckled. "Sort of. I'd like to pay a visit to the hospital where O'Neil worked."

"Not a problem. I'll let the powers that be know you'll be in town. Anything in particular feel funny to you?"

"Nothing I can put my finger on."

"Ahh, the famous Non-specific Rollins Brain Tingle."

"Go ahead and make fun. But O'Neil's sister said a nurse at the hospital where Tim worked might have some important information. A talk with her seems like a good place to start."

"Have at it. Let me know if I can help."

Nick hung up the phone. He sat at his desk, drumming his pen on its cluttered top.

No one lived a completely isolated life. Someone somewhere knew what had happened to Tim O'Neil and why.

Chapter Twenty-Three

Frankie's daily counting ritual had lengthened until it stole nearly three hours out of her morning. That should probably bother her more than it did. But life was, after all, made up of a series of tradeoffs. And the subsequent sense of temporary peace, albeit mingled with guilt and shame, seemed worth the ever-increasing cost to her self-esteem.

Between bites of breakfast, she reviewed her list of possible suspects in Tim's death, scribbling notes on a piece of notebook paper. On the first line she wrote *the two men who broke in to Tim's apartment.* She added *one with a pockmarked face, and one with a baby face. Motive: Unknown.*

She considered writing Mina's name in the second slot, but why would the nurse want Tim dead? Had they been romantically involved? That didn't seem likely. Mina's demeanor had been one of respect and admiration, not of a jilted lover. And Frankie was certain it had been two men in that pickup. If one of them had been a woman, she'd have had to put her hair up into a cap. Mina's hair was too thick, long, and heavy to manage that.

As for the other hospital employees, Mina said Tim was loved and respected by everyone with whom he worked. Everyone but Bellamy. Frankie jotted down the doctor's name as second on her list. Next to it, she wrote the words *Motive: jealous hack.*

In third place she wrote *Guy in the Camaro, Motive: unfinished business?*

She wrote Flatte's name in fourth place. But although he was a pompous narcissist, she could see no motive for Tim's attorney to kill him. Flatte might be compelled to murder someone he perceived as a threat to his social or financial status, but Tim certainly hadn't fit that bill. She scribbled a question mark next to Flatte's name.

As number five, she wrote: *Relatives of Esther Emory.* Although none were listed in the medical records, that didn't rule out their existence. She'd heard Tim complain on more than one occasion about errors in the records. But she'd only begin the process of ferreting them out if none of the other leads showed promise.

As suspect number six, Frankie listed Nick Rollins. She knew of no reason for him to kill Tim, but he worked in the area where the murder took place. But then, so did all of Eagle Nest. She jabbed her pen against the paper and scratched three question marks next to the deputy's name so forcefully the paper tore.

Her landline rang. Hoping it was Mina, she grabbed the telephone.

"Good morning, Miss O'Neil. Jeremy Flatte returning your call."

"Oh. Good morning, Counselor."

"Ouch," Flatte said.

"Sorry, I'm expecting another call. But I do appreciate your getting back to me."

"I won't take up more than a minute or two. I wondered if you'd have dinner with me tonight."

Surely Flatte had sensed her negative reaction to him during their first meeting. But maybe his ego buffered the input, and he figured he'd misread her vibes.

"This could be a working dinner if you like," Flatte added. "Can I pick you up at seven?"

"A working dinner sounds good. I do have a couple of things I'd like to run past you, but at your usual hourly rate."

Flatte chuckled. "If you insist. I'll see you then."

Frankie hung up the phone, wondering how she was going to pay for the attorney's time. Her mind flashed on the pile of gold coins in Tim's safe deposit box. The things were probably worth many thousands of dollars in today's market. But she couldn't see herself doing anything with the coins until she discovered where they'd come from.

"Man oh man, Tim. You left quite a mess."

Her brother's droll voice floated into Frankie's ears: *Hence the letter of apology.*

Frankie jumped when her cell rang, interrupting her thoughts. The caller identification listed a familiar number, though she couldn't place it.

"Miss O'Neil?" the male voice at the other end of the line said.

"Speaking."

"This is Hector Cordero."

"Oh yes, Mister Cordero. Thank you for getting back to me. I found your phone number in Tim's address book, and it looks like he had an appointment with you just before he died. I was hoping you could tell me what that was about."

The line went silent for a few seconds. When

Hector's voice came back on, it was softer, nearly a whisper.

"I asked him to meet me, yes. I had some medical questions and he offered to come by my work station."

"At seven in the morning on the day he was murdered?"

"Yes."

"And did he keep that appointment?"

"Yes. But Miss O'Neil, I cannot talk now, I'm at work. My wife called me with your message because she thought it might be important."

"I was hoping we could meet somewhere for coffee."

"I would be glad to meet with you. I may not be able to answer your questions, but my wife would love to meet the sister of the man who helped us so much. Please join us for dinner tomorrow evening. We always eat at six, but you're welcome to come earlier."

"I'd like that." Frankie jotted down the address and hung up.

If Hector Cordero had been one of the men in the green pickup, she might be walking into a trap. She didn't really think he'd hurt her in front of his family, but it was a chance she'd have to take. And he could be an important domino. She added Hector's name as number seven on her list of suspects.

****

Larry had settled into his usual spot in Frankie's tree just as a late model sports car pulled into her driveway. Some guy wearing a western shirt with pearl snaps, a black leather vest, designer jeans and ostrich boots climbed out of the car, walked up to Frankie's door and rang the bell. Although he didn't recognize the guy, Larry could smell his money. He drove a BMW convertible with its top down in spite of the cool autumn evening, and looked like he'd dressed to impress someone. Dressed to kill.

Frankie came to the door wearing denim jeans stuffed into brown leather, high-heeled boots, a gold colored jacket zipped up against the cold air, and a thick, fluffy scarf the color of her hair wrapped a couple of times around her neck. Larry's breath caught in his throat. And he knew all too well how the vision was affecting the butt-nugget standing there ogling her.

"I hope you're up for steak," Rich Boy said.

Larry strained to hear Frankie's answer but was too far away to understand her murmured response.

"Good. I'd like to try out that new steakhouse on Jefferson." The guy bent his elbow and held out his arm for Frankie to hold on to. Larry squelched a chuckle when she ignored it and headed toward the Beemer.

The sports car pulled out of the drive and sped off. For the next couple of hours, Larry tortured himself with images of Frankie and Rich Boy. He pictured the couple at dinner, gazing into each other's eyes. He could hear Frankie laughing at the dip-wad's jokes, a lock of her hair falling over her right eye as it often did. And he could see Rich Boy's eyes flashing on high beam as he weighed his chances of getting Frankie into the sack.

Larry began to hum an old song about a bad moon being on the rise. Yup, this was shaping up to be one of those bad moon nights, sure enough.

****

While waiting for the garden salad prelude to the pan-seared rib eye steaks, Flatte sipped Petite Sirah and

Frankie drank iced tea.

"How well did you know Tim?"

"I actually saw him in person only the two times he came to my office to set up his trust. I spoke to him on the phone a couple of times after that. Why?"

"Just trying to fill in some gaps. I'm talking to anyone with whom he came into contact the last weeks of his life in hopes they can shed some light on his death."

Flatte puffed out his lips, the expression on his face quizzical, as if she'd spoken in Urdu. "Don't you think you should let the police take care of that? That's what they get paid to do."

"You may be right, but so far the police haven't found any leads."

"But who would want to kill Tim? He seemed like a great guy."

"You said we could call this a working dinner. I need to ask you a couple of questions."

"Of course." Flatte leaned forward in his chair.

"Am I correct in assuming that anything I tell you will be held in confidence?"

"I'm your brother's attorney, and you are the executrix to his estate. Attorney client privilege about anything concerning his trust, within certain legal parameters, is a given. What can I do you for?" The words were followed by a smirk and a surprisingly lecherous grin.

Frankie ignored the double entendre and mentally kicked herself for not bringing her own car. But, she reminded herself, she could always call a cab. She just hoped the cab driver would take a credit card. "What if I found evidence of Tim's involvement in something questionable? How would I go about setting it right?"

A puzzled look flitted across Flatte's face. "Can you be more specific?"

"What if I found a stash of gold coins in his safe deposit box?"

Flatte nodded his head. "Good for your brother. Lots of people are investing in gold right now. And other than an in-floor safe, a safe deposit box is about as secure a place to store them as any."

"But Tim's bank records don't reflect any large purchases. And he hadn't started earning enough money yet to buy one gold coin, let alone a box full."

Flatte shrugged. "Tim struck me as a shrewd money manager. I'm sure there's a reasonable answer, you just haven't found it yet. But that reminds me, you remember I said there were a couple of things that needed attention? You'll need to send a statement of Tim's assets to the IRS. Although his estate is not large enough to require you to pay estate tax, you'll be required to pay taxes on any interest accrued from the time of his death."

"But that's just it. He didn't have a savings account or a retirement fund. Just the gold coins."

"Then you'll need to document where he got them, along with their current value. Nothing the IRS would like more than to bust someone for evading taxes."

"I'll need your help in getting his transaction records from the gold company." Frankie handed Flatte a paper upon which she'd written the gold merchant's phone number.

"No problem, I'll get my assistant to draw up the necessary documents in the next day or so. You said a couple of questions?"

Frankie nodded. "I also found some patient medical information on his laptop."

"And that struck you as strange in what way?" Flatte's voice assumed a patronizing tone. "Tim was a doctor. Doctors work with patient records every day."

"But do they make copies and take them home?"

The attorney held his hands out palms up. "There are several perfectly reasonable explanations for why Tim might keep track of some of the patients with whom he worked."

"Like what?"

"Like research for a paper he wanted to write, for one."

Frankie considered the attorney's comment. Maybe he was right about everything. Maybe Tim had done really well at something like day trading in the stock market and invested his profit in gold as a hedge against inflation. And as for the medical records, Frankie didn't know what comprised legal or illegal, ethical or unethical activities in medical circles. Maybe he'd done nothing wrong at all.

But none of her rationalized explanations explained either Tim's letter, or Mina's reaction to the spreadsheet. Suddenly, Frankie wished dinner would be over so she could get home and call the nurse.

****

By the time Frankie and Rich Boy returned, Larry had worked himself up into an emotional lather. His facial muscles felt tight, and his belly seethed. He strained to hear the conversation between the two as they stood on the porch. What would he do if Beauty invited the guy into her house for a long goodbye?

"Thanks for dinner and the consultation," Frankie

was saying.

"I did intend to pay for your dinner as well," Rich Boy said. "But I respect independence in a woman." Butt-nugget leaned toward Frankie, his intention to kiss her obvious.

Larry's pulse rate picked up speed. His vision blurred and blood rushed to his extremities. The primal urge to kill anyone perceived to be a rival for the favors of his woman beat rhythmically in the veins at his temples. Poised to spring on the guy, Larry held himself in check to see how Frankie would respond to his advances. He smiled to himself when she stepped back to put distance between the two of them and unlocked her door.

"I'll contact your office in the next few days to finish up."

"How about a cup of coffee?" Rich Boy took a step forward.

"Sorry, but I have several things to do yet, and I have an early morning." Frankie stepped through her door. She turned and said, "Please let me know as soon as you've contacted the gold company." She closed the door.

Evidently the guy rarely got turned down, because he stood on the porch, seemingly unsure of what to do next. Finally, he returned to his car, started the engine, and did something to make the roof glide back up into place.

Larry swung down from the tree and hot-footed it to his own vehicle. For the first time, he saw it as it must look to other people. To him, it had been an acceptable means of getting around, even with its dented fenders, cracked windshield, broken tail light, and nearly bald tires. But to people like Rich Boy it would be a joke. And he would be a joke for driving it.

His throat tight and blood pounding, Larry turned on the ignition and pulled onto the street behind Rich Boy.

Chapter Twenty-Four

As soon as Flatte drove away, Frankie checked her answering machine. The single flash sent her sprinting to the phone.

"Hey, Frankie. This is Mina. I'm sorry I haven't called earlier, but I wanted to double check a couple of things before getting back to you. You remember I said something about Tim's spreadsheet seemed off? Well I found a couple of—"

A doorbell rang in the background, and the nurse's voice grew distant as she turned her head away from the phone. "Just a minute," she yelled. The phone made jostling sounds as it was repositioned, and Mina's voice became clear again. "I'll try your cell. Call me as soon as you get this, no matter how late it is."

Frankie pulled her cell from its holster and checked voice mail and the incoming call log: nothing from Mina.

It seemed like hours before Frankie could quiet her racing mind and fall asleep. She couldn't stop speculating about what Mina had learned. And she couldn't stop mulling over what connection it might have to Tim's death.

When she woke up the next morning, she grabbed her paper and pen and scribbled: *Someone is hungry. Hungry and in a dark place. Feelings: Dread, fear, sadness.*

She went through her morning chores by rote, the feelings dredged up by her dreams hanging around her neck like Scrooge's dead partner Marley's chains.

Before driving to the Cordero home, Frankie stopped at a florist and picked up a bouquet of daisies and mums. She arrived at six on the dot and rang the bell. A lovely Latina opened the door, allowing the complex aromas of New Mexican food to pour out the opening. Frankie's mouth watered.

"Hello, Miss O'Neil, I'm Imelda. Please, come in."

Frankie handed the flowers to Hector's wife, who escorted her to the living room of the small, spotless home. A handsome, black-haired, dark-eyed man of about thirty rose from an overstuffed chair in the adjacent living room and strode toward Frankie, his hand extended.

"Good evening, Miss O'Neil. It's good to see you again. Seeing you is like seeing your brother."

"Thank you." Frankie shook Hector's extended hand. "And thank you for the invitation. Something smells wonderful."

A tiny, brown-eyed girl dressed in purple leggings and a purple and white-flowered tunic peered out from behind Imelda's legs.

"Hello," Frankie said to the pixie-faced child.

Imelda bent down and picked up her little girl. "Anna, this is Miss O'Neil."

"Hello, Anna," Frankie said. "I really like your dress."

Imelda put Anna down and held a hand toward an arched doorway. "Dinner is ready. Please come in."

Hector took his place at one end of the small dining table and motioned for Frankie to sit at the other.

Imelda brought out steaming bowls and platters of food, which she placed on hot pads strategically set out around a centerpiece of dried multi-colored corn and candles. The family offered grace and began to eat.

The meal was an amazing compilation of homemade tortillas, *chiles rellenos*, pinto beans, Spanish rice and pulled roast pork simmered in a thick red chile sauce. Dessert was a rich vanilla pudding called *natillas* topped with real whipped cream and fresh strawberries. Dinner conversation focused on little Anna's school work, on Frankie's concert schedule, and on an authentic New Mexican cookbook Imelda was preparing for publication. After dessert, Imelda shooed Anna to her room to do her homework, and Hector invited Frankie to the living room for coffee.

Hector sat down in the chair from which he'd stood earlier. The smile he'd worn since she arrived was replaced by a look of what appeared to be concern. Frankie took a seat on the sofa across from him.

"I've been thinking about my responsibility to your brother," Hector said. "I owe him a great debt. Whatever is in my power to do for you, I will do."

"Thank you. Did you know Tim was fired from his job at the hospital?"

Hector nodded his head. "Yes. We were all angry about it, but no one was surprised."

"Do you know why he was let go?"

Hector dropped his gaze to look at his feet. He slowly shook his head. "Doctor Bellamy and Doctor O'Neil often fought. It was just a matter of time before one of them had to leave."

"Would you be willing to tell me what your appointment with Tim was about?"

Hector's forehead creased as he considered his answer. "When Anna became sick we were beside ourselves with worry. We didn't know where to turn. Doctor Tim helped us, so it was only natural for me to think of him when I started having headaches. He said he'd look me over during my breakfast break."

"Did he say anything about what was bothering him?"

"Not that I can remember." Hector's gaze moved to the floor in front of him. He took a deep breath and let it out through pursed lips. "I gave him a small gift. Just something I thought he could use." He lifted his shoulders in a tight shrug. "Then he checked me and left." Hector moved his eyes to look directly into Frankie's. "Do you believe in God, Miss O'Neil?"

"Yes, I do. Why do you ask?"

"Do you believe vengeance is best left to Him?"

"That's what the scripture says. But I also believe in justice."

Hector nodded. "Your brother was a good man and I'll miss him. But nothing will bring him back to us. Our responsibility is to protect those we love who are still with us." He opened his mouth, closed it, clenched his jaw and remained silent.

"Hector, if you know anything about my brother's murder, please tell me."

"I don't know anything for certain, and it would be wrong to speculate. I can only tell you that our God is just. He will punish whoever killed Doctor Tim."

Hector stood and held his hand toward Frankie. "It's been good to meet you. We continue to pray for the peace of Doctor Tim's soul." As he shook Frankie's hand, he placed his other hand on top of it, the look on his face one of deep concern. "You must be careful. Whoever is responsible for your brother's death will not hesitate to hurt you."

Frankie thanked Imelda for the dinner, hugged Anna, told them all good night, and headed for her car.

It had been comforting to meet people who loved Tim, even if the evening had brought nothing new to light about his death. It had, however, offered a couple of intriguing tidbits. It left no doubt in Frankie's mind that whatever Hector's meeting with Tim had been about, it involved a lot more than headaches. And with all his talk of vengeance, it supported her theory that Hector was a domino.

But where did he fit in the lineup? Was he the first tile, or the last?

As anyone knew who'd ever set up a domino chain, one misstep, one fumble, could topple the whole thing prematurely. And when the falling process began, it would move with lightning speed until the whole thing lay in a heap.

Then, once all the dominoes were lined up, the most important thing was to thump the right one.

Chapter Twenty-Five

Frances, Frances wake up. Uncle Mike's voice made its way into Frankie's dreams just as the phone re-charging on her nightstand rang. As phone calls in the middle of the night tend to do, it shot her heart rate into the stratosphere and sent her bleary eyes darting toward her lighted bedside clock. Two-thirty. Her first thought was that it must be Tim calling. But then her sleep benumbed brain told herself, no, Tim was dead.

Frankie reached to turn on the bedside lamp, but instead knocked over a half-filled water glass on the nightstand beside it. Murmuring a string of imprecations that would have shocked the more conservative of her choir members, she sat up on the bed's edge, grabbed the phone, and unplugged the power cord from it.

"Hello," she said, her voice more croaking toad than human.

"Get out of the house." The whispered words sounded tense, distorted.

"What?"

"I said get out of the house." The voice increased in volume.

"Who's this?"

"A friend. No time for questions and no time to dress. Just get out." The caller hung up.

Fully awake, Frankie grabbed her robe from the

end of the bed. She slipped it on and slid her feet into furry, flip-flop slippers. The smoke alarm began pulsing its warning as an undulating yellow glow spilled into the hallway from the living room. Crackling sounds of burning wood soon became a low roar, and the air thickened with smoke.

Fear seized Frankie's stomach in an icy fist. Had she forgotten to bank last night's fire? Had Collette somehow managed to get beyond the fire screen and paw a glowing ember onto the rug?

She dropped her phone into her robe pocket and grabbed her purse, tote bag, and keys. With the flames lighting her way, Frankie lurched toward the front door. She disengaged the Katy bar and slid back the chain lock, but Collette's throaty growl of terror stopped her from stepping out into the night.

After a millisecond of internal debate, she closed the door, turned back toward the hall closet, and grabbed the pet carrier while calling the cat's name. But Collette didn't appear.

Intensely aware of the ticking seconds and billowing black smoke, she ran through the rooms not yet aflame, lowering her head to see under the roiling ceiling of black smoke. Her eyes watered, and her lungs heaved in an effort to draw in oxygen.

She should leave the cat to fend for itself, but the damned creature was helpless. It needed her, depended upon her.

She gave her life for an arrogant animal that couldn't have cared less. Too many words for an epitaph, but they might make for a good obituary. Frankie's self-mocking snort metamorphosed into a coughing spasm.

As smoke clogged her throat and swirled around her head, she ran to the living room, where Collette snarled at the world from her favorite hiding place atop the bookcase. Frankie reached for the animal, but the terrified creature shied from her touch. Hissing and growling, she pressed her body tightly against the wall and swiped at her owner's extended hand.

"You either come with me, or your next eight lives will be spent playing a harp in kitty heaven." Frankie made her voice as calm as she could. "And I'll be right there beside you, honking away on my harmonium." She held the open carrier in front of Collette as she had done at the kennel. "I'm counting to five. After that, you're on your own."

Collette surprised her by shooting into the pet carrier. Coughing and gagging, Frankie carried her through the front door and out into the night.

With the furnace-like heat at her back, the cold night air flowed over Frankie like ice water poured from a pitcher. She set the pet carrier down on the concrete of the driveway and reached into her pocket for the phone. Her shivering fingers grew numb as she punched in the emergency number and reported the fire.

The fire grew in intensity. Its dancing glow lit up the windows as its victory cry roared into the night stillness. The smell of burning wood filled the still air.

A list ran through Frankie's mind of all the things she wished she'd had the time and presence of mind to bring out with her. Important things like legal documents and family photos. Things like Tim's laptop containing his journal and notes.

Tim's laptop.

Frankie dropped her bags on the driveway next to

Collette and ran back toward the house. But the fire's heat reached her before she got near the door. The adobe construction of the house created an oven effect, making the fire so intense the paint on the outside of the door bubbled and the metal door handle glowed red-orange.

Tears that had nothing to do with the burning smoke sprang from her eyes. Her new home, her oasis from the world was disappearing in front of her. Her new furniture, her new window dressings, her clothes. All gone, along with her food stores.

Feeling as if she'd just been sucker-punched, she picked up the carrier and put it into the passenger seat of her car. She climbed in behind the wheel, backed out of the driveway, and parked a little way down the street to allow the fire truck easy access. She turned off the engine, stared out the windshield, and waited.

Several lights came on in neighboring houses. Heads appeared in doorways and drapes were pushed aside.

Frankie opened the carrier door, and the cat jumped into her lap. The two huddled together, watching their home burn.

Firemen, police, and emergency first-responders arrived less than ten minutes after her call. Bustling activity replaced the quiet stillness typical of very early morning. The roar of flames mingled with the shouts of the firemen as they moved in practiced efficiency, focused on their fight with the beast consuming her home. She got out of the car and approached one young fireman pulling tools from a truck.

"This was no accident," she said, her voice flat.

The fireman's head shot up, and his eyes locked

onto Frankie's. "And you are…?"

"The owner. This is my house. I'm Frankie O'Neil."

"Do you know how the fire started?"

"No, I don't. But someone called me and warned me to get out. Otherwise I'd probably still be in bed." Disbelief mixed with horror as the reality of her words hit her with the force of a sledge hammer.

The fireman nodded toward an older man talking into a phone. "Our fire officer will call an investigator. He should be here shortly."

Frankie nearly doubled over with a coughing spasm, and the fireman motioned for her to stay put. He stepped to a lidded box built into the side of the fire truck, and pulled out a blanket, which he threw over her shoulders.

A female paramedic carrying an oxygen tank approached. "I'm told you inhaled some smoke. Oxygen will help your lungs do their work."

After Frankie nodded her acceptance of the young woman's ministrations, the EMT slipped the oxygen mask over her face and turned on the valve.

"You're lucky you got out when you did. Most people who die in fires don't die from the flames, they die from smoke inhalation. But your color's already improving." The young woman snapped a plastic, clothespin-looking instrument onto the tip of Frankie's index finger. "Your blood oxygen level is not bad. But if you'd like, we can take you to the hospital for observation and some tests."

Frankie shook her head. "No, I'm feeling better…I feel okay." Besides, her insurance deductible was more than she could manage. The only way anyone was going to get her into a hospital was if she were unconscious.

When she could fill her lungs with air without coughing, she pulled the oxygen mask off. She thanked the young woman for her help, signed the form that would be used in the police report and sent to her insurance company as proof of services rendered, and made her way back to her vehicle.

She started the engine and turned on the heater. In a few minutes warm air poured through the vents. Frankie offered a prayer of thanksgiving for the genius who invented the marvelous thing.

A man approached, and she rolled down her window. Cold air poured in, displacing the warm bubble inside her car. The man nodded his head once by way of salutation, introduced himself as the fire investigator and questioned her. He asked her things like what time the call came, did she have any enemies, did she ever burn candles, and did she leave a fire going in the fireplace.

Then he pulled a paper from a green plastic folder and handed it through the window. He instructed Frankie to fill out the interview form and then write on the back her memory of events up to and including the time she received the call.

"We're nearly done here," he said. "Once everything has cooled down, we'll determine the cause of the fire. We'll most likely need to speak to you again. Do you have anywhere to go tonight, someplace to stay?"

Frankie's mind went blank. "I…I hadn't even thought about it."

"Any family close by? Someone we could call for

you?"

"No…no one." *You don't even have any close friends.* "I'll stay in a motel for a while."

The investigator nodded, and returned to the scene of the fire.

Several neighbors assembled in their yards. They stood watching the conflagration, their concern for the safety of their own homes nearly palpable in the flickering light. As if on swivels, their heads turned back and forth between her and the fire, their attention captivated by the destruction of someone else's life. A few cars drove slowly by, the drivers craning their necks toward the scene. Some slowed to a stop, but moved on as the police motioned them on.

The crowd of onlookers grew from a few to several. Some of the younger ones held cell phones above their heads, their tiny cameras turned toward the scene. No doubt they'd soon be frantically posting their videos on their chosen networking site in hopes of becoming the next internet star.

"So glad I could be a source of entertainment for you and your friends," Frankie murmured under her breath toward the human-shaped shadows jockeying for a position with an unobstructed view.

People can't resist scenes of destruction, Uncle Mike's voice whispered. *It's just human nature.*

"Yeah?" Frankie shot back. "Well, it's a different thing when it's your own life being destroyed."

It's just stuff, Frances. Stuff can be replaced.

Frankie stared at the mob milling around just outside the police barricade. Two faces caught her attention. One was a baby faced young man who stared into the flames, a look of pure delight on his face. The other young man, someone she'd seen but couldn't figure out where, stared intently and directly at her. When certain he'd caught her eye, he smiled and raised his hand in a mock salute.

Two young men. One with a baby face.

Frankie shoved open her car door and stumbled out. "Hey!"

A dozen faces turned toward her. Not caring how she must have looked to her neighbors, she hugged the fireman's blanket against her body and ran toward the two men. But one flip flop flew off her foot, and her bare flesh landed on the icy asphalt. A shock wave shot up her leg, forcing her to stop long enough to re-shoe.

A series of loud popping sounds erupted from the fire, and she instinctively jerked her gaze toward the blaze. When she turned back again, both men were gone.

A feeling moved up her spine as if an ice cube were being run along its bony ridge. Because she was certain the baby faced man was the one she'd seen peering at her from inside the Chevy Camaro. And the look he'd shot at her just before disappearing from the crowd was exactly the same as the one he'd worn while trying to run her down.

Frankie's neighbor, Lola, moved toward her from among the crowd. Murmuring words of comfort, she gripped Frankie's hand in her own bony fingers. "You're shaking like a leaf in a gale. You'll catch your death of cold. You should get back inside your car."

As if in a trance, Frankie tore her eyes from the fire to look at the only neighbor she really knew. "I don't...I don't seem to feel much of anything."

Lola nodded her head as if she understood. "In that

case, you stay here. I'll be right back." She walked to her house and returned with a tan wool jacket and fluffy plaid scarf. "These belonged to my Cathy. I think you're about her size."

"Bless you, Lola." Frankie slid the blanket off her shoulders and put on the proffered coat. She wound the scarf around her neck, grateful for its immediate warmth.

The old widow waved her hand dismissively. "Now listen, you're going to need a place to stay until things get sorted out, and I have an extra room. You're welcome to stay as long as you need." The old woman pressed a house key into Frankie's palm and folded her fingers over it. "This is to the back door. There's a stairwell just inside the entry and to the left that'll take you to an apartment over the garage. There's a bedroom, bath and kitchenette. I had it remodeled for my Cathy." The old woman turned to go, stopped and turned back. "And you can bring the cat," she said. "My Tommy got sick, and I had him put down. But I kept his food and water dishes, and a few toys."

To ensure every hotspot had been thoroughly doused, the firemen continued to drench the ruins of Frankie's home long after the flames had disappeared. The morning sun was rising by the time the soot-begrimed, tired men packed up their gear and left.

Neighbors retreated in gratitude to their homes. A couple of them threw glances back over their shoulders, as if reluctant to leave the scene of such devastation.

Frankie approached the burned-out shell of her home. Due to the rapidity with which the fire department responded, a couple of the outer adobe walls remained standing. But much of the sun-hardened mud now lay on the tile floor - her retreat from the world reduced in a few hours to a puddle of hot, steaming mud.

Her shoulders sagged and her fluffy, green flip flop-shod feet barely cleared the asphalt as she carried the pet carrier containing Collette toward Lola's house. The smells of smoke and burning plastic hung in the air, and the morning sun lit up the green and yellow paisley print of her satin pajamas like the neon of an all-night diner.

As Lola had instructed, she unlocked her neighbor's back door, walked up the stairs, and entered a small apartment. An electric space heater stood in one corner. Its red glowing filaments warmed the room and added an amber light to that cast by the bedside lamp. The lilac floral wallpaper, probably from the eighties, matched the filmy, lavender-colored curtains that framed the only window. Closed Venetian blinds partially blocked the rising sun's rays, dimming the room and casting shards of light onto the barely worn purple shag carpet.

The pungent smell of mothballs radiated from a free standing armoire located against one wall. Frankie pulled open the hinged door and moved her eyes over the clothes hanging there. Skinny jeans, carefully torn at the knees and frayed at the bottoms, a couple of tee shirts screen printed with the names of heavy metal bands, a well-worn jean jacket adorned with safety pins holding tiny swatches of fabric, and a pair of black spandex trousers proclaimed Lola's daughter to have had punk rocker leanings. A pair of leather, high-top Doc Martens rested on the armoire's floor next to a pair of sneakers.

From the way Lola spoke, Frankie had got the impression Cathy left home fairly recently. But based on the outdated, yet still new looking carpet and clothing, it must have been years earlier. Without a speck of dust or a single cobweb in its corners, the room felt like a memorial. More proof that sooner or later, people always lost the ones they loved.

She stepped over to a short bureau next to the armoire and pulled open the top drawer. Rows of neatly folded bras and matching panties lay side by side. The woodsy fragrance of cedar squares used as a deterrent to insects wafted into the room.

The pitiful sight of Cathy's intimate apparel, so carefully left in place, tugged at Frankie's heart. That and the thought of feisty little old Lola, hanging on to the hope that one day her middle-aged daughter would come home.

A litter box lay on a plastic placemat in the corner of the room. Two white ceramic dishes, one filled with kibble and the other with fresh water, lay on another. Briefly wondering about the expiration date of the kibble, she approached the bed.

The dark wood double bed appeared to be an antique. Covered with a thick, purple, down comforter, it stood high off the floor. Two or three changes of neatly folded clothes lay on top of the duvet, and a pair of tan leather slip-ons lay on the floor beside the bed.

When Frankie opened the door to the pet carrier, Collette shot into the room as if fired from a circus cannon. She made several circuits around the small space, jumped up onto the bed, shot a look at Frankie that could only be translated as a warning not to try to interfere with her plans, and chose a resting place on one of the pillows.

Frankie visited the tiny bathroom and then headed for bed. Careful not to disturb the snoozing Collette, she piled the clothes on a chair, and then slid under the covers. The pillow top mattress conformed to her body and muscle tension in her shoulders, neck, and back loosened.

But her mind swam with chaotic thoughts. Unable to lie still, the torque of her tossing body wrapped her in the sheets like a lavender colored mummy.

The caller had saved her life. But how had he known about the fire in the first place? How had he got hold of her unlisted number? And how had the two young men come to be in the neighborhood at exactly the time her home was burning?

It seemed she could almost feel the sulfurous wind of evil swirling around her, filling the air, enveloping her in its thickness. And just as with a hundred twenty mile-per-hour category three hurricane, the question was not whether the wind was blowing—the question was what the wind was blowing.

Chapter Twenty-Six

Larry sat in a chair in front of Bellamy's desk while Mel assumed his usual slumped position in the chair to his right. The two remained immobile as the doctor dialed a number on a burner phone. Bellamy drummed his fingers on the desk, and then stopped drumming, sat up straight and spoke into the phone.

"We heard about your unsuccessful attempt to torch our little Miss O'Neil," Bellamy said. "We appreciate your efforts, but cannot help wondering how well you covered your tracks."

Bellamy paused while the other person responded.

"If you didn't, who did?" Larry's boss leveled a look at him and Mel. He made a *tsk tsk* sound through his teeth, and turned his attention back to the caller. "That's too bad. We thought you might be showing a bit of initiative, regardless of how ill-advised."

The caller's voice grew louder, but the words remained unintelligible.

"Make no mistake," Bellamy's voice rested on the s like a hissing snake, "you will do exactly as you're told, and that includes carrying out any of what you refer to as our dirty work." He turned his office chair so that he squarely faced his two employees. "Name calling is a tool of the lower classes. Mel and Larry would be incensed if they knew you'd referred to them as mindless toadies."

"If you think I'm going to kill someone for you, you're out of your mind." This time the caller's words were loud enough to be understood in the otherwise silent room.

"That's possible, but beside the point. We'll be in touch with further instructions." Bellamy broke the connection and turned his head toward Larry and Mel. His eyes narrowed.

"Do either of you know anything about the fire that destroyed Miss O'Neil's house last night?"

Larry and Mel simultaneously shook their heads.

Bellamy snorted. "Bobble-heads." He stood and walked to the picture window. "We'll only say this once, so listen carefully. Nothing untoward will happen to Miss O'Neil until we say. No more acting on your own. We will decide what, when, and where anything will be done about her. Is that absolutely clear?"

"Yessir," Larry said.

Mel nodded his head once.

"Good. Lest there be even a hint of misunderstanding, hear this: if we learn that one or both of you have drawn attention to us by doing something other than what you are told to do, it will take the police weeks to fish the pieces of you out of the Rio Grande. That is, any pieces the catfish haven't eaten. *Capisce*?"

"Yes sir," Larry said.

Mel nodded. But as Bellamy turned away, Mel smiled his rare, crooked smile. It lasted only an instant, but that death's head smile told Larry all he needed to know.

He'd have to make his move quickly, before Mel could carry out whatever plan his messed-up brain was working on.

****

Frankie awoke to the fragrance of fresh coffee and sizzling bacon. Normally the smells would have made her mouth water. Instead, her stomach tossed bile up into her throat at the thought of the acid and grease soaked fare.

Her eyes felt rusty as old hinges. She could almost hear them squeaking as she moved them around the momentarily unfamiliar room. The taste in her mouth reminded her of the time-to-change-me-now fragrance of Collette's litter box, and her head throbbed. The smell of her burning home coated the insides of her nostrils and clung to her flesh.

"Frankie?" Lola's stage whisper through the bedroom door sounded conspiratorial. "Frankie dear, there's someone here about the fire."

"Okay. Give me a minute." Frankie threw back the covers and stepped out of bed. She stumbled into the bathroom. A small, clear plastic travel bag filled with bottles of creams, ointments, shampoo, deodorant and other necessities lay on the counter next to a faux tortoise shell comb and brush. Fresh towels and washcloths hung from the towel rack.

After splashing water on her face, she hurriedly brushed her hair, pulled on a pair of blue jeans and a pink cotton knit sweater from the clothes Lola had left on the bed. She slid her feet into the flip flops, and headed downstairs.

A heavyset man somewhere in his mid-fifties sat in one of Lola's straight backed cane-bottomed, wooden chairs. His khaki trousers looked two sizes too small, and his light blue dress shirt looked like he'd just pulled it out of a laundry hamper. With a cleanly shaven head, no discernible eyebrows, and a body shaped like a beach ball, the man looked like an alien being out of a science fiction movie. His ponderous thighs drooped over the sides of the chair, and he kept shifting his position. An unwelcome image blazed across Frankie's mind of the effect the waffle pattern on the chair's seat must have been having on the man's backside. He seemed relieved to have an excuse to stand up as she entered the room.

"Good day, Miss O'Neil. I'm Aaron Blinquet. I'm an investigator with the Violent Crimes Division of the Albuquerque Police Department."

Frankie's eyebrows arched. "Violent Crimes? You're not here about the fire?"

"Not so much about the fire, no." Blinquet bent his knees slightly and wiggled his ass in a motion Frankie had seen heavy men do to dislodge wedgied underwear. His face turning bright crimson as he realized what he'd just done in the company of two women, he emitted a couple of harrumphs and resumed his seat.

Nice. Tim's voice sounded in Frankie's ear. She smiled before she could catch herself.

"Did I say something amusing?" Blinquet said.

"No...I'm sorry, it's just—this has all been such a shock..." Frankie's voice trailed off.

Blinquet's lips puffed out, and his eyelids lowered to slits. "A shock, yes, I'm sure."

Lola politely cleared her throat. "Can I get anyone some coffee or tea? I have filtered water, if you'd prefer."

When neither of the other two accepted the offer, Lola positioned herself next to Frankie on the sofa.

"What's this all about?" Frankie said.

199

Like a pinpoint of light focused through the lens of a magnifying glass, Blinquet fixed his eyes on Frankie. "Can you explain how partial human remains came to be in your freezer?"

Frankie gasped as if every atom of air had been sucked out of the room. "What?"

"I said partial human remains were found in your freezer. Not the whole person, you understand, just the leg. The pathologist says someone with medical knowledge sawed it off just below the knee and right above the foot." Blinquet scooted forward in his chair, as if preparing to lunge at the women. "Evidently, the foot removal took place a year or so ago. But the leg removal took place just prior to death. Do you know anything about that?"

Frankie shook her head. "I'm sorry, but I'm blown away by what you're saying. I have no idea how a leg ended up in my freezer."

As soon as the words left her lips, Frankie flashed on Tim standing in her living room, asking off-handedly if he could keep something in her freezer for a few days.

A well-read man, Uncle Mike often said Frankie had a babbling countenance. Judging by Blinquet's hardening stare, there must have been something to that. Her face reddened as the man quietly waited for her to revise her earlier statement.

"In your freezer, yes," he prodded.

Frankie took a deep breath. "My freezer is filled with the fruits and vegetables I put up every fall. I'm sure I would have noticed a human leg."

Blinquet pursed his lips again. "I see." He squinted at the two women. With a sound like a whale clearing its blowhole, the rotund little man stood. The heaviness of his girth flopped over his belt, and his shoe leather creaked as if under intense pressure. "Is this where you'll be staying?"

"Lola kindly offered me a room for the night, but I don't know how long I'll stay."

The investigator pulled the requisite business card from his pocket and handed it to Frankie.

"If you remember anything, give me a call." Blinquet turned to go, stopped, and looked back. "It's only a request, you understand, but please let me know if you decide to leave town."

Lola followed Blinquet to the door and closed it firmly behind him.

She returned to sit next to Frankie. "I don't like the tone that man took with you. He treated you like you'd done something wrong."

"I can understand his thinking," Frankie's face twisted in a wry smile. "Here I am, claiming someone set fire to my house and then warned me to get out. That's pretty unbelievable. Not to mention my having a human body part nestled among my frozen veggies."

Lola made a dismissive movement with her hand as she walked toward the kitchen. "I'm sure the police will sort it all out. But my dear, it's well after noon. Are you hungry?"

"My stomach feels a little upset right now." Frankie patted her abdomen. "I don't think I can eat. But a cup of hot tea sounds wonderful."

Lola disappeared into the kitchen. She returned in a few minutes with a saucer upon which rested a china cup, steam curling up from its contents. Beside the cup she'd placed two slices of lemon. She handed the saucer and a paper napkin to Frankie and sat down next to her.

"My dear, I wonder if you've gotten caught up in something difficult."

Frankie opened her mouth to speak, but Lola silenced her with an uplifted hand. "You don't have to tell me. But if you ever need anything, you must not hesitate to ask."

"Thank you. And thanks for allowing me to spend the night here, but I can't stay. I believe someone set fire to my house to keep me from doing any more digging into Tim's death. If I stay here, you might be in danger as well."

"Don't you worry about me, kiddo. My daddy taught me to shoot when I was knee high to a grasshopper. I can break down a pistol, clean it, oil it, and put it back together in under five minutes. Got my .45 under my pillow. No one's going to get the drop on me." Lola put her hand on Frankie's arm. "But if you're in danger, you must tell the police."

"Tell them what? That I believe someone is trying to kill me? You heard Blinquet. He didn't actually say so, but he thinks I set the fire to cover up something horrible."

"But my dear—"

"I'll be okay. You've done a lot for me already." Frankie patted the old woman's hand. "And thanks for not asking me questions I don't want to answer."

Lola stood. "If you must leave, at least take some clothes. There's a suitcase in the armoire in your room. You can return everything after you've gotten settled somewhere."

Frankie thanked her neighbor again, returned to Cathy's room and packed a couple of outfits. She managed to get Collette into the carrier before hauling everything out to her car, where she sat staring out the window. For the first time in her life, she had no place to go.

After several tries and at least thirty minutes later, Frankie found a motel that would accept pets. Grateful for the new credit card she'd applied for and received a couple of days before, she packed up Collette, along with the clothes and toiletry items Lola pressed on her.

At the motel, Frankie agreed to the hefty deposit required for the cat, and the two of them settled into a room on the second floor.

Decorated in the style of countless other motel rooms across the country, the space contained the standard mass-produced furnishings. A large, faux cherry wood desk stood against the wall in the corner of the room. A lamp and telephone rested on its top, along with a cardboard brochure attesting to the room's broadband capability.

A matching entertainment center stood next to the desk. Frankie opened its two accordion-type doors to reveal a large, flat screen television. Two drawers under the television invited her to unpack her things and make herself at home.

Although fairly pricey, the room did not smell pleasant. She requested a nonsmoking room but the unmistakable smell of old cigarette smoke hung in the air. No matter how motel management tried, they could never completely eradicate the smell of human byproducts left behind by its clientele. She remembered seeing a documentary in which scientists measured the levels of bodily emissions, oozings, drippings and spurtings flung around even high-end motel rooms by countless human bodies. She shuddered.

"Laundering the bedspread regularly and steaming the carpet would be a good start," she said to Collette. "But we'll make it ours in no time." She placed the litter box in the bathroom, glad she'd had the presence of mind to stop at a pet store on the way to the motel and purchase the large reservoir, self-feeding food and water dishes that held enough to make it unnecessary to refill them more than a couple of times a week.

Except for the occasional blink, the cat sat unmoving on her new perch atop the entertainment center.

"I don't blame you. I'd stay off the bed, too, if I were you." Frankie picked up her purse and headed for the door. "Try not to disturb the neighbors."

Collette assumed her meatloaf position. With her unblinking stare, she looked like one of those odious stuffed replicas found in some gift shops.

What kind of brain had come up with the idea of life-sized faux kittens coiled up on plush little mattresses? Cats that never moved, never blinked, never made a sound. Creepy, taxidermy-specimen, marble-eyed things.

"At least they don't poop or scratch up the furniture." Frankie rubbed her hand along Collette's rounded back. The kitty shot a condescending look at her and made a strange sound in the back of her throat.

"More a grumble than a purr, but I'll take it." Frankie closed the door behind her and headed for the car. It was time to find Mina. And this time, she'd not take no for an answer to her questions about Tim's spreadsheet.

Chapter Twenty-Seven

"Excuse me," Frankie said to the young man behind the counter of the hospital nurse's station. "Could you tell me where I might find Mina Landowski?"

The young man raised his head from the computer upon which he'd been furiously typing and mouse-clicking. "Mina no longer works here."

"What?"

"She left last night before her shift ended."

"Was she ill?"

"Didn't seem to be…more like upset. Said she wouldn't be back."

"Did she say where she was going?"

The young man spoke over his shoulder to a group of other staff members. When no one answered, he shrugged. "Sorry."

Apprehension skipped across the back of Frankie's neck as she returned to her car. Maybe one of Mina's resumes had paid off and she'd found employment elsewhere. Maybe she was even now packing her things to move out of town. But to leave before her shift was over?

No, that didn't make sense. And she'd have bet her last dollar Mina would not blow someone off after promising to call.

She rummaged for the sympathy card she'd

received from the nurse and tossed into her tote bag. She looked at the return address, started her car, and headed for the exit.

Just as she was about to pull out of the hospital parking lot and into the street the old Chevy sped past, nearly sideswiping her vehicle. Even though the baby-faced driver was so focused on maneuvering the car into the parking lot he didn't see her, she recognized him. In fact, the image of his face contorted with rage had begun showing up in her dreams. A mixture of emotions blazed along her spine, none of them pleasant.

Oblivious to other drivers, Baby Face parked his car and got out. He stood for a second, swiveling his head around atop his otherwise motionless body as Frankie lowered herself into her seat. She wondered if she should call the police. And tell them what? No, her credibility had suffered enough. She had to have something solid to take to them.

After Baby Face entered the hospital, Frankie backed her car up. She found a parking spot where she could wait without being seen, and sat.

The young man returned to his car about twenty minutes later. At the same time he started his engine, Frankie started hers. When he pulled out of the lot, she counted to five and followed.

The vehicles made their way through the downtown, the suburbs, and into the industrial area of south Albuquerque. Light traffic made it easy for Frankie to keep the Camaro in sight, but it also made it difficult to stay out of the driver's range of vision.

The Chevy merged onto Interstate 25 going south and continued out of the city limits. Frankie didn't relish the idea of following the guy on what was beginning to look like an innocent road trip, but there was no way she was going to let him out of her sight.

Baby Face exited onto a gravel county road and drove down a wide, gated drive. In peeling black letters on a once-white background, a warped metal sign announced the entrance to Bellamy's Fresh Egg and Poultry Farm.

Wary of tipping the young man off to her presence, Frankie kept driving for about one hundred yards, made a U-turn and pulled over next to a group of huge, old cottonwood trees. She turned off the ignition. While waiting, she tore the aluminum wrapping from a granola bar and munched her lunch.

Over the next hour, a parade of vehicles entered and exited the farm. Most bore the logos of local landscaping nurseries and eating establishments. All came and went within a matter of minutes. But Baby Face didn't reappear.

A white panel truck slowed and turned into the farm entrance. Acting again on impulse, Frankie started her car and followed it into the compound. When the truck parked in front of a small green building with a sign over the door that read *Farm Store*, Frankie pulled in next to it.

The driver's door opened. Kinky red hair exploded from under the young driver's baseball cap. Bombardier-style headphones encased his ears, and his screen-printed tee shirt screamed that mean people suck. Moving his head in time to whatever music spewed directly into his ear canals, the young man walked around to the rear of the vehicle. He pushed up the truck's scroll-type rear gate and pulled out a hand truck, which he rolled into the store. In a short while he returned loaded with cardboard boxes, the stenciling on the sides of which proclaimed them to contain Bellamy's farm fresh eggs. The driver deposited the boxes in the back of the truck and went back for another load.

When Frankie got out of her car, a smell unlike any she'd ever before experienced assailed her. With no breeze to move it, the stench hung in the air like a fog.

The farm appeared to be a fairly small concern. Besides the long confinement buildings where the chickens lived, a large barn, a bunkhouse, and several small outbuildings stood in an apparently random pattern.

The sight of the Camaro sitting in front of the bunkhouse shot adrenaline through Frankie's body. Trying to be inconspicuous, she sauntered toward the building. Busy making purchases or delivering supplies, no one even glanced her way.

She peered through the grime coated, curtain-less bunkhouse windows. Baby Face sat at a card table, a cup of something in front of him. He took a sip from the cup before replacing it on the table. A thoughtful look on his face, he inserted his right index finger into his nose. After some fairly vigorous digging, he withdrew the finger, peered at it, wiped it on his pant leg, and took another sip from the cup. Frankie's lip twitched and her stomach did a pirouette.

Baby Face turned his face toward her, and Uncle Mike's voice belatedly rang in her head. *Never look directly at someone you're hiding from or trying to sneak up on. That person will subconsciously sense another human presence and look toward his watcher.*

Frankie ducked her head, bent her body at a right

angle, and walked until well away from the window. When she straightened back up, the barn lay directly in front of her. The barn's position in relation to the bunkhouse and farm store made its entrance invisible from any incoming and outgoing traffic.

Telling herself she could probably be charged with trespassing, she made a snap decision and swerved toward the barn door. After sliding the door open barely wide enough to slip through, she squeezed her body through the opening. She pulled the door closed behind her, and instantly became enveloped in darkness.

An old familiar fear clawed its way up Frankie's stomach and into her throat. She breathed deeply and slowly, counting each breath as Angela had taught her. Eventually, her pulse rate slowed and her eyes grew accustomed to the scant amount of light sifting through a tiny overhead skylight.

Along with the expected odors of burlap, grain, and chicken-farm ambiance, a hint of another smell caught her attention. Most likely trapped dead mice or rats in need of disposal. She wrinkled her nose and let go a barrage of sneezes.

The builders had sprayed the interior corrugated metal walls of the barn with yellowish liquid foam insulation, which had hardened into bizarre, melted-wax shapes. Various farm implements hung suspended from a series of hooks fixed to steel crossbeams. Some of the implements were recognizable as of the same type Uncle Mike had used on his ranch. Others looked strange and fierce. Storage bins lined one long wall, and an assortment of machinery lay scattered around the floor.

Unsure of what she might find and not knowing

quite why she felt compelled to do so, Frankie made her way through the barn. She peeked inside receptacles and raked her fingers through the grain stored in open fifty-five gallon drums.

Toward the back of the barn sat a large, tarpaulin-covered object. More out of idle curiosity than anything else, Frankie lifted a corner of the heavy fabric, exposing the front wheel well of a vehicle. Perhaps someone's vintage automobile awaiting eventual restoration.

At that moment the barn door opened. Sunlight exploded into the darkened space and illuminated the partially uncovered vehicle. Frankie stared down at the green pickup driven by the two men who shot Tim.

Chapter Twenty-Eight

"Well, well, lookey what we got here," Baby Face said. He advanced on Frankie, his arms slightly bent, his fists clenching and unclenching. "If it ain't the trouble-making bitch herself. Now that you know who killed your poor brother, what're you going to do about it?"

"I'm going to see you fry." Frankie glared into Baby Face's eyes, surprised at the emotions chasing each other through her solar plexus. In all the time she'd spent looking for the men who killed Tim she'd never given any thought as to what she'd do once she found them. And now that she stood in front of one, the primal emotions infusing her gut nearly took her breath away.

"You think so?" The young man's face turned deep red-purple as he strode toward Frankie. He stopped in front of her and stared into her bi-colored eyes. "Well Freak, I asked you a question. You think so?"

Frankie wanted to rush at this monster who killed her brother. She wanted to tear at his hair and claw at his face. She wanted to pound him into a mass of jelly. But instead, she pulled herself up to her full height and spat in his face.

Fighting an enraged man focused on doing serious damage is a far cry from the benevolent self-defense instruction Frankie received at the hands of her loving

Uncle Mike. This was not an action packed movie fight scene in which blow after blow is sustained by the good guy with minimal effect. Even one solid punch to Frankie's head would addle her, leaving her completely at the mercy of her attacker.

Look for a weak point.

In the instant following Uncle Mike's words, Frankie spotted the man's strangely shaped little finger. She grabbed it and jerked backward as far as the webbed flesh would allow.

Baby face yelped and tried to jerk his hand free, but Frankie's hands and arms were strong from years of playing the organ. She held on tight.

Her attacker writhed. He shifted his balance and grabbed a fistful of her hair with his free hand. Tears spurted into her eyes as he jerked her head from side to side.

With no time to think or plan, Frankie had only milliseconds in which to act. She allowed her instinct to take over and the muscle memory from her uncle's training to kick in. The man grabbed her by the throat and tried to position his thumbs on her windpipe. She clapped the palms of her hands over his ears. If she couldn't pop his eardrums, perhaps she could at least cause enough pain for him to loosen his grip.

This maneuver might have worked had her aim been better. But the man moved his forearm upward and partially deflected the move. Her attempt served only to further enrage him.

Baby Face snarled. The raw sewage odor of his breath enveloped Frankie in a stomach-churning cloud. He dug his thumbs into her neck and pinpoints of light burst in her vision.

In one fluid movement Frankie straightened her arms down at her sides, brought them up, around, and above her assailant's arms. She brought her forearms down with all her might on top of Baby Face's straightened elbows. He relaxed his hold just enough for her to wriggle from his grasp at the same time she drove her knee into his groin. He grunted and bent over at the waist, giving her the opportunity to bounce her forehead against his nose in a perfectly executed head butt.

Stars swam into her vision at the same instant blood spurted from the man's nose. He yelped and grabbed the air where Frankie had been standing, but she was already running toward the open barn door.

Before she'd gotten further than a few feet, her adversary tackled her from behind. He catapulted her face down on the ground, positioned himself astraddle her back, and pinned her arms down with his knees.

As if her hair were the rubber band attached to a toy punching ball, he grabbed a fistful and repeatedly slammed her face into the dirt. With barely enough time to register gratitude for the softness of the soil, flashes of light burst against Frankie's retinas. She tasted blood and realized she'd bitten her tongue.

As a strategy of last resort, she stopped struggling and lay inert. Baby Face stopped his attack.

For several seconds, he sat unmoving, breathing heavily. "You can stop playing possum now." He stood, reached behind his back for a pistol, which he pointed at her. "You'd better be glad I got to check with Bellamy before I get to play with you, because it'd sure enough be my pleasure to make you dead. Get up, and don't do nothing stupid."

"Doctor Bellamy?"

Baby Face cocked his head sideways. "Yep, Doctor Bellamy. Looks like Miss Smarty Pants ain't so smart after all. Get up."

When Frankie didn't move, the young man motioned with the barrel of the pistol. "I can empty this into places that won't kill you, but that'll sure as hell hurt," he said. "Now get up."

****

The sun had climbed well over the Sandia Mountains by the time Nick pulled into the hospital parking lot. He'd left Taos early that morning after a long, restless night. It was as if he stood in front of one of those arcades where fifty cents bought a chance to get a stuffed animal, but the loose mechanical claw always dropped the coveted item before it got to the chute. Something vital to the case was staring him in the face, but just when he thought he had it in his grip, it slipped away.

He'd first talk to the hospital personnel whose statements he'd read, then he'd chat with Dr. Bellamy. He knew he was grabbing at what might turn out to be a fistful of smoke, but someone might let something slip. Or might remember something they'd forgotten to mention in an earlier statement. A rock climber before his tour of duty, all he needed was a tiny outcropping or indentation to put some weight on. Even a slight unevenness in someone's response to his questions might get him moving in the right direction.

He made his way through the hospital doors. Too early for the information desk to be open, so he took the elevator to the second floor in hopes of finding someone who could point him in the right direction.

Anyone who might know a nurse named Landowski.

After walking down a long corridor, he came upon a nurses' station, behind which sat a young man, his head bowed over a computer. The young man took his time finishing the sentence he was typing, sighed, and looked up at the deputy.

"All I can tell you is what I told the woman who was here earlier…Mina no longer works here."

"The woman you're talking about, was she short, with auburn hair and different colored eyes?"

"Yes, that's her. She got really upset when I told her Mina had resigned. I got the feeling she was going to Mina's house when she left here."

Nick swiveled on his heel and headed for the exit. "Thanks," he said over his shoulder.

Once back in his pickup, he reached for the manila folder on the passenger seat and found the nurse's address in his notes.

"Twelve twenty-three Richardson," he said into the GPS sitting on his dash. While the directions downloaded to his pickup, he headed for the hospital parking lot exit.

He should have used stronger language in telling Frankie to leave the investigation to him and Pritney. He should have threatened to charge her with interfering with an investigation. But it had seemed the more reasonable he tried to be, the more obstinate she became. And now she wasn't answering her cell.

Fighting down the urge to floor the gas pedal, he followed instructions from the vaguely British female voice telling him to make a right turn at the next light.

****

Frankie's eyes darted around the farm. But the

215

bustling business of just an hour earlier looked like a ghost town.

"Too bad, so sad," Baby Face intoned the children's singsong taunt. "This place closes down at two o'clock. Nobody here now but us chickens. Get it? Nobody here but us chickens?" He slapped a hand against his thigh. "Oh man, sometimes I just kill myself."

"Now there's a thought."

"Funny." Baby Face hawked, and spat out a gob of coagulated blood. He drew the back of his hand across his blood-smeared face. Looking into Frankie's eyes, he gagged, spat again and giggled. "We're going to have us some fun. I'm going to teach you some of the lessons of life."

"What you're going to do is answer for my brother's murder."

Baby Face snorted again. "Not any time soon. Now walk, go on, over there."

Several feet from where they stood lay the dome of an in-ground cistern used for water storage. About seven or eight feet in diameter, the dome resembled a huge upside down salad bowl. A round, chimney structure, perhaps ten inches high and twenty-four inches in diameter had been welded onto the cistern's top. A metal manhole-type lid fit tightly into the opening through which farm staff would drop buckets and draw water in time of drought.

"Open it up and get in."

When Frankie made no move to obey, the man lifted the gun up to her face. He grinned and pressed the barrel into her cheek, grinding the flesh against her teeth. Immediate and intense pain shot through her face and up her temples. "We don't keep water in it nowadays, so you won't drown. Now I said get in, or the first one will be through your face. In one side and out the other, maybe take a few teeth with it. It won't kill you, but you'll sure bleed." He grinned. "The good news is it'll make both your eyes the same color—black and blue." Baby Face hooted again and clapped his hand against his thigh.

Frankie walked to the cistern and bent over the lid. Perspiration beaded on her upper lip, and her stomach muscles went taught. Once inside the metal enclosure, her chance of escape would be nil. She pretended to struggle with the lid. When Baby Face came closer, she threw the heavy metal cover at his head, turned, and ran.

After a couple of steps, gunshots rang out and puffs of dust blossomed at Frankie's feet. She froze in place.

"You mess with me one more time, and I swear I'm going to kill you and tell Bellamy you just up and disappeared. He'll be pissed, but he'll get over it, you hear me?"

Frankie walked back to the cistern. She squatted down on her haunches, slipped her feet over the lip of the opening and sat on the rim with her feet dangling into the interior. The thin edge of the metal dug painfully into her buttocks as she bent forward and gripped the metal rim of the stovepipe opening. She began to lower herself into the cool darkness of the cistern. Pain shot through her hands and down her upraised arms as the full weight of her body came to bear on her fingers, the lip of the opening digging into the digits.

Extending her arms to their full length, she dropped

into the blackness, her knees bent to avoid breaking her legs. She hit bottom almost instantly. Dust filled her nostrils and she coughed.

The air in the cistern smelled stagnant and foul. The horizontally rippled, galvanized steel walls of the cylindrical tank rose above her head. Shards of sunlight slanted through the opening, but the rest of the interior lay in darkness.

Baby Face's head appeared in the circle of light, a black oval blotting out the sun. "You're nothing special. We'll see how pretty you are after a few days in here."

"I thought you needed me alive."

"I do. But how much alive is up to me." Baby Face giggled as he slid the metal cover back into its sleeve.

The clang of metal striking metal set up a deafening echo. The ensuing darkness was thick enough to chew.

Chapter Twenty-Nine

Nick knocked on the door of Mina's condominium. He waited for several seconds before knocking again, harder. When the door moved a fraction of an inch, he pushed it open.

"Hello," he called out. "Mina Landowski? Deputy Nick Rollins. I need to ask you some questions."

Like a family of spiders backpacking to his scalp, a funny feeling started at the base of his neck—a feeling he knew all too well from his tour in Afghanistan. He unsnapped the strap on his holstered sidearm, rested his hand on its handle, and stepped further into the unlit condo.

A table lamp lay on its side on the carpeted living room floor, the bulb shattered. Something made of bright blue glass had either been dropped or thrown on the brick hearth in front of the cold fireplace. Rust colored splotches and smears marked a path from the wet bar back to the door.

Nick grabbed his phone and punched in a number. "Ted, it's me. The nurse's condo has been trashed. She's not here, and there's a good bit of blood splashed around."

"I'll call it in." Ted broke the connection.

Nick scanned the room. An open handbag lay on its side on the coffee table. A cell phone, lipstick, comb and other feminine items lay scattered around the purse.

A piece of white typing paper lay on the coffee table, as if someone had been sitting on the sofa studying it.

After snapping on the latex gloves he always carried when on duty, Nick lifted the paper by its corner. Printed on it was a matrix of names, dates, and strange abbreviations. Someone had circled four of the entries in red ink.

Hadn't Frankie said something about finding a spreadsheet of patient information? Nick's stomach formed into a hard knot. Wherever the nurse was, he had a sinking feeling Frankie was with her. And he couldn't shake the feeling that time was running out for the two women—if it hadn't already.

The image of Frankie O'Neil's face swam into his vision. The determined set of her jaw. The light of battle in those compelling eyes.

Nick folded the paper and put it into his breast pocket. He ran back to his pickup, punching in Ted's number again along the way.

****

Frankie struggled to stay calm. Her eyes felt as though they were bulging from their sockets in search for even a tiny ray of light. Her heart pounded and her breathing came in short gasps.

She choked back the scream she recognized as the precursor to a full blown hysterical frenzy. What if something happened to Baby Face before he came back for her? Or what if he decided to just leave her there? She would die of thirst. Or starve.

Uncle Mike had said the average adult could live for about five weeks without food. But that same person would die within a week without water.

Knowing what took place in the human body under

conditions of extreme deprivation told Frankie it would be better to starve than die of thirst. The process of dehydration did horrifying, painful things to the human mind and body. Even then, she felt comforted in the knowledge it would be quicker than having nothing to eat. And people could get awfully hungry.

Her thoughts flashed on her stores of provisions and her pitiful attempts at home security. All gone. No help to her in this place.

What about Collette? How long before someone at the motel realized something was wrong and broke open the door to her room? She didn't allow herself to think of what would happen when the cat's food and water ran out.

Frankie closed her eyes and forced herself to breathe deeply. Hyperventilating would waste air. And as to how long the air in a container this size would last, she hadn't the foggiest.

When she'd calmed a bit, she poked and prodded her arms, legs, and ribs. Nothing seemed to be broken, and no fresh wetness indicated an open wound. Hopefully, she'd sustained no internal injuries either during her struggle with Baby Face or her subsequent fall into the cistern. Any one of several wouldn't kill her quickly, but would slowly incapacitate her, making escape impossible.

Dust filled her nostrils and sent her into a coughing spasm. She tore a strip about four inches wide from the bottom of her cotton knit shirt, filled her mouth with saliva and spit into the cloth over and over, wetting a small area. She tied the makeshift air mask around her head so the moist area covered her mouth and nose. Although some dust sifted through the weave, most of it caught in the damp fabric. The panic that came with being unable to get enough air into her lungs subsided.

Based on her brief view of the cistern before Baby Face shut the lid, it was perhaps eight feet in height. Its diameter would render a chimney climb impossible, and she couldn't jump high enough to pull herself out through the opening, even if she could somehow dislodge the tight fitting lid. If she removed her jacket and rolled it into a tight ball, she might add a couple of inches to her reach. But she needed a lot more than a couple of inches.

She moved her hands over the bottom of the cistern. The low lying spots in the warped metal floor held a fine powder of dust, and every movement stirred up a new cloud. She ran her hands in widening circles, her movements smooth and slow.

Within a few inches from where she knelt, Frankie's searching fingers ran up against something hard. Hoping the thing could be used either as a weapon or to help her escape, she grabbed it with both hands.

But what she held was not a potential weapon, it was a shoe. A shoe on a foot attached to a very cold leg.

****

When Larry's cell phone rang, he didn't answer. Bellamy and Mel were the only people with his number, and he didn't want to talk to either of them just now. Especially now. Just a couple more days, that's all he needed.

Larry liked to think of himself as a planner. Just because some of his ideas never actually panned out didn't keep him from coming up with them. And lots of his ideas worked just fine. He'd read somewhere that failing to plan was actually planning to fail, so from that moment on he'd done very few things on the spur of the moment.

He closed out his checking and savings accounts, packed his belongings, and sold what wouldn't fit in his car. The subsequent heaviness of the zippered bank bag felt reassuring as he stuffed it into the glove compartment of the Mercedes.

Larry smiled in anticipation of a new life. "Our new life," he said out loud.

****

Once back in his hiding place in the tree at Frankie's house, Larry pulled out his phone. Beauty wasn't home yet, but he'd wait. He pressed the voice mail button and listened to Mel's recorded message.

"I found her sneaking around the farm." Mel's digitized voice sounded high pitched and agitated. It was a tone Larry recognized all too well. "She spotted the pickup. I called Bellamy, and he told me to bring her in."

Larry broke the connection, jumped down from the tree and ran to his car. No time for a change of plan—what the old geezer called *poo* had hit the fan.

****

Frankie shrieked and jerked away from her discovery. She crab-scuttled across the cistern floor until she slammed up against the corrugated metal wall, sat up, pulled her knees to her chest, and folded herself into a ball.

"Is someone there?" Her muffled voice sounded pinched and thin, like dough extruded through the tiny holes of an angel hair pasta maker. She commanded herself to slow her breathing.

The form on the floor neither spoke nor moved. No

sound but the echo of Frankie's own voice rang in the hollow darkness.

As she struggled to regain control of her trembling body, snapshots of her life tumbled over one another in a cacophony of light and sound bites. She heard the plastic-against-plastic click Uncle Mike's reading glasses made when he closed them and put them into their case. And she remembered the look on Alma's face when she entered Frankie's childhood room amid gales of laughter only Frankie could hear, the laughter of people only she could see. She felt again the joy of being surrounded by countless family members, of playing hide and seek with twin cousins who'd died centuries earlier, and of listening to stories about things that happened before the human race started writing things down.

Willing herself to dissolve into nothing, she bowed her head and pressed her face against her tightly folded knees as something shifted in her mind. She crossed an unseen barrier and became a child again. Panic bubbled up from the wellspring of repressed memory as the cistern morphed into a basement, the darkness of which had haunted her nightmares for years.

I'm afraid. Jenny's voice.

A baby wailed from somewhere overhead.

Don't you want to be with Jenny and Timmy? A woman's voice, flat, devoid of emotion. *I'll be back. You wait here.*

"Mommy?" the adult Frankie cried into the darkness. The single word bounced around inside the cistern, ricocheting off the metal walls.

Shut up, the neighbors will hear. My Jonathan would never have enlisted if not for the three of you.

Always needing this and that, and never enough money. You're the reason he's dead.

Like a boat rhythmically bumping against its mooring, Frankie's mind nudged the barrier between sanity and madness. It would be so easy to give in to the emptiness beckoning her. To feel nothing and know nothing. To become nothing.

The image of Tim's spreadsheet came into her mind. In vivid detail she saw it lying next to Esther Emory's original medical records. Suddenly, she knew why Mina had become so agitated. And she knew that if she didn't manage to escape and tell the police, more people would die.

A flash of heat kicked up the pulse in Frankie's blood. It began at her sternum and coursed through her insides—so potent her flesh grew warm. It flashed through her brain, sharpening her thinking and helping her focus.

Commanding her emotions to shut down for as long as necessary in order to do what she had to do next, she took a deep breath and moved back toward the body.

Chapter Thirty

Nick sat in his pickup, his cell phone pressed against his ear. In his left hand he held a black plastic ink pen which he manipulated, weaving it around each finger until it circled his pinkie, and moved back to his thumb, a skill he'd taught himself in high school to impress the girls.

"We got people headed for the nurse's place," Ted said. "And I'm on my way there now."

"How long've we been friends?" Nick said. "Eight, ten years?"

"Oh, about that. Since Camp LeJeune, why?"

"Just making a point. You know how I work."

"I know your instincts are pretty good. What gives?"

"I can't shake the feeling that Miss O'Neil and Miss Landowski are in trouble. I'm going to talk to the neighbor where she stayed when her house burned. She may know something."

"Okay, but you need to know that Blinquet in Violent Crimes has been brought in on the investigation."

"What's that about?"

"It seems partial human remains turned up in Miss O'Neil's freezer. But I told Pritney all this yesterday."

"What human remains?" Nick stopped twiddling his pen, dropped it, and sat up straight.

"The arson investigator found a partial human leg. By the way, tell Pritney I'm sorry I missed her call this morning."

"Wait, wait, a partial human leg?"

"You heard right. It was in her freezer.

"Jesus, Mary and Joseph."

"That's not the worst part. Don't know if you knew, but we've had a couple of recent disappearances. Blinquet has a theory that one or both of the O'Neils were abducting people and keeping them imprisoned somewhere."

"Oh come on. Where'd they keep them? From what I understand, Miss O'Neil only recently moved into that house."

"Hey, that's Blinquet's theory, I'm just the messenger."

"What did Miss O'Neil have to say about the leg?"

"Blinquet's trying to find her so he can bring her in for further questioning," Ted said. "He's thinking in terms of a kind of Jeffrey Dahmer scenario, like maybe they ate on people a little at a time before they finally killed them."

"Good God."

"The missing people had one thing in common: they both worked at the same hospital as O'Neil. Blinquet's thinking he's finally caught a break in that case. He's trying to get permission to take the cadaver dogs to Miss O'Neil's half acre backyard."

"I don't care how this looks, there's no way she could have been involved in something so messed up."

Ted snorted. "How well do you know her anyway?"

"I know her type."

"We've been in law enforcement long enough to know that anyone is capable of anything, given the right circumstances."

Nick sighed. "The problem is we're at a standstill on the brother's murder. The stuff going on now may be in your jurisdiction, but I know in my gut it's all connected."

"Blinquet's calling the brother's death accidental. He thinks the sister claims it was murder to make it look like she's being targeted. Like she's the victim of some nefarious plot. He's clamped down on this like a crazed bulldog."

"If she did make all this up, wouldn't it make more sense for her to get rid of the leg before setting the fire? And wouldn't she leave the dead bird and chalk threat on the porch to back up that story? It's a good thing the inquest verified her account of her brother's shooting or someone would be charging her with that as well."

"Blinquet figures she forgot about the leg. And you know as well as I do, criminals often make stupid mistakes. Most of them are not real bright."

"Yeah, but she's not stupid. And she's no killer. She's an intelligent, capable woman."

"Well, well, listen to you. Tell me before you break into poetry and I'll dig out a tissue."

"I'm serious, Ted. Life has dealt Frankie O'Neil more than her share of body blows. She's tough, I'll give her that, but she's also bull-headed. I think she's in way over her head."

"You've fallen for her." Ted chuckled. "You do know that Karla has run through all her single female friends trying to fix you up, right? And now here's the take-em-or-leave-em bachelor Nick Rollins talking like a love-struck kid. And without Karla's help? She'll be ticked."

Nick's face grew warm. He wished he could think of an appropriately acid comeback, but his mind teemed with images of Frankie smiling at him over her salad at Kate's. Frankie with the miss-matched eyes and the deviated septum that made her little nose sit a bit crooked on her face.

"Need I remind you," Ted was saying, "that you've been wrong about women before?"

"One woman. I was wrong about one woman."

"Yeah, and it nearly got you killed."

"Yeah, yeah, and if you hadn't come along when you did, I'd have bled to death—as you seem to never tire of reminding me."

"And it left you with a permanent limp."

"Your concern for my welfare is duly noted. Listen, you told me I could stay at your place if I ever needed to. Does that invitation still stand?"

"Sure, when are you coming?"

"I won't get to your place until later this afternoon," Nick said. "I'm hoping the neighbor knows something."

"Let me know what you learn…the Captain's pressing me for details."

"Agreed."

"Lisette will be thrilled to see you. You know you're her favorite adult male in the world."

Nick chuckled. "That's because I always bring her treats."

"No, that's because you're a terrific godfather. I'll call Karla and let her know you're finally taking us up on our invitation."

Nick hung up the phone and sat back. An old woman's leg in Frankie's freezer? What in God's name was that about? Had he been so far off base about her? He'd brushed up against some pretty cold-hearted people, both as an MP in the military and as a county deputy. Some of them had been perfectly capable of smiling warmly into your face while wielding the knife to disembowel you. But Frankie O'Neil?

Nick dialed another number into his phone and Deputy Pritney answered after a couple of rings.

"Are you busy?" he said.

"Not really. Served Tom Jasko his divorce papers this morning, so there's nothing else pressing. What's up?"

"I need you to do some digging for me."

"Is this about that O'Neil thing?" Pritney said.

"Yeah, it is. I need you to find out everything you can about the Cottonwood Hospital in Albuquerque."

"You want me to work on something outside our jurisdiction?"

"I think it's connected to our case."

"What kinds of things are you looking for?"

"Backgrounds on all the administrators and staff. Anything you can learn about the operation."

"That's going to take some time," Pritney said. "I hope you're not in a hurry."

"Actually, I am. I'd do it myself, but I'm going to look for Miss O'Neil."

"Why don't you just call her?"

"I've tried. She's on the horn four, five times a day. Suddenly she stops calling and no one's seen her for a while. Something's up."

"It's an APD issue now," Pritney said. "Besides,

she's a suspect in an arson investigation."

"I never knew you to be so territorial."

"It just seems like you talk about her a lot. Your mind's not on your other work, that's all."

"By the way, when were you going to tell me about the leg in her freezer?"

Pritney paused a couple of beats. "I haven't seen you long enough to give you an update for the past few days. But I was going to—"

"What's going on, Judy?"

During the two or three years they'd worked together, Nick had never seen Pritney as keyed up as she'd been over the past few weeks. She'd developed a tightness around her eyes and mouth that gave her face a sharp, grim look. More than once, she'd quickly hung up her phone when he walked into the office and been evasive when he asked about the calls.

Pritney breathed into the phone, the resulting plosive loud in his ear. "It's just that I've been under a lot of pressure lately. My grandmother's sick and I'm the only family she has left."

"Want to talk?"

"Nothing you can do about my situation. But it seems to me that you've put more time into this O'Neil shooting than you should. Especially since there isn't any new evidence to justify it."

"There are too many things happening to the sister. This whole thing smells. Are you going to help or not?"

"I'll do whatever I can. Where are you?"

"I'm going to stay in Albuquerque for a while. I'm taking some personal days. I'll call you tomorrow."

Pritney didn't respond.

Nick hung up and started his engine.

****

The absence of odor meant Frankie's cistern companion had died within the past twenty-four hours, give or take. And the cool, dry, ambient temperature in the belowground tank served as an additional bonus. At least she wouldn't have to deal with the smell of rotting human flesh. It also meant the body had not decomposed to the point of being useless for her purpose.

With her hands against the corpse's torso, Frankie half pushed, half rolled the body over to the side of the cistern. Other than a bit of stiffness from remaining rigor, the body rolled easily. Gratitude, horror, and fear formed a slurry in her stomach. She swallowed hard.

Squatting beside the corpse, she gripped its shoulders. After several minutes of struggling, she managed to prop the body into a sitting position against the cistern wall. She put one hand on each shoulder and pushed downward in an effort to wedge the body tightly into place.

Long hair brushed Frankie's hands and something hard and sharp scraped against her arm. Hoping for anything that might prove useful, she ran her fingers through the thick tresses. Her fingers sank into a concave area and shards of bone stabbed her fingertips. Hair wrapped like tentacles around her searching fingers. She swallowed the gorge that shot up into her throat.

Bracing the head against the palm of one hand, she slowly ran her other hand around it until her fingers made contact with a metallic object. She pulled the thing free, and ran her fingers over its outline.

Made of what felt like metal, rays radiated out of a

solid center in a starburst pattern. An image flashed across her mind's eye of Mina in Dr. Bellamy's office self-consciously touching her heavy barrettes.

Frankie slid the barrette into her pants pocket. She hugged Mina's body, sobbed and rocked back and forth. "I'm so sorry," she said over and over.

Enough. It was Uncle Mike's drill sergeant voice.

"Don't you understand? I'm the reason she's here. I'm the reason she's dead."

You don't know that. But you do owe it to her to get out of here and tell someone.

"That's easy for you to say." Frankie gritted her teeth. "If you weren't already dead, you'd know there's no way out of here."

Then make a way. Use what's at hand, like I taught you.

For several minutes Frankie considered her uncle's words. The only thing at hand was a corpse. Then, like light dawning in the East, she understood what he'd meant.

Again, she propped Mina's body up against the cistern wall. When satisfied with its position, she stood. "Help me do this."

But attempt after attempt to use the body for a ladder failed. When Frankie put one foot onto a shoulder, the weight of the head either pulled the body forward, or Frankie's weight on the shoulder would make it angle downward toward the floor and pull the body over onto its side.

For the next several minutes she mulled over possible solutions. Finally, she pulled Mina's body away from the wall and turned it onto its stomach. Then she doubled the body so it rested on folded knees. In this position the nurse's body would add perhaps sixteen to eighteen inches to her reach.

She stepped onto the nurse's back and ran her hands up the corrugated metal wall, straining to reach as high as she could. But her fingers encountered only the uninterrupted near-flatness of the cistern's dome.

Since she had no clue as to the opening's location, she had to move Mina's body around the perimeter of the cistern several times. Each time, she dragged the corpse a few inches to her left, stood tiptoe on bent back, and felt for the cistern opening.

With each re-location of the body, Frankie's muscles objected more and more strenuously. She grew alarmed at how all the stooping, tugging, and pulling on the dead weight of Mina's body was sapping her strength.

Her throat constricted. She could die in this dark hole.

"Stop it. You can do this…" Her voice had become an unrecognizable whine, but its echo somehow strengthened her, bolstered her determination. She began to sing the words of a childhood song, her voice growing in strength until she was virtually shouting the words, "The wheels on the bus go round and round, round and round…"

Again she stepped onto Mina's folded body. This time her outstretched fingers encountered the inside of the cistern's opening sleeve. With a burst of renewed energy, she stood on her tiptoes and stretched. Her fingertips touched the lid, but just barely.

After several jumps that ended in her sliding off Mina's back and onto the floor, she managed to dislodge the cover from its sleeve. The metal set up a clanging reverberation as it bounced off the cistern's rooftop and fell to the ground.

Exhausted, Frankie crumpled to the cistern floor beside Mina's body and looked up.

The starlit evening sky told her she'd been in the cistern for at least four or five hours. So where was Baby Face? How long could it possibly take him to talk to Dr. Bellamy? Either something had happened to him, or he was making good on his promise to leave her in the cistern for a couple of days.

Frankie rested, willing her body to relax, knowing her next move would require every ounce of strength she could muster. She removed her tennis shoes and thick cotton socks, replaced the shoes on her feet and slid the socks onto her hands like gloves.

"Okay Mina. Let's try again."

Again Frankie stepped onto the corpse. All too aware that she had only enough strength left for a couple of tries, she launched herself off the nurse's back.

This time she cleared the opening by just enough to hook her fingers over the rim. With the socks offering some protection for her fingers and the horizontally corrugated metal walls offering toeholds, she walked up the cistern walls. The muscles of her arms quivering from the strain, she finally managed to pull herself up and through the opening before collapsing onto the ground.

Every breath a ragged gasp, her heart hammered so it seemed ready to jump through her ribcage. Instinct screamed for her to get going, to escape. But her tortured muscles twitched and jerked so violently, she couldn't even stand.

Finally, she managed to get to her feet and stumble toward her car on legs that felt like gummy worms that had been left in the sun in July. But she'd only taken a couple of steps when something hit the side of her head. Her knees gave way, and she sank to the ground.

"Thanks for saving me the trouble of having to haul your skinny ass out of that cistern," she heard Baby Face say as everything went dark.

Chapter Thirty-One

When Frankie regained consciousness she was lying on her back. The inside of her mouth tasted like she'd been chewing on a handful of copper pennies. Her throat was dry and her eyes felt too big for their sockets. A continuous buzz hummed in her ears, as if a phalanx of worker bees had moved in. Her head throbbed with each heartbeat.

With what seemed like an inordinate amount of effort, she lifted her head. But waves of vertiginous nausea caused her to drop her head back down. Tears sprang to her eyes as an evident head wound made contact with sharp, curled edges of cracked naugahyde covering the old hospital gurney upon which she lay. Salty drops rolled down the sides of her face, stinging when they came into contact with the scrapes she'd sustained in her fight with Baby Face.

Padded leather straps at Frankie's wrists and ankles held her tight, seriously inhibiting blood flow. She commanded her fingers to move, but had no way of knowing whether or not they responded.

She tried to call out, but only a muffled moan made its way through something covering the lower part of her face. Duct tape? Panic pushed bile into her throat. Unable to open her mouth, she could choke to death on her own vomit.

Frankie jerked against her bindings. The buckles

rattled, but they'd been pulled so tightly, her range of motion could probably be measured in millimeters.

She took a slow, shuddering breath, and let it out through her nose. Once her gut calmed a bit, she moved her gaze around the small, unfamiliar room.

Paint the color of dried green peas peeled and flaked off the walls. Something dark had been spattered on one and then halfheartedly wiped off. About halfway up the discolored wall sat an oblong window of frosted glass crisscrossed by a reinforcing wire grid. Iron bars outside the window cast vertical shadows on the floor as bright morning or afternoon sunlight fought its way through the glass and metal barrier.

How long had she been unconscious? One day? Two?

The room's only door had been fitted with a small window. Made of clear, wire-reinforced glass, the window's position offered those outside the room the ability to observe whatever went on inside.

The ceiling was of a type often found in schools and hospitals. It consisted of acoustical, mineral fiber squares, each patterned with tiny round holes and suspended in a metal grid. Frankie remembered a kid in middle school throwing pencils straight up like spears and sticking them into the same kind of ceiling.

A cabinet with a sink and faucet ran along one wall. A soap dispenser flanked the sink on one side, a roll of paper towels lay on the other. The smells of mildew and disinfectant hung heavy in the air.

"Hello, Beauty."

Frankie spun her head toward the sound. Too fast. Flashes of light went off behind her eyes and bile shot up into her throat.

"Whoa," the voice said. "Best to stay still for a while. You'll be okay in a bit. I brought you some water."

A young man's familiar face swam into Frankie's field of vision. She recoiled at the smell of the same cologne she'd smelled in her house.

"You don't need to be afraid of me." The young man stroked her hair. "I'll take the tape off, but you can't make any noise or we'll both be in trouble."

Frankie nodded in agreement, and the man tugged the tape from her mouth. Even though he obviously made an effort to be gentle, the tape took flesh with it and left her lips raw and hurting.

The young man lifted Frankie's head slightly and held a plastic, sipper-lidded water bottle to her mouth. As he bent forward, the sleeve of his blue chambray shirt rode up and exposed a silky blue ribbon knotted around his wrist. "You got yourself a bad concussion," he said. "I can't let you have too much water or you'll get sick. Kind of swish it around in your mouth and let it trickle down your throat like."

"I've seen you before." Frankie's voice sounded raspy, like she'd been smoking for the past fifty years or so. "What's your name?"

"Mister Larry H. Littlefield, at your service." Larry stepped back a bit and performed an awkward Sir Walter Raleigh bow.

"You were there when my house burned."

"Yeah, but you've seen me a lot more'n that. I been going everywhere you went. Filled my car with gas at the pump next to the one you used. Opened an account at your bank while you were talking to a teller. I even said good morning to you while you shopped for

239

clothes a couple of days ago, but you never spoke to me." The young man moved his face close to Frankie's. "It kind of made my stomach feel funny, you know, kind of like you were ignoring me. But then, I figured you were just being your lady self. Ladies don't talk to strangers."

"Where are we?" Frankie said.

Larry moved his hand in an arc. "This here is what's left of the old hospital. It's supposed to be torn down sometime or other, but Bellamy still uses it some."

"Are you the one who warned me about the fire?"

"I am the very one." Larry smiled beatifically.

"Did you start it?"

"It wasn't me, I'd never hurt you. That was Mel."

"Mel?"

"I figure it was him brought you here. You've seen him before, too. He was right there watching your house burn."

"Baby Face?"

"Yup." Larry shook his head. "I'll say this about Mel, if there's one thing he's good at, it's sneaking. I always said he could sneak away before his own shadow knew he was gone. I saw him coming down off your roof. I saw the flames through your picture window."

"He was on my roof?" Frankie frowned. For some reason her brain seemed to be working in slow motion. All her precautions and her security—all for nothing.

"Yessir," Larry said. "He poured a couple quarts of liquid candle wax down your chimney and threw in a match. It's a trick I taught him. I'm kind of surprised he remembered it. Lucky for you I fell asleep in my hiding place or I'd have been at home in my own bed. Sad to say, you'd be history."

His hiding place?

"But why would Mel want to kill me? I don't even know him."

"I guess Bellamy told him to. Or maybe he just took a notion. Mel has been known to take some pretty serious notions." Larry rubbed his chin, a thoughtful look on his face. "But it needed some figuring for him to set that fire, and Mel isn't too strong on figuring."

"I'm glad you're here." Frankie moved her arms up and down against the restraints on her wrists, rattling them. "Would you please unbuckle these? I must be a mess, and I'd like to clean up."

"All in good time."

"Please, Larry. I really need to go to the bathroom." Frankie struggled to stay calm. Every cell in her body shrieked that time was running out.

The young man seemed unperturbed. He combed his fingers through Frankie's hair. "Your hair's so pretty." He pointed to the scrap of ribbon on his arm. "I wear this everywhere. You recognize it?"

Frankie started to shake her head, but thought better of it. Every action, every word had to be chosen with care. "It makes a nice bracelet for you."

"It's not much to look at now, not good enough for you to wear in your hair again." A strange look came over Larry's face. "But I'll never take it off, no matter what."

Before Frankie could respond to that, someone shoved the door open. The hollow metallic sound as it ricocheted off the wall set her head pounding with renewed vigor. She closed her eyes and reopened them as Mel strode into the room.

Mel's nose was covered with flesh-colored bandaging, and his nostrils bulged with packed white gauze. Without even so much as a glance at Frankie, he strode over to Larry.

"Where've you been?" Mel said. If it hadn't been for the dark look in his eyes, the voice would have sounded almost comedic as it worked its way through the packing in his nose. "You said you'd come back to the farm."

"I got busy with other things."

"Bellamy thinks you skipped out. You know what he'll do if he finds you here?"

"He won't. I checked his schedule and he's in surgery."

"Are you coming back?"

"No, Mel, I'm not coming back."

"Then what're you doing here?"

"I came for her." Larry motioned toward Frankie.

"You can't take her."

"You don't want to try and stop me. You know what he'll do to her."

"Yeah, I know." Mel grinned. His eyes moved to Frankie's midriff, a portion of which lay uncovered by her shortened tee shirt. He rubbed his disfigured little finger. "But she can't go. She knows enough to make bad trouble for all of us. Besides, she's a freak. Hey, maybe there's other freaky parts. I mean, maybe she has two belly buttons—or three tits." He giggled, the sound like something out of a B rated horror movie.

Larry put a hand on Mel's shoulder and gave it a little shove. "Come on, man. Don't talk like that in front of her."

Mel kept his eyes glued to Frankie's midriff. "Maybe you know something I don't, what with watching her undress and all."

"I said shut up." Larry shoved Mel again, harder. As Mel stumbled backward, Larry turned toward Frankie and began unbuckling the strap at her right wrist.

"She's not leaving." Mel reached for Larry's arm and tried to spin him around.

Larry gripped the hand clamped on his arm and twisted the other man's fingers until he let out a howl. "What's gotten into you?" The look on Larry's face was one of incredulity.

"You and me've been friends a long time," Mel said. "It's always been just us, you watching out for me and me watching out for you."

Larry shook his head. "One thing we've never been is friends. I let you hang around 'cause you had nowhere else to go. But you're a slob and you got no people skills. I'm moving on."

"This ain't you talking, it's her. She's got you hippertized."

Mel jerked his fingers free of Larry's hold and the two grappled. They moved around the room in a macabre dance, each one struggling to gain control of the other. Flailing arms knocked a tray of surgical instruments off the counter. Metal rained down on linoleum tiles, the clatter adding to the charged atmosphere. A flying elbow knocked over a black examination lamp. Its high power light bulb exploded against the floor with a pop, and tiny shards of razor-sharp glass skittered across the room. A knee bumped into a cabinet door. Boots thumped and rubber-soled shoes squeaked as they slid across the floor.

Then as suddenly as it had begun, the fight ended. The sounds of blows, grunts and cursing ended with a final thud as something soft and heavy fell to the floor.

Mel lay on his side next to the cabinet, his face turned toward Frankie. A pool of blood oozed from his head onto the floor beneath it. Bloody hair and pieces of flesh smeared the protruding corner of the Formica-topped counter above him.

A look of stunned surprise on his face, Larry stared down at the dying man. "Dammit. Dammit-all Mel. Now look what you made me do."

Mel's eyes were riveted on Frankie's. The hatred reflected there made her blood run cold.

She watched his light dim, and then wink out. The smells of feces and urine filled the room.

Frankie's stomach convulsed. She turned her head toward the wall and vomited.

Larry pulled a handful of paper towels from the holder and dampened them under the faucet. Gently, he wiped the vomit from Frankie's face and clothes. When he'd cleaned her up to his evident satisfaction, he turned his attention to Mel's body. He studied the scene for several seconds, seemed to reach some resolution, and without another glance at Frankie, left the room.

Within a few minutes, he returned with a canvas laundry hamper. He reached inside it and retrieved what appeared to be a box of dark green lawn and leaf bags, along with a roll of gray duct tape. He pulled two plastic bags from the box, and slid one inside the other. He folded Mel's body into a fetal position, then rolled and slid the corpse until he finally managed to get it completely inside the plastic bags. He twisted the tops, taped them closed, and wrapped duct tape around the bundle several times.

While Larry's attention was diverted from her, Frankie contorted her hand inside the loosened leather binding, bending her wrist at a nearly impossible angle until it felt it would break. If she could just pull her fingers a little further back…

Larry squatted next to Mel's body, secured a grip on the corpse's elbows and knees and struggled to lift the bundle into the laundry hamper. When the plastic bags began to tear, he laid the laundry hamper over on its side and rolled the body into it before lifting the whole thing onto its wheels. With what appeared to be a look of satisfaction on his face, he opened the door and pushed the hamper into the hall. The door closed quietly behind him.

Chapter Thirty-Two

Nick turned on the pickup's radio to crowd out the images he'd begun envisioning after his chat with Ted. Although tempted to turn on his lights and siren and kick his speed into the stratosphere, he kept to the limit. A tic started up in his left eyelid, the flesh jerking in sync with the rhythm of the music pounding into his cab.

Maybe Pritney would be able to find something helpful. The more Nick had dug into the workings of the Cottonwood Hospital and the attached convalescent center, the more worried he had become.

Although there was nothing he could put his finger on, something about the setup felt wrong. On the surface, the locally owned inpatient facility subscribed to an altruistic approach to medical care. Very low income individuals and vagrants received topnotch care. The costs not covered by Medicare or Medicaid were often paid for by funds from a foundation set up by several local philanthropists.

The hospital specialized in geriatric and terminal illnesses. Through its body, organ, bone, and tissue donation and retrieval programs, patients unable to pay for various high cost, life changing surgeries could now access them.

But it seemed to Nick that an inordinate number of the patients were dying. Added to that was the much higher than average number of lawsuits, ranging from simple patient negligence to wrongful death.

Nick had called the state medical examiner's office. Unable to make direct contact with the person who held that position, he'd left an extended message and requested a return call. If he didn't hear back soon, he'd pay the M.E. a personal visit. But first he had to find Frankie.

He pulled into Lola Bridger's driveway, turned off his engine and stepped out of his pickup.

"Frankie told me she'd stay in touch," Lola said to Nick as he stood on her front porch. "I offered her and Collette a room, but she said it wouldn't be safe for me if she stayed here."

"Have you heard from her?" Nick said.

"No. She was going to stay at a motel until she could find someplace to lease while her house is being rebuilt. I haven't heard from her since she left just after noon yesterday. And I'm a little worried, especially after what she said about someone coming after her. I called the police, but they can't do anything until she's been missing longer."

Nick frowned. "She called me yesterday. But I was out of range, and now she's not answering her cell. Do you have a phone book I could borrow?"

"Sure do. You come on in and sit down, I'll get it."

Nick followed Lola into her living room. He sat for a few seconds before his twitching nerves took complete control of his body and he jumped up. He paced back and forth in front of the sofa.

The phone call he'd received from the state medical examiner's office a few minutes ago had disturbed him. The family of an elderly man was suing the hospital's director and main surgeon Dr. Bellamy for malpractice and wrongful death. The family members insisted their father's health was fine two days prior to a needless kidney removal, the complications from which resulted in his untimely death.

The lawsuit was not for the removal of the healthy organ. In fact, Nick was surprised to learn it was not illegal to wrongfully remove a healthy organ or to amputate a healthy limb. About twenty percent of all appendectomies performed by even the best surgeons would be on healthy tissue. Any more than twenty percent indicated excessive caution on the part of the surgeon, while less than twenty percent meant not enough.

According to the M.E.'s office, a nurse had called claiming to have firsthand knowledge of illegal activities. An investigation into the hospital was pending. And now Frankie had vanished.

Nick's body sizzled with the need for action. He drummed the fingers of his right hand on his thigh.

When Lola returned, she carried a stack of various white and yellow-paged phone books. She placed them on the coffee table and pulled a phone from somewhere inside her bra.

Nick sat on the sofa and opened an Albuquerque phone book. "I'll start with the A's. Why don't you begin with the last entry and work your way forward. Hopefully, by the time we meet in the middle of the list, we'll have found the motel where she's staying."

The two bent their heads over the phone books, and began making calls.

****

The noise from the room known as the lockup drew

Hector's attention away from his work. More out of curiosity than anything else, he walked up the hall toward the sounds of struggle. But by the time he neared the area, the uproar had already died down.

As the lockup door began to open, Hector dropped down on one knee behind an old metal desk awaiting a trip to the dump. He knew all too well the atrocities that sometimes took place in this part of the hospital, and had no intention of bringing trouble down upon his own head by making his presence known. At least, not until he found out what was going on.

When Larry stepped through the door, Hector smiled in relief, glad to see his friend alive and well. Especially since rumor had it that Bellamy either had him killed, or he'd fled the country.

Hector knew Larry had done some bad things. But he also knew only too well how a man could get caught up in things beyond his control.

Larry had always treated the cutters with respect. He often stopped by to drink a soda and talk about sports or his latest money making idea. He even occasionally pitched in to help when the cutters got swamped.

So when Larry pushed a bulging laundry hamper out into the hall and closed the door behind him, Hector stepped out of his hiding place.

"*¿Qué pasa, Ese?*"

Larry spun around, his arms instinctively assuming a combative posture. Hector took a step back at the look on his friend's face.

"What's going on?" Hector lowered his voice to a whisper. "Are you in some kind of trouble?"

Larry pointed toward the laundry hamper. "They

don't make trouble any worse than I got. Mel and me had a tussle, now he's dead, and I got to get rid of him." Larry described what had happened.

"An accident, *amigo*. You got nothing to worry about. Besides, the world is a better place without *El Dedo*."

"Yeah, but I was with him when he did something bad. I'll go to prison for sure if the police find out about it and connect me with him."

Hector patted Larry's shoulder with one hand while he reached for the hamper with the other. "Let me take care of him for you."

Larry gripped the hamper tighter. "I can't let you get mixed up in this stuff, you having a family and all. If the police find out what you been doing, you could go to jail too. Then who'd take care of your little girl?"

Hector gently disconnected Larry's hand from the laundry cart. "It would be a gift for you to allow me to dispose of this *cochino*. But what are you going to do?"

"I'm leaving town tonight, I got me a girl and we're going to get married."

"Congratulations, my friend. I wish you years of happiness." A beatific smile on his face, Hector pushed the hamper with its grisly contents toward the cutting room.

****

When Larry returned to the lockup he was pushing a wheeled bucket of water from which jutted the wooden handle of a mop. He grinned shyly at Frankie and set to work mopping the floor.

After he'd scoured the Formica counter top, he replaced the scattered instruments. Then he pulled a can of aerosol room deodorizer out of a metal storage cabinet, aimed the nozzle into the air, and sprayed. The sweet fragrance of apples and cinnamon co-mingled with the stench of feces, urine, and vomit.

Frankie's stomach heaved, and she retched again.

****

Deputy Judy Pritney sat at her desk and stared out the window of the sheriff's office. Her right leg bounced up and down on the ball of her foot like a piston in an eighteen-wheeler going ninety miles per hour.

She pulled a pencil from among several kept in a wire mesh holder atop her desk and tapped it on the flat wood surface while chewing on her already-raw bottom lip. She studied her reflection in the polished surface of the thermal, stainless steel coffee mug her grandma had given her for Christmas a couple of years ago. The distorted, fun-house face glared back at her.

"What are you looking at?" she said to her image.

How had she managed to get herself so deep into this horrible mess? Stupidity, that's how. But then, no one had ever accused her of being the brightest bulb in the neon sign of life.

Pritney scowled again at her reflection. Even after three years of working together in close proximity, Nick had never once looked at her the way he looked at Frankie O'Neil the first time he saw her.

Did he not know how she felt about him? He was such a good detective, how could he not have figured that out? She took such pains with her makeup and hairdo. She'd even taken to wearing perfume, and that was saying something. But Nick never even noticed.

Although Pritney didn't have the delicate beauty of Frankie O'Neil, she'd always had her share of men panting after her. Always had them staring at her round, muscular ass and drooling.

But not Nick. No, he'd been blinded by that bouncy little church-organist bimbo, while Pritney had hated her on sight. It was more than her beauty, although that would have been sufficient reason. It was something about the way she dealt with the shit-sandwich life had handed her. Pritney would have railed against the heavens, cursed at the police and threatened lawsuits. She'd have taken to the streets, guns a-blazing.

But Perky-tits appeared to have taken all the crap in stride. She'd gritted her teeth and dug in her heels. And that had impressed the hell out of Nick.

Pritney couldn't accuse her partner of any loss of professionalism and courtesy in his dealings with the O'Neil woman. Just the opposite. His behavior had always been completely appropriate. Everyone who knew him respected him.

He'd never made even one pass at Pritney. And that was the problem. No matter what she did, he'd always treated her like she was just one of the guys.

It was obvious to anyone in the room that Nick had loved that stuck up little O'Neil witch from the minute he first saw her in the Eagle Nest Café. It had shown in his eyes. Never mind that, as far as he knew, the little bitch might be a mass murderer.

But she wasn't a mass murderer, was she? No, not her. Miss Priss had probably never even jaywalked.

What would Nick think of his partner if he found out what she'd been up to? He'd hate her, that's what. He'd hate her and then arrest her. And rightly so.

Deputy Pritney sighed. She sat for several minutes,

motionless, unseeing. Then she opened a desk drawer and pulled out a pen and notepad. For the next forty-five minutes she wrote.

When the letter was done to her satisfaction, she went through all the drawers in her desk. She removed her belongings, and put everything into the cloth tote bag she'd used to transport homemade bread to the office—another attempt to get Nick's attention.

After unbuckling her belt, she placed it on top of her desk along with her side arm and shield. She propped the notepad against the terra-cotta colored coffee cup on Nick's desk, placing it squarely in front of his chair so he'd see it first thing.

With a look of determination on her face, Pritney pulled her jacket and cap off the rack that stood in the corner by the front door. She zipped the jacket, tugged the knit cap over her head, and took one last look around the office.

Her gaze came to rest on Nick's desk. Tentacles of emotion tugged at her heart as she studied the photo of a younger Nick and his now-dead father on horseback, herding cattle to pasture.

Two equally handsome men. Nick would age well.

But he wouldn't be growing old with her. Nope, that was a done deal.

The civilian Judy Pritney took in a long breath and slowly let it out through pursed lips. She slung her purse over her shoulder, picked up her tote bag, opened the door and stepped out into the cold mountain air.

Chapter Thirty-Three

"It wasn't me killed your brother," Larry said to the still-bound Frankie. "I told Mel not to shoot. But like I said, he sometimes takes a notion and does things on his own."

Frankie didn't respond. The way Larry kept referring to them as a couple made her flesh crawl.

One litany of the many from Uncle Mike's survival training ran through Frankie's mind: survive, evade, resist, and escape. Keep your thinking in resistance mode, but do whatever is required to survive while looking for an opportunity to escape. And at least one opportunity will usually present itself. She just had to watch for it and be willing to do whatever it took to capitalize on it.

"I believe you, Larry." Frankie carefully modulated her voice. There could be no patronizing, no false note to her words. If Larry thought she was manipulating him in any way, he might decide to leave her there.

Larry's smile was shy. "I got plans." He glanced at his watch. "Got to go."

Frankie struggled to hold down the hysteria that kept creeping up her throat. "Larry please unbuckle my hands. Dr. Bellamy could come in at any minute."

"He's doing an amputation, so he'll be a while. I got to go get the car, but I'll be right back. I want us to be on the way out of town within the next half hour."

"But I really need to clean up. I won't feel comfortable until I do."

"Plenty of time for that once we're on the road."

"Please…don't leave me here."

But Larry was already out the door.

The *shush* of the door closing behind Larry was immediately followed by a muffled thump. Frankie's ears strained for other sounds, but when the noise was not repeated, she set to work on the partially loosened restraint.

Although most likely only a few seconds passed, it seemed several minutes before she could pull her right hand free. She shook off the leather strap and reached to unbuckle her left hand just as the door was pushed open and Dr. Bellamy entered.

"Brava." Bellamy applauded in pseudo-adulation. "You had poor Larry eating out of your adorable little hand."

Dressed in blood-spattered green surgical garb, Bellamy carried a small fire extinguisher to the counter. When he set it down, several drops of a thick red liquid dripped onto the counter top.

He turned toward Frankie, his eyes devoid of expression. "Don't expect the lad to come to your rescue. Sadly, we had to dispose of your knight errant."

Think the unthinkable, Uncle Mike's voice sounded in Frankie's head.

If Bellamy would just move a few inches closer…

As if on cue, the doctor took a couple of steps toward the gurney. Like a coiled spring, Frankie's hand shot toward the doctor's crotch, her fingers poised to clamp down and twist with all her might. But the experiences of the past several hours had taken a toll on her speed and strength, and Bellamy recognized her intention before she could complete the move.

"No, no, no." The doctor chuckled and danced backward. "Mustn't hurt the visitors." Bellamy grabbed Frankie's wrist and forced her hand back down to her side.

She struggled, but he soon had her tightly buckled down again.

"We hate to mention it, dear, but you really do smell. Judging by the smears on the floor, Larry did at least try to clean you up before we arrived." Bellamy compressed his lips. "Your meddling has cost us a great deal of energy. Energy put to better use helping people who are in need."

"I may not know everything about what you do, but I know you're not helping people."

"You wouldn't begin to understand. We take in people no one wants, people either without family or whose families can't be bothered to see after them. We feed them and take care of their medical needs."

"Right. You're just a misunderstood philanthropist. I know better…I know about Esther Emory."

Bellamy arched one eyebrow. "Sarcasm? Impolitic, in light of your current situation. You have no idea the kind of work to which we have dedicated our life."

"I know you're responsible for my brother's death and for an attempt on my life. What you are is a liar and a delusional egomaniac."

"My, my. So pompous." He moved his face to within inches of Frankie's. "Your dear, departed brother was heavily involved in our little side business. Was, in fact, happy to receive money from it."

"Tim would never willingly be part of anything

illegal or unethical."

Bellamy shot Frankie a look filled with mock sympathy. "And now who's delusional? When we approached Tim with the idea of selling the body parts surgical hospitals are required by law to dispose of, he was happy to become our partner."

"You're lying."

"Really? Have you found his stash of money yet?"

Frankie's face must have mirrored her reaction to those words, because Bellamy continued his onslaught.

"Where did you think he got it? You must have known he couldn't possibly have saved that much from his paltry resident's income." Bellamy's lips twisted in a sneer. "However, on to the issue at hand."

The doctor walked to the counter and studied the instruments there. He moved the pieces around on the cloth pad upon which they lay. Metal clinked against metal as he sifted through them.

He made a *tsk-tsk* sound through his teeth. "All this disorder. We really must speak to the help." He selected an instrument, returned to the gurney, and looked down his nose at Frankie. "We usually allow Mel to participate in matters of this nature. He'll be disappointed when he learns what he missed, especially after what you did to his nose. But he is apparently off doing God-only-knows-what to God-only-knows-whom." Bellamy turned the metal object over in his hands. "It's probably just as well. His work is generally too messy for our taste. And we wouldn't want to do anything to mar that lovely face."

Frankie's eyes opened wide.

Bellamy chuckled, a reflective look on his face. "We would have given a month's income to see you in action. What did you use on him, a palm-heel strike to the nose? A straight-on punch? Perhaps a head-butt?" The doctor bent slightly and peered into Frankie's face, as if looking through a microscope at some new-found species. "But now that we are aware of your apparent expertise in hand-to-hand, we'll be doubly vigilant."

Bellamy held his chosen instrument in front of Frankie, rotating it so she could see it from all angles. The gleaming silver metal thing consisted of a handle of the same type found on scissors at one end, and a drinking straw body that ended in tiny pincer jaws at the other. He worked the handle, opening and closing the razor sharp instrument like a hungry little mouth.

"This marvel of engineering is so small, yet can inflict such pain. Ever heard of what the ancient Chinese called the death of a thousand cuts? In this case, it would be a thousand tiny bites." The doctor caressed Frankie's lips with the cold metal. "Now, where shall we begin?"

Frankie looked directly into the man's eyes. She'd regained her composure, and other than her tightly fisted hands, nothing indicated she'd heard his words.

"You are in possession of some things your suddenly-sanctimonious brother took from us." Bellamy's face reddened at Frankie's continued silence. "Please do not waste our time denying it. We are aware that the police are in possession of the leg. But it means nothing without the accompanying documents. And according to our very reliable source, those are in your possession. You will tell us where to find them, or we will dissect you one millimeter at a time."

Gorge rose in Frankie's throat, and she swallowed. The resultant gulp was loud enough for Bellamy to hear, because he smiled.

"Let's see, perhaps we'll begin with the tender parts between your lovely toes."

Frankie could refuse to answer Bellamy's questions. But he would torture her until she'd be ready to tell him anything he wanted to hear, and kill her anyway.

"Okay."

A look of something akin to disappointment flashed across Bellamy's face. He frowned down at the biopsy tool as he opened and closed it several more times.

"I said okay. I'll give you what I have."

Bellamy sighed. "Of course you will." He stood up. "Where is it?"

"It's in my brother's safe deposit box. But I'll have to get it; they know me at the bank."

Bellamy leveled a suspicious look at his captive. He walked to the cabinet, replaced the tool, and left the room. When he returned, he'd removed the surgical garb and was wearing a yellow dress shirt and dark brown slacks.

The doctor bent over and pulled up his left pant leg. When he stood, he held a derringer in his right hand. He pointed the weapon at Frankie.

"Not to worry, we have a concealed carry permit. Wouldn't want to do anything illegal." Bellamy laughed, or at least that's what Frankie thought he meant to do. The sound made her flesh crawl.

The diminutive handgun appeared similar to one in Uncle Mike's antique firearm collection. Although the weapon looked like a toy, each of its two stacked barrels would hold one deadly round.

"Precious, isn't it? Less than five inches long." Bellamy held the weapon up for Frankie's inspection. "So small it is lost in our palm, nearly invisible."

The doctor pointed the derringer at Frankie's face. "This little sweetie is an American made .38 Special. Notice the chromed frame, fixed sights and big bore. What you can't see is that it's loaded with two copper jacketed, hollow point rounds. Do you know why we use hollow point bullets, Miss O'Neil?"

Frankie raised her chin, commanding her face to remain devoid of expression. "The hole in the tip of the bullet makes the projectile expand upon impact. It results in the widest wound path possible."

Bellamy's eyebrows rose. "Superior response. It would be such a pity to have to kill you. However, we will not hesitate if you do not do as you are told, understood?"

Frankie nodded her head. "I don't have the key to the safe deposit box with me."

The doctor again brought his face to within inches of Frankie's. "Where is it? You're beginning to piss us off, Miss O'Neil."

"It's at the motel where I've been staying since my house caught fire."

"Ah yes, we heard about the fire. Do the police have any leads?"

"If not, they soon will. You can't think I'd be stupid enough to track you down on my own, do you?"

Bellamy smirked and shook his head. "Such a clumsy attempt. But no matter, we've had our own personal exit plan in place for a good while. By the time anyone figures out what has happened, we will be sunning our oiled body and sipping mojitos in an undisclosed, non-extraditing location."

Wordlessly, the doctor walked back over to the counter and picked up the roll of gray tape Larry had left there. He returned to the gurney and loosened the restraint on Frankie's left hand.

"Now loosen the other hand." He paused. "Take the tape and pull out a length of about twelve inches. No, no, don't tear it off, keep it attached to the roll."

Frankie complied.

"Wrap the free end of the tape around your right wrist a couple of times, that's right. Now hold out both hands, wrists together." Bellamy wrapped duct tape around both her wrists with one hand while keeping the derringer pointed at her temple with the other.

"Now undo the restraints at your legs."

After several seconds of struggling, Frankie managed to sit upright. She fumbled with the buckles at her ankles, her fingers moving like thick sausages.

Bellamy backed out of kicking range and motioned for Frankie to stand. She slid her legs over the side of the gurney and sat on its edge. Her vision swam, and her bound wrists caused her arms to stick out awkwardly in front of her.

"If the things your brother took from us were to come to light, we would spend a great deal of time in prison. We share that information with you so you will understand that we have nothing to lose by ending your earthly existence. Do not make us shoot you, Miss O'Neil."

Frankie sat for several seconds before slipping off the gurney and standing beside it. Bellamy motioned toward the door, and the two exited the room. They stepped over Larry, who lay crumpled next to the door.

Blood slowly dripped onto the floor from a gash on the side of his head. He didn't appear to be breathing.

Frankie walked ahead of Bellamy through the rear exit of the hospital and out into the darkness of night. The well-lit staff parking lot was dotted with a few other vehicles, but there was no one else in sight.

The doctor motioned toward a black, late model Jaguar parked at the far end of the lot.

"You drive."

"You're kidding." Frankie held her bound hands toward him.

Bellamy ignored her protest and opened the door on the driver side. "We never kid. Get in."

Frankie managed to slide into the driver's seat. She rested her bound wrists on top of the steering wheel while the doctor climbed into the passenger's seat.

"Start the engine." Bellamy dangled the car keys in front of Frankie's face.

"You can't seriously expect me to drive with my wrists taped like this. I can't even hold on to the steering wheel. Besides, the seat is too far back—I can't reach the pedals."

"You are in no position to make demands. However, as they say, safety first."

Bellamy stepped out of the car and walked around to the driver's side. With the derringer unwaveringly aimed at her left eye, he adjusted the seat then returned to the passenger side.

"Hold out your hands." Making no effort to be gentle, he removed the tape bindings. He smiled as several layers of Frankie's flesh come off with it. "You will not exceed the speed limit, nor will you do anything to attract anyone's attention. We assure you that we are quite willing to shoot anyone who approaches us."

During the drive to the motel Frankie considered one escape plan after another. Perhaps she could speed so a policeman would pull them over. Maybe she could drive into a lamppost and take her chances on getting out of the wreckage ahead of Bellamy. Or maybe she could drive straight to the police station and lay on the car's horn. But Bellamy had a weapon. And she had no doubt he would be all too happy to kill one or two innocent bystanders.

She glanced at Bellamy. "The key to my room is in my purse. And unless Mel took it, it's still out at the chicken farm." She pulled into the motel parking lot, parked the car in the slot in front of her room, and turned off the engine. "I'll have to get another key from the desk."

"So you say." Bellamy sat still. Frankie could nearly hear the wheels of his mind grinding as he tried to decide how best to proceed.

"Okay, Miss O'Neil, we shall go in together. Is there any need for us to repeat our threat?" Bellamy put the hand carrying the derringer into the pocket of his trousers.

"No need."

The two walked side by side to the front desk. The young man behind the counter initially smiled in recognition of Frankie, but as they neared the desk and the young man got a closer look, his smile faded.

Frankie could only imagine her appearance. Her torn clothes were filthy with dust from the cistern and stiff with Mina's blood and her own dried vomit. Her hair had heaven-only-knew what kind of creepy crawlies tangled in it. She must smell like something dragged out of a landfill.

"Hello." Frankie addressed the desk clerk in a conversational tone. "I have a problem…I lost the key to my room. Could you make another one for me?"

The young man's eyes slid back and forth between Bellamy and Frankie. Regardless of her appearance, Bellamy's impeccable dress obviously impressed him.

"Sure thing. No problemo. Room two seventy, right?" The kid looked meaningfully at Bellamy, the look on his face telegraphing words to the effect of: *whatever butters your biscuit.* "And will you be needing a second key?"

"No," Frankie said, "just the one."

The young man keyed a new magnetic keycard and handed it to Frankie. She thanked him and slid the key into her pants pocket. She and Bellamy walked outside.

Located on the second floor, Frankie's room was only accessible via the outside stairs spaced about every thirty feet. She walked toward the stairs nearest her room with Bellamy close behind her.

As they approached the door to her room, Frankie stuck her hand into her pocket for the key. Something pricked her finger, and pain shot up her hand. Mina's barrette.

Frankie withdrew the key, her mind swirling with ideas of how to use the small metallic weapon to her advantage.

Bellamy motioned for her to unlock the door. "You will not make any sudden moves."

Frankie inserted the key card into the lock. When the tiny green light on the keypad blinked, she pushed the door open.

Bellamy shoved the barrel of the derringer into her back. "After you."

Frankie considered smashing the door back into Bellamy's face, but he stayed too close on her heels for that move. His proximity also negated her closing the door before he could get in.

But as the doctor walked through the door, Collette leapt at him from her perch atop the entertainment center. With the full force of her thirteen pounds, the cat hit Bellamy's shoulder, instantly pushed off again and disappeared into the bathroom.

Bellamy yelled something that sounded like "Whaa," and tossed the derringer in a high arc to his right.

The weapon hit the wall and fell to the floor. Frankie and Bellamy simultaneously dove for it, but the doctor was a nanosecond quicker.

In desperation, Frankie reached into her pocket and pulled out Mina's barrette. She stepped toward Bellamy, closing the distance between them. By the time he straightened and turned back toward her, the two stood nearly face to face.

Surprised by Frankie's proximity, Bellamy did not take time to aim but precipitously pulled the trigger so rapidly the two shots almost sounded like one. Something tugged at Frankie's sleeve as the first bullet nicked the fabric and buried itself in the wall. But the second bullet found its mark in her shoulder. A red hot poker screamed its way through her flesh as the superheated projectile expanded, searing and masticating tissue at the same time gun powder stippled her neck and cheek.

A low growl started up from somewhere deep

inside her chest. It gained strength as it rose in her throat, turning into a full throttled battle cry. She shoved the sharp metal points of the starburst barrette into the base of Bellamy's neck. The heavy metal spikes sliced deep, piercing flesh and muscle.

Dr. Bellamy squealed, dropped the derringer, and backed away. His eyes wide, he tugged at the still embedded barrette, but realized too late his mistake. With nothing to hinder its flow, blood seeped through his fingers and down the front of his shirt.

One hand pressed against his neck, Bellamy half ran, half crawled toward his car. Drops of blood marked his progress down the stairs and along the sidewalk.

Frankie's vision blurred, but she forced her body into action. Warm blood trickled down her arm and ribs. Her legs felt like they were tethered to sandbags. But she ran after Bellamy.

The doctor whimpered and kept glancing back over his shoulder. With his free hand he opened his car door, fell onto the seat and jammed the key into the ignition.

Only a few feet from Bellamy's car, Frankie's eyes went out of focus. Her knees buckled and she fell forward onto the asphalt.

Chapter Thirty-Four

When Larry regained consciousness he was lying on a hard, cold, flat surface. His head throbbed in rhythm with his heartbeat, and the roar of pumping blood filled his ears. He lay still for a few seconds and waited for the chaos in his mind to clear a bit. When it did, he opened his eyes.

Every movement shot fresh pain through his head, but he sat up. Nausea tickled at his insides and his vision blurred. He tried to stand, but his legs refused to hold his weight and he plopped back down onto the floor. The contact with the hard floor jarred his head and he nearly lost consciousness again. He hand-walked up the wall, leaning against it for support.

"Is that the best you could do, you old bastard?" he said to the empty hallway.

Larry staggered toward the lockup. Steeling himself against what he might find, he opened the door. But other than the empty gurney, the room looked the same as when he'd left to go for the car. He was relieved to see no blood or any other indication that Bellamy had hurt Frankie.

That was the good news. But as soon as Bellamy got his hands on what Tim took, he'd have no choice but to kill her.

"Not my Beauty." Careful not to move his head more than necessary, Larry slid his hand along the wall and wobbled toward the cutting rooms.

Hector and the other cutter were standing at their work stations when Larry stumbled into the room. Hector put down his boning knife and walked toward his friend, while the other cutter went back to slicing pieces from the red mass in front of him.

"I thought you'd be gone by now," Hector said. His mouth opened wide when he saw the blood on Larry's clothes and the gaping wound on his head.

"So did I," Larry said. "But I got sidetracked."

Hector pulled his bloodied apron off and tossed it into an empty chair. He peeled rubber gloves off his hands and threw them on top of the apron. "What happened?"

"Bellamy hit me and took off with my girl. I'm going to get her back, but I don't want to attract attention. Folks see me all bloodied up, someone's going to ask questions. Might even call the police."

Hector examined Larry's head. He clicked his tongue a couple of times and walked to a white metal cabinet against the wall. He wet a handful of cotton balls with some kind of brownish solution and dabbed at the wound. Larry winced.

"You need stitches. Scalp wounds bleed bad."

"That's why I'm here." Larry glanced at the other cutter, who kept his head down and eyes on his work. "I need you to sew me up."

"I can, but I don't have anything to deaden you. It'll hurt."

"Can you do it fast?"

Hector nodded. "My mother taught me. She said I was better than any doctor." He grabbed sutures out of a cabinet and told Larry to sit in a chair. After he'd put several stitches into his friend's scalp, he doused the area with the brown liquid that burned like fire.

"That's going to hurt pretty bad for a couple of days." Hector held out two white tablets. "Extra strength aspirin will help some."

Larry put the pills into his mouth and chewed.

Hector began to take off his blue and white striped pullover. "Take off your shirt. You can wear mine." He tossed the shirt to Larry then put his black rubber apron on over his white undershirt.

Larry put his own red flannel shirt into a nearby trash can and slowly pulled Hector's shirt over his head. "Thanks."

"*De nada.*"

"I'll name my first boy after you." Larry headed toward the door.

Hector beamed. "Go with God."

"Give little Anna a hug."

As fast as his pounding head would allow, Larry walked toward the exit through which Bellamy and Frankie had passed a short time earlier.

****

Nick drove like a madman toward the motel where he'd learned Frankie was staying. In the event he was over-reacting and she was okay, how would he explain his presence to her? He couldn't just show up out of the blue and tell her he'd come because he couldn't stop thinking about her—that he couldn't work, couldn't eat, and couldn't sleep because of her. Or that he was terrified the blood in Mina's apartment was hers.

As he neared the motel what began as a tickle at the base of his neck blossomed into full-fledged alarm at the shriek of sirens growing louder and louder. He pulled into the parking lot just behind the ambulance from which the sirens whooped.

The emergency vehicle's lights bounced in eerie strobe patterns off the brick front of the motel. The ambulance headlights lit up the parking lot, bringing into sharp detail a tableau straight out of a television crime show.

Two patrol cars had arrived earlier and secured the area for the safety of the emergency response personnel. Motel guests stood in clusters watching the action. Several of the younger ones held camera phones pointed toward the scene.

A black Jaguar stood in a cordoned-off area, its driver side door open. A man half sat, half reclined behind the wheel, his legs splayed with one foot inside the car and the other outside. The man's head leaned back against the headrest, his eyes open and staring. His hands lay in his lap. Blood formed a puddle around the man's shoe where it rested on the carpeted floorboard. Blood, now coagulated, had poured from a red line encircling the man's throat and onto his shirt front.

Frankie lay face down on the asphalt a few feet from the car, her hair fanned out into an auburn halo around her head. Unable to tell whether or not she was breathing, Nick gritted his teeth as his stomach clenched into a hard ball.

Two paramedics, bags in hand, jumped out of the ambulance and split up. One moved toward Frankie and the other toward the man in the car.

Nick identified himself to the police officers, one of whom he recognized. He explained his presence, and after some discussion was allowed to move closer to Frankie.

One paramedic dropped to his knees beside her still form. He checked her vital signs and called out information to the other paramedic.

"Is she going to be okay?" Nick said.

"It's too early to tell," the paramedic said. "Are you a relative?"

"No, I'm a friend."

"She's been shot in the shoulder and has lost some blood. Her pulse rate's a little weak and she's in shock. Our best bet is to get her to the hospital ASAP."

"This one's gone," the paramedic attending the man in the car called out. He picked up his bag and moved to help his partner. After a few more minutes, they packed up their gear, put Frankie into the back of the ambulance and sped away, sirens blaring and lights flashing.

Chapter Thirty-Five

Larry had run inside the motel at the sound of approaching sirens. He'd hurried through a rear door and into the nearest men's restroom, where he spent the next several minutes washing blood from his hands and the front of Hector's shirt. He washed the blood from his knife, folded it back up and put it into his pants pocket. Careful to avoid contact with his head wound, he ran dampened fingers through his hair to straighten it, and exited the restroom. He blended in with a gaggle of motel guests that were filing out of the building and into the parking lot, loudly speculating with each other as to the nature of all the excitement.

A large crowd soon gathered in the parking lot. The police held the watchers a distance from the scene, where they milled around, craned their necks and exclaimed.

The usual, Larry thought. Gawkers. Probably not one of them had a real life. They just sucked energy from the crap that got dumped onto other people's heads.

Someone tapped Larry on the shoulder, and his heart rate instantly shot sky high. He turned toward the person who was trying to get his attention.

"What's going on?" an elderly man said.

Larry shrugged. "Not sure. But it looks like someone got what was coming to him."

The paramedics bent over Frankie. Relief washed over Larry when one of them said she was still alive, and a smile of satisfaction creased his face when he heard Bellamy was dead.

Some tall guy wearing cowboy boots, blue jeans, and a western shirt got out of a white pickup and approached the police. They let him pass through the cordon and approach the paramedics.

After Larry overheard the paramedics tell Cowboy the name of the hospital where they would take Frankie, he slipped away from the crowd and headed toward the darkened rear of the motel where he'd parked.

Warm feelings of pride and pleasure suffused his body. His Beauty had lit up that old doc pretty well.

When Larry had first arrived at the motel, Frankie lay in the parking lot a few feet from Bellamy's car. The doc sat behind the wheel, sobbing like a baby as he tried unsuccessfully to get the engine to turn over. He was talking to the car for all the world like it could hear him, like he couldn't believe the thing would dare ignore his commands to fire up.

At the sight of Frankie lying there so still Larry's head felt like it would explode. He'd sure enough lost it. He ran right up to Bellamy's car and yanked open the door. The doc was bleeding some, but the injury was not fatal. So Larry made it fatal.

The expression on Bellamy's face was priceless. It seemed kind of comical how his look of hope changed from pleading to terror as he recognized Larry's intention.

"You failed to properly plan your escape," Larry had said into the dying man's face. "You should have just packed up and left."

The ambulance pulled out of the parking lot, the blare of its sirens jerking Larry out of his reverie. He ran back to his car. A maelstrom of mixed feelings churned at his gut as pieces of a new plan came together in his mind.

****

Frankie opened her eyes to a dream world. She stood on a grass-carpeted pathway that meandered through a meadow of the deepest green imaginable. The fragrance of a million flowers filled the shimmering, sparkling air. Trees of exotic appearance and flowers of every imaginable color moved their fronds and branches in time with music such as she'd never before heard. Complete, unconditional love engulfed her.

People poured into the meadow from every direction. They stood with their faces turned toward her, eyes sparkling and alight with welcome. Although they must have numbered in the thousands, and even though all but a few of them had died long before she'd been born, Frankie recognized each one.

Great Grandma Malloy stood beside Uncle Mike and his Grandma O'Neil. Her dad stood atop a small hillock, waving and smiling at her. A pair of Ó Mórdha cousins raised their hands in greeting. Row after row of Frankie's Irish forebears nodded in welcome.

A handsome, dark-haired man named Aedan, her grandfather several times great who'd lived during the sixth century, began singing in a clear tenor voice:

Ar scáth a chéile a mhaireann na daoine.
Saol fada agus breac-shláinte chugat.

Although Frankie had no memory of ever having heard the ancient Irish tune, she recognized the haunting melody and understood the Gaelic words that

274

told of people helping each other to survive, and blessing the listener with a long, healthy life.

Movement drew Frankie's gaze to her right. Tim stood near a particularly tall tree, a child of about five beside him. Both their bodies were outlined in a brilliant white light.

"Hello, Sis," Tim said.

"Hi, Peepers." It was Jenny's voice.

At first, Frankie couldn't speak for the emotion that blocked her vocal chords. Tears stung her eyes and rolled down her cheeks. Her brother and the child she now recognized as her older sister smiled. Their eyes filled with infinite gentleness.

"Where's Mom?"

"Don't try to talk," Tim said. "You need your energy to get well."

"But I want to meet her. Where is she?"

Tim held up his hand, palm out. "Look, Sis, I don't have much time, and you have to go back to your life."

"I don't want—"

"You'll come back here when it's time." Jenny smiled. "But not until you've finished running your race."

Tim nodded. "Life's too short to live in regret of the past and fear of what might happen tomorrow. You can choose to open your heart to love—it's the only thing that never dies—or you can slug it out alone through years of loneliness. Your choice."

The beautiful world grew fuzzy, like a video camera going out of focus.

Tim nodded his head, as if agreeing with some unspoken voice. "Or you can continue to isolate yourself and become a bitter, angry old woman who'll die alone."

A sudden rushing wind filled the garden. Tim, Jenny, and all the generations of Frankie's gene pool dissolved as she was pulled backward through a long tunnel.

"She's lucky to be alive," a clinical voice said from somewhere to her left. "She lost a great deal of blood."

Frankie's shoulder throbbed. Something was hooked over her ears, wound down her face and looped under her nose, forcing air up her nostrils. She tried to swallow, but something was stuck down her throat, and when it moved, it irritated the already raw tissue. She gagged.

"She's choking," Lola said. "Those tubes are clogging up her throat."

"Those tubes are doing the breathing for her," the clinical voice said. "They'll be removed once she regains consciousness and can breathe on her own."

"How long will that be?" Nick said.

The sound of his voice made something funny happen in Frankie's stomach. But this time she didn't push the feeling away.

"It depends on several things," the clinical voice answered. "The bullet entered just below her right collarbone. The damage would have been much worse had the weapon been further away. As it is, the bullet miraculously missed any major blood vessels. The fragments that didn't make it all the way through her flesh became embedded in the scapula. We removed the pieces and repaired her collarbone."

"She's a fighter," Kate said.

"What was that sound?" Lola said. "I'm telling you, she's choking."

Frankie opened her eyes. She tried to speak, but the result was a cross between a bark and a gargle.

Everyone was ordered from the room while the breathing tube was removed and other adjustments made. They were allowed to return after Frankie had been made comfortable.

"Look who's awake," Nick said. His smile almost too wide to get through the door, he strode to stand beside the bed. He looked into Frankie's eyes and stroked her cheek with the back of his hand. His touch was feather gentle.

Black stubble covered Nick's face. His clothes looked like they were made of that pre-wrinkled fabric people bought so it wouldn't wrinkle later. He combed his fingers through his hair several times, his efforts to control the thick locks mostly unsuccessful. It was a look Frankie could get used to.

*Make every day precious...*Grandma O'Neil whispered.

Frankie mouthed something. Nick bent over to bring his ear close to her mouth as the air in the room crackled with anticipation.

Suddenly, Nick blew a puff of air out through his nose in a soft snort, nodded his head, and laughed. He clapped his hand on Kate's shoulder and smiled. "She says she hopes you brought some of your marvelous pecan pie."

Chapter Thirty-Six

The morning sun was barely up when Hector awakened. Although he'd slept only a couple of hours, he cheerfully got out of bed and dressed for work. He walked out of the bedroom he shared with his wife, his head held high and his shoulders squared for the first time in months. He whistled a melody from his boyhood as he entered the kitchen.

Imelda smiled up at Hector. The sight of her made his chest swell with pride and love.

Anna stopped coloring the picture of a unicorn she had nearly finished. She squealed "Papi," and ran into her father's arms.

Hector's heart was overflowing. *El Dedo*, the demon henchman of the evil Dr. Bellamy, had been sent back to Hell.

"The evil, dead Doctor Bellamy." Hector repeated the sentence over and over to himself, savoring the flavor of the words on his tongue.

Imelda placed a plate of bacon and eggs on the table at her husband's place. She put a filled tortilla-warmer in the center of the table and a butter dish next to it. "Come to breakfast, *mi amor*."

Hector took his seat at the head of the table. The family offered a simple prayer of thanks for the food and began to eat.

A few blocks away, the colony of flesh-eating

beetles scrabbled over fresh meat. For the next several days they would work diligently, patiently, eating all the soft tissue from the newly introduced cadaver, the right hand of which had a curiously misshapen pinkie finger.

****

Larry pulled the green pickup onto an empty lot outside of Mountainair, a village about ninety minutes south of Albuquerque. The land had cost him close to half his savings, but it suited him just fine. The nearest neighbors lived a good three or four miles up the dirt road, and the rolling hills would render him fairly invisible to anyone driving on Highway 55.

He unloaded lumber, bags of concrete, nails, insulation and other building supplies, which he stacked beside a staked-off area. He pulled a wheelbarrow, hammer, hand saw, and two saw-horses from the pickup, placed them atop the lumber, and covered it all with a tarpaulin.

The finished building would be big enough for a twin bed, wash basin, and table. A Bunsen burner would do double duty for cooking and warmth. And a green, plastic bag-lined five gallon bucket would serve as a latrine.

It took two more trips to the lumber yard before Larry had everything he needed. With only a couple of hours of daylight left, he pulled a shovel from the pickup bed, headed to the marked-off area, and began digging out the foundation trench.

When it grew too dark to work any longer, he removed his cap and leather work gloves. He dusted off his brown nylon wind breaker and blue jeans and climbed into the pickup. He pulled a can of baked beans, a can opener, and plastic fork out of a paper bag, cut open the can, and began shoveling great gobs of the smoky sweetness into his mouth.

A bit of syrup dripped from his chin onto his jeans, but he didn't mind. Here he was, sitting on his own land, eating a can of cold beans. But an inch thick, prime rib steak wouldn't have tasted as good.

After Larry scraped the last drop of syrup from the can and licked the fork clean, he put them both into a plastic trash bag. He kicked off his boots and unrolled a brand new, down-filled sleeping bag. The flannel lining smelled a mite musty, but it was soft and warm. It'd do him just fine.

Larry slid into the bag until his feet butted up against the passenger door. He pulled the flannel fabric up to his chin. Although he'd have to sleep on his side to avoid the floor-mounted gear shift, he heaved a sigh of contentment. The warmth of his cocoon seeped into his muscles and he dropped off to sleep, visions of the future swimming in his head.

****

When the doctor pronounced Frankie alert enough for questioning, Blinquet and a homicide detective entered her room. Nick looked on as both men took turns questioning her. They asked many of the same questions over and over, squinting into her face as if trying to divine some deep, inner secret.

Frankie told them about her trip to the chicken farm. She described her fight with Mel and how she'd found Mina's body. She told the officers about awakening tied to a gurney in the hospital, and Mel's subsequent death at Larry's hands. She explained how the leg came to be in her freezer and about Tim's journal.

"And I found medical records for someone named Esther Emory in Tim's safe deposit box. There is a discrepancy between her original medical records and the spreadsheet that I copied from Tim's laptop. One indicates she had diabetes, and the other indicates heart trouble. I don't know which is accurate."

"We'll need those records," the homicide detective said.

"They're in the tote bag in my car. Unless someone moved it, it's still at the chicken farm."

Blinquet and the detective exchanged glances. The detective left the room.

Frankie's body felt as if Gulliver's Lilliputians had sneaked in and tied her down with thousands of constricting bands. Even the smallest movement required all the energy she could muster.

She pushed the button on a small pump and medication flowed through a clear plastic intravenous tube and into her arm. The throbbing pain in her shoulder lessened slightly as she answered Blinquet's last questions.

"No, sir, I didn't know what was in the duffle. Yes, I was curious. I asked Tim about it, and he brushed it off, so I didn't push."

The tone of Blinquet's voice, the stare he leveled at her and the way he pursed his lips when she spoke left little doubt as to how he felt about her story.

"The Medical Examiner confirms that you wounded Bellamy with the barrette found at the scene," Blinquet said. "But that's not what killed him. His throat was slashed so violently, he was nearly decapitated. Can you tell us about that?"

"Nearly decapitated with a barrette? That's ridiculous." Frankie sat up straighter. "Wait a minute, are you insinuating I murdered him?"

Nick, silent until then, got up from the reclining chair in which he'd slept and taken meals for the past few days. He walked to the bed and stood beside Frankie.

"If she cut Bellamy's throat, what did she do with the knife? Did you find it at the scene?"

Blinquet pursed his lips again. "Not yet, but we're still investigating."

"Miss O'Neil was so weakened from loss of blood she wouldn't have had the strength to inflict the kind of wound you've described. Besides, Bellamy had to be twice her size."

"I chased him into the parking lot," Frankie said. "He was bleeding, but not bad. Next thing I know, I'm here."

"What about this Larry guy?" Nick asked. "Have you talked to him?"

Blinquet puckered his lips. "Nowhere to be found. But we've put out an APB."

Nick looked at Frankie. "It's only a suggestion, but I recommend you not answer any more questions until you've spoken to an attorney."

Blinquet frowned, reiterated his order for Frankie to stay in town and left.

Frankie slept for the next eighteen hours, waking only when her shoulder pain forced her to surface. Each time she roused, her eyes went to the uncomfortable-looking reclining chair in which Nick tried to sleep, his eyes flying open at her every movement.

All the female nurses developed an obvious crush

on the handsome deputy who kept watch over their charge. One brought him a hospital blanket and pillow, another brought a disposable razor, and still another brought him visitor meals from the hospital cafeteria.

Hector and Imelda Cordero brought flowers and a note from Anna—a page torn from a coloring book. Under the brilliantly-colored picture of a unicorn, Anna had written the words *Get Well Soon* in purple crayon.

Kate dropped in with goodies from her café a couple of times.

Pastor Dan and Frankie's choir members all came to visit, leaving the hospital room awash in flowers and stuffed animals.

Lola came to repeat her offer of room and board, and to assure Frankie that Collette was fine and living the high life in her house. "Nothing's too good for Collette. She saved your life, Dear One."

Chapter Thirty-Seven

Larry nailed the final piece of plywood into place and moved his eyes around the living space he'd just completed. Without windows it might be dreary, but it was low-ceilinged and well insulated. It would offer good protection from the harsh winter common to these parts. And later, if everything worked out according to plan, he could add on a room or two.

He pulled a mattress, card table, and two molded plastic chairs from the pickup, which he carried into the shed. Next, he retrieved several bulging shopping bags, the contents of which he lined up on a shelf he'd built along one wall.

Baked beans, soup, spam, sardines, and a box of crackers sat next to two plates and coffee cups. A small, square pan held two cheap stainless steel spoons. It would be wise to keep the forks and knives in the pickup—at least for a while.

A wide smile creased Larry's face as he placed a small, square tin on the shelf beside the dishes. Jasmine tea. Exotic, just like his Beauty.

For the umpteenth time that morning, he examined the eyebolt affixed to one heavily reinforced wall. He grabbed the heavy eight-foot chain hanging from it, yanked as hard as he could, and smiled when it held fast. Its attached leg iron sounded a solid *thunk* against the wood flooring when he dropped it.

He'd have to figure out some way to pad the inside of the iron. Otherwise, it'd injure the leg to which it was bolted. And he had no desire to hurt that precious leg.

Larry pushed open the door and stepped outside. In the spring he'd replace this door with one that had knobs on both sides. By then, if all went according to plan, he'd be an expectant papa.

He slipped the padlock's retractable bar through the u-bolts on the outside of the door, slid the key into its slot, and turned it. Metal-striking-metal sent birds flying from the surrounding trees, twittering their fright to each other.

No one was getting past all that reinforcement. At least, not without some heavy duty metal cutters.

"Tick tock, the game is locked. Nobody in, nobody out." Larry hadn't spoken for several days, and his voice sounded strange.

He headed for the pickup. His body taut with excitement, he hummed a happy tune.

It was finally time.

****

Dressed and ready to leave the hospital, Frankie was sitting on the edge of the bed when Nick returned from the cafeteria.

He plopped down in the chair and rubbed his belly. "I had scrambled eggs, ham, pancakes, and coffee for breakfast. What about you?"

Frankie pointed toward the rolling tray-table she'd moved against the wall. "I always thought jokes about hospital food were cliché. I think the brown stuff is supposed to be an egg, but I don't know what the sticky gray stuff is. I ate the toast and applesauce."

Nick chuckled. "I just met someone you know."

"Who?"

"A man by the name of Flatte. He said he's your attorney."

"He was Tim's attorney, but I might wind up needing him if Blinquet doesn't let up. What's he doing here?"

"A hit-and-run driver nearly killed him a couple of weeks ago."

Frankie gasped. "Is he okay?"

"Now he is, but I gather it was touch and go for a while. He said it happened right after he took you home from your dinner date."

"It wasn't a date. Do the police know who did it?"

"No, but they have a description of the car. Someone told them they saw an old Mercedes speeding away."

The blood drained from Frankie's face. "That's what that guy Larry drives."

Nick was suddenly all business. "I'll call the APD and ask them to beef up patrols through Lola's block. At least until he's caught."

The look in Nick's eyes right then, the straight lips, the square jaw, all reminded Frankie of the pictures in one of Uncle Mike's illustrated books of warriors throughout the ages. The men and women in those paintings, sketches and photos, were from all over the world and different centuries. But they all had that same look—the look that meant bad news for their enemies.

For the first time in months, Frankie felt safe.

The doctor arrived for one last examination. He warned Frankie not to lift anything heavier than two pounds or to do anything strenuous, wrote out a couple of prescriptions and pronounced her well enough to go home.

The duty nurse came in for one last smile at Nick. She offered some additional advice about shoulder wound care, and after an eyelash flutter in Nick's direction, she left.

"I'll bring the pickup around to the exit," Nick said. "The nurse said she'll take you downstairs in a wheelchair and wait with you there." He headed for the door, stopped, and swiveled his head over his shoulder. "Lola says she'll have a nice brunch and plenty of hot tea waiting for you. She said you'd probably be ready for a good meal."

After Nick left, Frankie walked to the window, pulled up the blinds and looked out at the Albuquerque skyline. With only two or three nurses working the floor, she figured she had several minutes to wait. She was surprised when only a couple of minutes had passed before her door opened and someone came in.

"Hello, Beauty."

Frankie spun around. Larry stood just inside the door, holding a revolver pointed at her. The ribbon-bracelet still encircled his wrist, but its edges were frayed into tiny scallops and stretched out of shape. Its faded color was barely discernible beneath a layer of grime.

"I come for you, like I promised."

If it hadn't been for Larry's voice, Frankie would not have recognized him. Even more slender than he'd been the last time she saw him, a patchy red beard now mottled his gaunt face and his hair hung in greasy strings over his collar. In grimy blue jeans and a filthy windbreaker, he smelled of dirt and old sweat.

Scratches and cuts crisscrossed his hands and black dirt outlined his jagged-tipped fingernails.

But it was his eyes that caught Frankie's attention. Something had shifted in his eyes. She shivered.

"I'm sure enough glad to see you're all well and stuff. You're tougher than you look."

Frankie's eyes darted around the room. Her ears strained to hear anyone in the hall who could help. "The nurse is bringing a wheelchair."

Larry nodded his head. "You won't be needing it. I'm your ride, especially now that Cowboy's pickup has developed a few problems." Larry giggled, the sound strange and ugly.

He strode toward Frankie, grabbed her bandaged arm and jerked her toward him. Pain shot through her shoulder and she cried out, but Larry only squeezed her arm tighter. "I thought you were a lady. But real ladies don't take up with every man that looks at them twice. First Rich Boy, now Cowboy. You and I are going to come to an understanding."

"Larry, I—"

"Shut up. I killed Bellamy for you, and that means you belong to me. You'll do as I say."

Frankie tried to tug free from Larry's grip, but the intensity of the resulting pain made her vision go gray. She fell into step beside him.

As they moved through the door of the hospital room, Larry stuck the hand holding the revolver into the pocket of his windbreaker. He made a point of pressing its barrel against the fabric so Frankie could see it was aimed at her mid-section.

"I don't want any trouble. But I'm sure enough ready for it. Come on now, we got to make tracks."

Larry pulled Frankie into the hallway and toward the stairwell. She allowed herself to be towed, her mind a fury of activity. When the two began the descent down the three flights of stairs, Frankie feigned weakness and stumbled. Larry automatically made a grab for her at the same time she placed her foot in front of his legs and shoved. Waves of pain shot through her wounded shoulder.

Larry made a frantic but futile grab for the handrail and tumbled head over heels down the concrete steps. He rebounded off the gray cinder block wall at the bottom of the stairs and lay on the landing, his legs crumpled underneath his body. Blood seeped from under an old scab on the side of his head.

Frankie cautiously walked toward the semi-conscious form. She squatted, trying not to jostle her throbbing shoulder, and picked up the fallen pistol. Wetness seeped into her blouse and trickled down her abdomen.

The stairwell door above them burst open and Nick rushed to her side. He took the pistol from her trembling hand and pointed it at the now-stirring Larry.

"Are you okay, Frankie?"

"How did you know he was here?"

"There's an old gray Mercedes in the parking lot, and someone slashed my tires. I radioed the police from my truck."

Frankie's knees buckled and she sagged. Nick wrapped his arms around her shoulders and pulled her into his chest.

"My precious Little Warrior."

They were still sitting there when the police arrived.

Chapter Thirty -Eight

Frankie, Nick, Kate, and Lola sat around Lola's dining table sipping coffee and eating crumb cake. Collette eyed the four friends from atop Lola's roll-top desk, her posture radiating pleasure at her newly acquired fiefdom.

"Larry hasn't stopped talking since his arrest." Nick took a sip from his second cup of coffee. "He said Tim discovered Bellamy was altering medical records to cover up the unnecessary deaths of too many of his patients. That's a felony."

"Bellamy told me Tim was his partner," Frankie said.

Nick nodded. "That seems to be true." He reached for Frankie's hand and covered it with his own. "Your brother wanted to help those without access to medical care, so when Bellamy approached him to help sell off amputated parts, it probably made sense. But when Tim found out Bellamy was performing needless amputations and harvesting healthy vital organs, he couldn't keep quiet."

Lola slowly shook her head, her facial expression sad. "I remember reading that every thirty seconds another poor soul has a foot or leg amputated as a result of diabetes. I wondered at the time what happened to those body parts."

"Tim's medical career would have been over for

his part in that," Frankie said.

"The difference between Bellamy and your brother is that Tim wanted to help people," Nick said. "Bellamy was motivated by pure greed. The bones and organs he didn't sell, he collected. APD found a huge cache of body parts hidden in his basement. It was such a horrific scene the department brought in a psychologist to talk to the guys who discovered it."

Silence descended on the three as their minds processed the images Nick's words elicited.

"But why did Tim have Esther Emory's original medical records?" Frankie said.

"Bellamy evidently generated his own copy of the records to make it look like she died of complications from diabetes. We're not sure how Tim got hold of the originals and Esther's amputated leg, but she didn't have diabetes. During the surgery to remove the leg, Tim administered anesthesia to her without realizing she had a bad heart. That's what actually killed her."

"No wonder he looked so awful when he came to my house. He would have been devastated to know he'd caused someone's death, even if it wasn't his fault."

"Bellamy might have deluded himself into thinking he was doing a good thing, at least at first. He brought indigent people in off the street and gave them medical attention. Of course, they didn't realize the occasional limb or organ would be removed and sold as payment for their care."

Kate put her hand to her cheek. "My God. He was parting people out like a human chop shop."

Nick nodded. "The whole thing began to implode when Mel and Larry shot your brother before they could find where Tim hid Esther's leg and medical records."

"Poor Esther." Frankie shook her head. "She'll never know how her death helped pull the plug on Bellamy's hideous business."

She knows, Tim said. *And she says to thank you.*

"Larry will be charged with Bellamy's murder," Nick was saying. "And he'll have to answer for running Flatte down."

"Has Mel's body been found?" Frankie asked.

Nick shook his head. "Larry won't talk about that. Ask any other question and he blabs nonstop. I think he's shielding someone."

"And Mina was killed because I asked her for help." Frankie's voice was low, filled with remorse.

"Not your fault," Nick said. "She called the state medical examiner's office about the time Tim was fired and suggested they investigate Dr. Bellamy. Word got back to him, and that's when he began to see Mina as a threat. He spotted her snooping around his files and ordered Mel to make her disappear."

Kate peered at Nick over the rim of her cup. "What about the other hospital employees? How could something like that go on and no one know about it?"

A snapshot of Hector's sincere face flashed in Frankie's mind. Hector with the lovely family, and with a dark and troubling secret. She remained quiet.

"I have some suspicions," Nick said, "but no one's talking. The good news is that thanks to the money Frankie's donating from Tim's life insurance, the local foundation will continue to provide health care for some of our most needy locals. By the way, I don't suppose any of you would consider a career in law enforcement, would you? I'm going to need a partner."

"What happened to Pritney?" Frankie said.

"Pritney was in league with Bellamy. She gleaned tidbits of information from her contacts in the Albuquerque Police Department and exchanged them for health care for her grandmother in Bellamy's convalescent home." Nick looked at Frankie. "She left the bird and chalk message on your porch."

"And cleaned it up while I called the police. Risky, but effective. It nearly convinced me I'd completely gone off the chart, something I'm pretty sure the police already thought."

Nick chuckled. "Let's just say the APD is grateful to have this case put to rest. You made quite a name for yourself. Someone nick-named you *The Tiny Terror*."

Frankie's face heated up. "I was never very good at just giving up and going away."

"Bellamy hinted to Pritney she was going to have to dispose of you. That's when she realized things were out of control."

"What'll happen to her?" Lola said.

"She's being held pending a full investigation," Nick said. "No one would have known of her involvement if she'd kept quiet, and that'll work in her favor. But she knew Bellamy was into some bad stuff and said nothing."

"It's all just so damnably sad." Lola's subsequent sigh was loud in the small room.

"By the way," Nick said, "human DNA was found in the feed grinder out at Bellamy's chicken farm. Microscopic bits of human flesh mixed in with the chicken feed."

Frankie nodded. "That explains the smell in the

barn."

"It seems Mel used the feed grinder to dispose of a couple of disgruntled employees who threatened to blow the whistle on Bellamy's operation. DNA tests should confirm the bits as our missing persons."

Kate took a sip of coffee and turned to Nick. "Didn't Bellamy sell eggs and dressed chickens to local eating establishments?"

Nick nodded at the three horrified faces turned toward him. "A recall has been issued. But there's no way of knowing how much DNA from the ground up employees has already made its way onto the breakfast and dinner plates of the local population."

"And what'll happen to the farm?" Kate said.

"It'll be closed down—the chickens will be destroyed."

Lola picked up the dishes and took them to the kitchen. Glassware clinked as she stacked them on the kitchen counter.

Leaning toward Frankie, Nick lowered his voice. "Have you told Lola yet about your plans to hire a private detective to find her daughter?"

Frankie shook her head. "I don't want to get her hopes up. I'll tell her when and if he finds anything."

"I might be able to help you with that, especially now that I'll be spending my free time in Albuquerque."

"Help with what," Lola said as she entered the room.

Frankie stammered. "Nick was saying—"

"Nick was saying he's going to help Frankie re-establish her garden," Kate said.

Frankie cut her eyes sideways at Nick. "I can

always use the help." Warmth spread through her body and she smiled. "How are you with a shovel and rake?"

Lola and Kate beamed at each other for a second before Kate winked at Nick. "Oo-rah."

"So what will you do now?" Lola said to Frankie.

"The next thing I have to do is to write checks to the people on Tim's spreadsheet."

Lola cut another piece of coffee cake, handed it to Nick, and then turned to Frankie. "You mean the ones whose body parts were sold?"

"Yes. I've contacted a firm that buys gold, and the good news is that the coins will sell for a lot more than Tim paid for them. I'm going to divide the money equally among those still living and among the family members of those who are not."

Uncle Mike would have liked Nick, Tim said.

"Yes," Frankie murmured, "he would."

"Who would have what?" Lola said.

Kate beamed at Nick. "The girl's been alone too long. She's gone to talking to herself."

Frankie squeezed Nick's hand. Maybe this whole being-alive thing would be manageable after all.

Chapter Thirty-Nine

Although coated with a thin layer of soot and smelling of smoke, Frankie's garage had remained relatively untouched by the fire that destroyed her home. She was thrilled to find the storage boxes still intact.

The two metal filing cabinets stood just as she'd left them. Uncle Mike's ruminations about life, the journals chronicling his years in Special Forces written in his own handwriting, his medals and letters of commendation from the United States government, along with the recipes he'd clipped from newspapers and magazines—none were even scorched.

One by one, she made her way through the folders, laughing and crying at the memories their contents evoked. Two hours later she found a thirty-two-year-old newspaper clipping from a small town newspaper in Texas. Tears streamed down her face as she read the article for the second time.

A Plainview woman is in police custody after allegedly drowning one child, a five year old girl, and trying to drown her other two children; a three year old female and a male infant. Kelby Stanton was taken to the Central Plains Mental Health Hospital where she will undergo a court-ordered psychiatric evaluation. The police report indicates the two surviving siblings show signs of malnutrition and long-term abuse. Stanton's brother Mike O'Neil reported that he became concerned when he could not raise anyone in the house, even though he could hear the baby crying from outside. He stated that he broke in the front door and entered the bathroom just as Stanton put the baby boy into the bathtub, which already contained the drowned five-year-old. The three-year-old girl was found in the unlit basement, where she told police her mother often made her stay. Stanton's relatives say she had been fighting depression since the death of her husband several months earlier.

A scab of memory sloughed off and remembered anguish spilled out of Frankie's subconscious, painful yet cathartic in its eruption.

"Why didn't you tell me, Uncle Mike? Why did you keep all these secrets?"

"At least I saved the paperwork. I figured you'd find it sooner or later."

"But you let me think I was losing my mind."

"You weren't ready for the truth, Frances. When you were little, I was afraid you would blame yourself for what happened to you, Jenny, and Timmy. Little kids tend to blame themselves for the evil that surrounds them. But none of that was your fault. You didn't make it happen and you couldn't have stopped it. As you got older, I just couldn't bring myself to go back into that darkness."

Careful not to damage the brittle newsprint, Frankie replaced the article in the folder and returned the folder to the cabinet. She pulled her cell phone from its holster and punched in a number.

"Good morning, Nana Alma. Would you allow me to buy you lunch tomorrow? No more secrets. I want to talk to you about my mother. But mostly, I want to talk to you about a little girl named Jennifer Stanton—my big sister Jenny."

"I'm so very pleased to hear from you," Alma said.

"Is it my choice whether or not to accept this gift—this fae thing?"

"Yes, but to refuse it would be about the same as cutting off your left hand. You could get along without it, but you wouldn't be whole."

Frankie considered Alma's words. "At least I'm not just your ordinary nut job. Besides, it might be kind of nice to know I'll never be completely alone. See you tomorrow." She broke the connection.

"The rules are fairly easy," Uncle Mike said. "You'll learn as you go."

"Welcome back, Peepers," Jenny said.

Scores of voices offered words of welcome. Some spoke with a heavy Irish-English accent, while others spoke Gaelic, and others in more ancient languages. Like sun-warmed water from a tropical island waterfall, the sound soothed her spirit. It was as if Frankie had returned home after a long trip. As if everything was finally normal.

A word about the author...

Olive Balla makes her home near Albuquerque, New Mexico, with her husband Victor.
Visit her at her website:
http://omballa.com